REED MEMORIAL LIBRARY
3 2827 00185 8123
W9-AEU-610

SACRED COWS

This Large Print Book carries the
Seal of Approval of N.A.V.H.

SACRED COWS

Karen E. Olson

Thorndike Press • Waterville, Maine

This book is a work of fiction. Names, characters, places, and incidents are the product of the author's imagination or are used fictitiously. Any resemblance to actual events, locales, or persons, living or dead, is coincidental.

Published in 2006 by arrangement with Warner Books, Inc.

Thorndike Press® Large Print Mystery.

The tree indicium is a trademark of Thorndike Press.

The text of this Large Print edition is unabridged.
Other aspects of the book may vary from the original edition.

Set in 16 pt. Plantin by Elena Picard.

Printed in the United States on permanent paper.

Library of Congress Cataloging-in-Publication Data

Olson, Karen E.
Sacred cows / by Karen E. Olson.
p. cm. — (Thorndike Press large print mystery)
ISBN 0-7862-8377-7 (lg. print : hc : alk. paper)
1. Women college students — Crimes against — Fiction. 2. Women journalists — Fiction. 3. New Haven (Conn.) — Fiction. 4. Escort services — Fiction. 5. Large type books. I. Title. II. Thorndike Press large print mystery series.
PS3615.L7525S23 2006
813′.6—dc22 2005034627

To Chris and Julia:
You are my life,
and I can't imagine
this ride without you.

National Association for Visually Handicapped
serving the partially seeing

As the Founder/CEO of NAVH, the only national health agency solely devoted to those who, although not totally blind, have an eye disease which could lead to serious visual impairment, I am pleased to recognize Thorndike Press* as one of the leading publishers in the large print field.

Founded in 1954 in San Francisco to prepare large print textbooks for partially seeing children, NAVH became the pioneer and standard setting agency in the preparation of large type.

Today, those publishers who meet our standards carry the prestigious "Seal of Approval" indicating high quality large print. We are delighted that Thorndike Press is one of the publishers whose titles meet these standards. We are also pleased to recognize the significant contribution Thorndike Press is making in this important and growing field.

Lorraine H. Marchi, L.H.D.
Founder/CEO
NAVH

* Thorndike Press encompasses the following imprints: Thorndike, Wheeler, Walker and Large Print Press.

Acknowledgments

First and foremost, I must thank Kristen Weber, Susan Richman, and Les Pockell at Mysterious Press/Warner Books for choosing *Sacred Cows* as the winner of the Sara Ann Freed Memorial Award. I'm very honored and thrilled by their enthusiasm.

Second, I must thank my agent, Jack Scovil, who's traveled much of the long road with me and never wavered in his encouragement and belief in my work.

I would never have found Jack if it weren't for writer Thomas Fleming and a long-ago interview on his front porch in Westbrook, Connecticut. Tom made good on his offhand comment to help me out someday, probably not realizing I'd call him on it.

Where would a writer be without those critiques and kudos from fellow writers and friends: Kerri Pedersen, who told me after seventy-five pages that it wasn't a piece of crap and I should continue; Eleanor Kohlsaat and Liz Medcalf, my first readers; my writers' group buddies, Liz Cipollina, Roberta Isleib, Chris Falcone, Cindy Warm, and Angelo Pompano, whose help I couldn't have done without; Tara York and Maria Garriga, fellow journalists who boosted me during difficult times; and my sister, Sandy Corr, and friend Melanie Stengel, who pointed out things no one had noticed in myriad readings.

Much thanks go to Michael Barbaro, intern extraordinaire who's made it to the Big Time, for his lengthy and entertaining tour of Yale, and to Webkazoo's Mike Jones and Barbara Kagan for a super Web site.

Newspapers and the media in general have gone through some tough times in the last few years. I would be remiss if I didn't acknowledge those I've worked with throughout my career, especially for their support and senses of humor, which make this business still worth it for me. But no, you won't recognize yourselves on these pages, so don't even try.

I have taken some literary license with locations, but most of them are intact and where they should be. New Haven has never had a CowParade; this is merely my vision of what it might be like if it did. Thanks to Harriet Dobin and Ron Fox of CowParade Holdings Corp. for amusing cow puns and assistance.

And finally, my husband, Chris, and daughter, Julia, get big gold stars for their patience, smiles, and hugs when I needed them the most.

Chapter 1

My hand closed over the cold steel in that second between hearing the phone ring and before my eyes opened. I squinted at the clock, the red numbers glowed 3:42, and I pushed the drawer shut, my paranoia possibly the result of too many beers. I knocked the phone off the table, and I could hear "Hello? Hello?" as I fumbled for the receiver on the floor.

"Yeah?" was the only sound that I could force through the fog of sleep.

"Get out of bed, Annie. There's a dead girl in the road in front of University Towers on York Street. She took a dive."

I heard the click, then the dial tone. Asshole, I thought as I pulled myself up on my elbows in an attempt to do what he said, but the room started to spin and I had to stop for a minute. What had I been thinking? I don't drink like that anymore. It's too dangerous, in too many ways.

A dead girl, that's what Marty said. In the road. I'm not the fucking cops, they're not going to tell me anything anyway, but I dragged my sorry butt into the bathroom. I almost screamed when I saw my reflection: my hair hanging in tangled clumps, lipstick smeared across one cheek, mascara smudged under my eyes. I was naked, but that wasn't anything new.

A blast of water was what I needed, even though I'd probably miss something by not leaving the house sooner. But if I didn't shower, get myself sobered up some, I'd miss more.

I grabbed a pair of leggings out of the laundry basket and pulled on a big sweatshirt. It was almost 4:00 a.m., for Christ's sake, and she was dead. No one was going to call the fashion police on me. My hair still hung in a clump, but at least it was clean and the alcohol haze had faded.

I stuffed my notebook in my bag and went out into the dark for the second time that night, the rain startling me as it slammed into my forehead. I cursed Marty for the umpteenth time, the dead girl for being dead at such an ungodly hour. I knew nothing, I was going into it cold, I hated this job.

The blue and red lights flashed against

the black backdrop of the narrow street. I double-parked next to a cruiser; they'd be pissed, but what did I care, they weren't leaving before me anyway. The yellow tape stopped just where the cops stood talking to one another, their notebooks getting soaked. I still hadn't taken mine out of my purse.

I saw her before any of them saw me. She was facedown, the rain beating into her bare back, her body slumped over the sidewalk and into the road, her hair a waterfall into the catch basin. Her arms were at her side, her fingers spread, clawing the pavement. The spotlight accentuated her white skin, the pool of dark liquid under her head. Someone had put a raincoat over her bottom half, but a mangled leg peeked out from underneath.

The rain was washing all the evidence away.

I looked up at the balconies over me, my eyes finally resting on the barbed wire fence between the sidewalk and the building.

I caught bits and pieces of conversation around me, but I ignored them, finally seeing the detective I knew would be there.

"Hi, Tom," I said, my voice still husky from the booze.

"What cat dragged you in?" He chuckled.

"Got a call. Thought I'd stop by."

"Didn't think you'd be up to it." He winked, and I could still feel his mouth on mine as he said goodbye. He was gone by the time Marty called; I hadn't heard his pager, but that's not a surprise, considering.

"I'm always up for it, you know that."

"I like your outfit." His Paul Newman–blue eyes caressed my body, and I struggled to bring myself back to the matter at hand.

"What happened?"

"She fell or she jumped, who knows?"

"Who is she?"

He shrugged, and I could see him putting on his armor. "Don't know yet. No ID."

"Where'd she fall from?"

He smiled patronizingly and put his hand on my shoulder. "Why don't you go home? I'll call you when we're done here."

Yeah, and then I'd never get any information. We'd been playing this cat-and-mouse game for a year now, and he still didn't get it. This was my job, I had to be a pain in his ass.

"Where'd she fall from?" I asked again.

He sighed. "We don't know. We're checking every apartment."

A row of balconies loomed over us. She had to have been on one of them.

"She bounced off the fence," he said wearily.

I didn't want to think about it. At least she hadn't gotten impaled. I forced myself to get my train of thought going in a different direction. "What time did she take her leap?"

"Coroner's guessing she's been here about an hour."

"Who found her?"

Tom glanced across the sea of officers at a tall woman teetering on high heels. One of New Haven's better-known prostitutes, her name is Patricia, but I think it used to be Peter. "Coming home from a late date?" I guessed.

"If you want to hang out, okay, but you have to let us do our job. Can you do that?" Tom began to walk away from me, the story of my life.

"Does it look like she fell or jumped?" I tried to keep him talking, but he just shook his head and kept moving out of my line of fire. He hadn't done that three hours ago.

"What happened?" I heard the voice behind me. I almost could feel his breath on the back of my neck.

"Who called you?" I demanded.

Dick Whitfield held up his portable scanner. "Heard it on this. Thought I might get a head start."

"This is my beat, now get the fuck out of here." I couldn't blame my attitude on my hangover, I always talked to Dick this way. It was the only way he could hear me, I swear.

"Wow," he muttered as he stared past me at the girl. "What happened?"

Exactly what I wanted to know, and exactly what I wouldn't tell him even if I did.

"Seriously, Dick. Go home, I've got this covered."

"Is that your boyfriend over there?"

I grabbed him by the arm and dragged him a few feet away. "Listen, I'm not in the mood for this right now. Marty called me, I'm here, you can go home."

Dick Whitfield was the newsroom boob, but the editors liked his "enthusiasm." Even Marty. If he got wind of this confrontation, I'd be dog meat. I wished I hadn't had so much to drink, it was making me even more cranky than usual. I took a deep breath and tried to compose myself. "There really isn't anything for you to do. I've got it covered."

A shout from above and my head moved back so fast I saw double for a second and thought I was going to throw up.

Someone was shouting, waving, and out of the corner of my eye, I saw Tom run into the building. That was it, that was the balcony, now how was I going to get rid of Louis Lane here? But when I looked at him, I saw his eyes were blank.

I glanced back over at Patricia, she was still talking to the cops. It was worth a try. "See that woman over there?"

Dick nodded.

"She found the body. We need to get some quotes from her, can you do that?"

If he were a dog, his tail would be wagging. It was pathetic. I watched his long, skinny frame lope through the rain, and my wet hair dripped into my eyes.

The night had started out better than this. I had a new dress on; it was black and slinky and sexy. The cold beer slid down my throat as Tom's hand caressed my knee under the table. We both knew what was going to happen; it always did, at least for the past year. Before that, it was just a lot of fantasizing and cold showers.

He shouldn't be seeing me, either. It was a conflict of interest for both of us, since I was the cop reporter. But the attraction was too strong. Not enough for more than what it was, neither of us wanted to get tied down, but we were monogamous in a weird sort of way. I didn't see anyone else, and neither did he. At least I liked to think so.

I wasn't sure why I got drunk, but I suppose it was just the whole scene, piano player banging out great jazz, candles flickering, the light making me look younger than my almost forty years. Sure, it was a great night. Until now. Wouldn't you know I'd have an editor who was an insomniac and kept his scanner on all the time.

I slipped in past the cop at the door; he was too busy interrogating some guy with a dog who wanted to go out. I could've been anyone who got caught in the rain. One elevator was stuck at 14; it seemed like a good place to start, so I took the other one up, the jolt stirring my stomach. When the doors opened, I was met by a patrolman who wouldn't let me out. I stuck my hand across the door so it wouldn't close.

"This is a crime scene, ma'am."

I could've forgiven anything but the "ma'am." It really pissed me off. "Let me out, goddammit. People live here, you know. You can't keep me from my home." I prayed Tom was too far away to hear me. I pushed my way out and moved down the hall, like I really lived there, and when the officer turned around, I made a beeline for the apartment with the open door and sounds of cops inside.

It had been tastefully and inexpensively furnished by IKEA. A plush sofa edged up against a sleek Scandinavian coffee table large enough to seat a family of five; a couple of chairs perched on the corner of a dark blue rug covering the standard beige apartment carpeting. A print of Gauguin's Tahitian women splashed the room with much-needed color. A big-screen TV stretched across one wall; a glass cabinet housed a sound system.

A few candles were scattered on the coffee table, all in various sizes, their wicks charred. A small pile of books lay like dominoes on a small table next to the couch. There were no strewn newspapers, no dirty laundry, no signs of life.

A galley kitchen was off to the right, the countertops gleaming, the stylish stainless steel dish drainer empty.

They were out on the balcony and in the bedroom. I bumped into Tom as he came down the hall with a pair of jeans in a plastic bag.

"How the hell did you get up here?" But

he was distracted. He didn't focus on me; his eyes were darting around like mine, taking in the scene, wondering what happened to that girl, how did she end up on the pavement.

"Come on, Tom, give me something and I'll leave. I promise."

He snorted. "Yeah, right. You never leave."

When I thought about it, I realized he was right. He was always the one who was gone in the morning, not me. But we were usually at my place.

"Are those hers?" I asked, pointing to the bag in his hands.

He nodded.

"Any ID up here?"

He sighed, biting his lip, and I wished I could bite it for him. "Yeah."

The wall was up, and I could be any reporter asking the questions. "Come on, can you give me anything?"

"You're not supposed to be here," he said roughly, trying to get past me.

"Any sign of anyone else here?" I was pushing it, and he glared.

"Leave. Now. You know about next of kin notification. Let us do our job." He gave me a little push toward the door.

"Okay, okay. Don't have a coronary. I'm gone."

The cop at the elevator gave me a dirty look but didn't say anything. I thought about shooting him the finger as the doors closed between us, but I was too tired.

There was no sign of Dick Whitfield when I stepped back outside. The rain settled on my sweatshirt, drops rolling down my neck. The coroner was bent over the body; the flash blinded me as someone took pictures. Cops mingled everywhere, curious people formed a circle outside the yellow tape. It's funny how a crime scene will attract people at the oddest hours.

"How'd she die?" I yelled over the tape.

The coroner looked up, his mouth twitching with the unpleasantness of his task.

"I'm with the *Herald*," I offered.

"Call me tomorrow." He turned back to the body.

I sidled up to another cop, Tim something-or-other. "Anyone else see it?"

He shrugged. "Canvassing now." He turned away, back to his colleagues.

I couldn't see what else I could accomplish. It was too late to get a story into the paper, too early to go to work. I could still get a couple hours of sleep. I wondered if Dick Whitfield ever slept.

My car was cold and had barely heated

up when I pulled up in front of my brownstone. Once inside, I stripped down to my birthday suit and crawled back under my comforter. Even though I liked Tom in my bed, it was nice to sprawl out in the middle all by myself.

I think I fell asleep in about a minute.

Chapter 2

I forgot to set the alarm. Both times I went to bed. The first time, I could see how I'd been forgetful. After all, Tom had been undressing me and I had been undressing him and somehow the clock slipped my mind. The second time, I'd been hungover, and I'd had to deal with Tom in a completely different way, the way I hated.

So it was 8:00 a.m. and the phone was ringing again. This time, I knew it was Marty, where are you, tell me what's going on, what happened, how much did you get? I wasn't in much better shape than I'd been during our first call, but he hadn't given me a chance to talk then. When I opened my mouth to tell him what I knew, such a sound came out that I was startled. God knows, Marty was speechless.

"What happened to you last night?" he finally asked.

"I had a rough night," I managed to croak. "Lay off."

"Dick is already here."

"Fuck Dick." I said it before I thought about it.

"He says she was found about three o'clock by that prostitute who hangs out near there." I was glad he ignored me, but it could come back and bite me on the ass if I wasn't more careful. "But the cops wouldn't tell him anything else. You have connections, you get anything?"

I hated it that everyone thought I had "connections" just because I was fucking a detective. We weren't exactly sharing job-related information during sex.

"She's a Yale student. Melissa Peabody," Marty said when I hesitated, his words hanging between us for a few seconds.

"No shit?" This was an interesting twist.

"We should find out if it was her apartment." Marty's voice was grim.

I doubted it. It was way too clean for a college student's apartment. But if not, then whose apartment was it? Who was she with, and why was she there? Another thought leapt across the fog into my brain: Maybe she jumped. Maybe she was one of those kids who just couldn't hack it. Maybe there was nothing sinister about this.

But she had been naked. If I was going to off myself, I don't think I'd strip first. The indignity would be a little too much.

Marty's voice brought me back.

"You know how this screws everything up." He meant because she was a Yalie. I could feel for him. Our publisher didn't like bad things to happen at Yale because it meant the prestigious Ivy League institution would have to be slapped across the front page with a 100-point headline about death. Who would want to send their kids there then? New Haven wasn't exactly standing on its own merits.

Two calls would be made to the publisher: one from the powers that be at the university lambasting us for publicizing something they'd claim was "private business"; the other from City Hall, lambasting us for ruining the city's "image." I didn't envy Marty, having to go upstairs to that office that I'd been in once and explain that the dead girl on the pavement was some rich, smart kid who was only visiting our fair city while she got the best education money could buy.

I swung my legs over the side of the bed, thankful that my middle-of-the-night outing had somewhat cleared the hangover web from my brain.

"I need a shower, then I'll get back out there. Cops are probably still there," I told Marty.

I heard the phone click, he'd done his job: He'd gotten me out of bed, he'd threatened me with Dick's presence. I wasn't sure I cared enough about this job anymore to worry about some asshole moving in on my territory. There were way too many kids at the paper now, not like it had been fifteen years ago when I started. I was the kid then. I'd joined a crack reporting team, but only three of us were left. Others had moved on, to the *Hartford Courant*, the *Chicago Tribune*, the *Philadelphia Inquirer.* I hadn't updated my résumé since I'd started at the *Herald*, more laziness than anything else. But lately I was getting too cynical, even for me. Maybe it was time for a change. This would be the best time, before I got too old and no one would want me and I'd be stuck at the *New Haven Herald* until I died.

What a pathetic thought.

I stood in the shower for the second time in four hours, washing away the crime scene. I could always go work for my father. He'd said that a million times. He'd give me some cushy job at the casino he managed and I would have weekends and holidays off and probably make a helluva lot more money than I was making now. But could I be a flack in Las Vegas? It's too hot and dry, lights flashing 24/7, glowing in the sunlight, every shabby facade showing its flaws, like all the old prostitutes who dared to bare it all anytime, anyplace.

When he got the job there, my mother said Vegas was no place to raise a child, so I grew up with a part-time dad. I was in middle school, and my mother and I waited for his weekend visits in our house in Westville, a neighborhood with a large Jewish population, New Haven's very small-scale Upper West Side with great delis and a synagogue. My mother grew up there in the house we lived in, a big white behemoth that towered over rose gardens and apple trees.

In high school I started rummaging through desks when no one was home and found old black-and-white pictures of my dad with his arm around strangers in suits, ties, and hats, sitting around the table, cocktails in front of them, cigarettes in unsmiling mouths. One woman in a long, sequined dress, her hair falling into her eyes, her hand on her hip, seemed glamorous, but I wasn't that naive. Dad grew up in New Haven's Little Naples, now called Little Italy for those tourists who may not know where Naples is, over on the other side of the city, which is known as the safest neighborhood because of its "connections." That's where I live now.

My mother endured the long-distance relationship with my dad for several years, but finally divorced him when I went to college.

Technically, I wasn't really his daughter. My mother divorced my biological father when I was two, and he died a couple of years later, some sort of construction accident. Being a reporter, I could look into it, but my curiosity extends only to those things outside my family. Otherwise I just don't want to know.

I shook myself out of my ruminations and gazed longingly at my jeans but pulled on a pair of khakis and a white shirt. The paper was cracking down on the dress code. Too many people coming to work like slobs, the memo said, Fridays were dress-down days. But no jeans, even then.

Too many rules.

I didn't go to the office, but drove straight down Chapel Street. I found a parking spot near the Yale Art Gallery, but only after I'd driven around the block three times. I slipped my press card onto the dashboard, and I walked the rest of the way down to York.

It always amazed me how on one block, the Gothic buildings of Yale towered over the street, but on the next, the neighborhood started getting seedy; thus the barbed wire that surrounded the apartment building where Melissa Peabody had taken her last breath.

The cops were still there, the yellow crime scene tape damp from the rain. Thank God the sun was shining today.

The TV vans were in full force, reporters from the state's three major stations jockeying for the best position in front of the apartment building, cameramen doing a balancing act with the equipment, the satellite dishes high above the telephone wires. I snorted as I wove between them. Where were they this morning, when the real news was going on? And where would they be after this? Waiting for the press conferences to get their handouts from the cops, less than a minute on the air to muster up some sympathy and outrage from the public.

The body was gone, but I could see where it had been. My stomach growled, reminding me I could've grabbed a coffee and a scone at Atticus, no one would've minded. Tom came out of the building, alone. I made my move.

"You're back," he said before I thought he even knew I was there.

"Like a bad penny."

"You have to talk to the chief."

I stared at him. "What?"

"This one's a little too sensitive."

The city police department would get a call from Yale, too, but with a lot more pressure about solving the crime and keeping details out of the press as long as possible.

"Come on, Tom, give me a break. I'll never get anything but a 'no comment' out of the chief."

He shrugged, his big shoulders moving slowly, his hand running through his blond hair. At least I got some sleep. "I'm not supposed to say anything. If I do, and you write about it, then everyone will know I told you."

So we haven't exactly been discreet.

I spotted Dick Whitfield coming toward us on the sidewalk. "If you tell me something, I'll make sure he gets out of your way." It sounded like a good deal to me.

"Oh, shit, he doesn't know what he's doing. He's harmless."

That's what he thought.

"I really can't tell you anything, Annie." I watched him move away from me, but instead of getting mad, I just wanted to jump his bones. Go figure.

I'd just have to use my other sources on this one. But then Dick was next to me.

"They're being pretty tight-lipped today," he said jovially, as if we were equals.

"Why are you here again?"

"Marty said I should help you."

I made a mental note to let Marty have it when I saw him. Marty knows I work alone. Yeah, we'd had the "team player" talk again recently, but I didn't really think it applied to me. The new kids, well, they didn't want my help and I certainly couldn't rely on them. It was a me vs. them situation, but neither side minded. It was only Marty, who somehow thought because of my experience I should be some sort of mentor. He should know better. He's known me a long time.

Dick stood in front of me, salivating. He was hungry, hungrier than others, but he was such a moron. If he chilled out a little, maybe he wouldn't be so bad. I needed to give him another job, get him out of my hair.

"Maybe you can find out whose apartment it is."

I got a blank stare.

"We don't know if it was her apartment or not," I continued, wondering if he was even more stupid than I thought.

A grin swept across his face. "Okay. I'll see what I can find out."

I didn't want him nosing around Yale. I wanted to find out about her first, talk to her friends to see if they knew anything. Sure, I wanted to know who owned that apartment and why she was there, but this way he could pick up half the legwork and I could put it together later.

I mulled this over a little. Having a slave might not be too bad.

The registrar wasn't exactly forthcoming when I asked about Melissa Peabody, what class she was in, where she was from, what dorm she lived in.

"I'm not allowed to give out that information." Her mouth sagged with displeasure, wisps of white curls accentuating her wrinkles. Would I look that old someday? "You have to talk to our public information officer."

I wouldn't get shit out of that guy, and she knew it. The school had closed up tighter than a clam.

My stomach was still growling when I

got back out on the sidewalk. The image in my head of Melissa Peabody's naked body faded as I thought about breakfast at Atticus. It's a small bookstore with a fabulous coffee bar and wonderful muffins and sandwiches. Before I knew it, I was sitting at the counter, nibbling on a blueberry scone, sipping my coffee as if I didn't have a care in the world.

"I can't believe it," I heard from somewhere in my vicinity. "I saw her last night. She seemed fine."

News travels fast, almost as fast as my head turned to see who was talking.

Three kids sat a couple of tables away, their expressions grim. Bingo. I hit the jackpot. Having no respect for anyone's personal space if I could get any information, I picked up my coffee and scone and moved to their table.

"I couldn't help but overhear," I started, "but it sounds like you knew that girl, Melissa, who died last night." I almost said "took a flying leap," but in that split second between saying something entirely inappropriate and the right thing, I chose wisely. I don't always.

I put my coffee down and pulled one of my cards out of my bag. "Anne Seymour. I'm with the *Herald*. I saw her, well, after."

I tried to sound meek, and I think I was pulling it off. They sighed collectively and asked me to pull up a chair.

"Was it really awful?" the girl with the red hair asked. "I mean, well, you know."

Fortunately I knew exactly what she was asking and nodded. "Yeah. It was pretty bad. Since you all knew her, could you tell me something about her? I have to write a story, and I hate having to write the gruesome stuff. If I could describe her, make her real, maybe the cops will really push to find out what happened to her." It was all bullshit. I was surprised they couldn't smell me coming a mile away. They were Yalies, after all. They were supposed to be smarter than me. I went to a state school, majored in beer and pot and Led Zeppelin. I kept *CliffsNotes* in business. Who had time to read?

"She was a sophomore." The red-haired girl obviously was the leader of this group. She wore pretty silver-framed glasses, and her hands were folded neatly on the table. "I knew her from bio. Biology class," she added, obviously knowing I didn't have the SAT scores she did. "She was going to be a doctor." Weren't they all?

I didn't pull out my notebook, but instead turned on the tape recorder in my head. No need to make it formal just yet. I took a sip of coffee and a bite of scone. If I kept my mouth shut, something I'm not known to do on a regular basis, I knew they'd talk. They wanted to.

"She was so pretty," blurted the other girl, a blonde with unfortunate skin. "No wonder David wouldn't leave her alone."

"David?" I prompted.

The red-haired girl fidgeted with a ring on her finger. "Oh, a guy we know. She went out with him for a little while but broke it off. He had a problem accepting that."

The blonde snorted, an ugly, wet sound that made the remnants of my hangover lurch back into my stomach. "A problem accepting that? Are you kidding? He was constantly calling her and trying to see her."

A stalker. I liked that. It could be easy. Girl dates boy. Girl rejects boy. Boy throws girl off balcony. Or something like that.

"It's not what you think." The boy, who sported a pierced eyebrow, finally spoke. He was good-looking in that punk sort of way, spiky hair, brooding eyes. If I was eighteen . . . well, I wasn't.

"What is it then?" I shook myself back to the matter at hand.

"She led him on, even after. She called him sometimes, asked him for help moving furniture, getting notes from a class, help with her lab stuff."

I knew the type. I was that type. Didn't really want him around, but it was nice to have someone paying attention. Okay, so nothing's ever simple.

"You saw her last night? Was David with her?" I gave them a nudge. My coffee was almost gone but I needed more information, and I needed it faster.

I felt a rush of cool air on the back of my neck and turned to see the door closing. He was standing at the counter, hands in his pockets, staring at the writing on the blackboard as if it was Greek. He was a Dunkin' Donuts guy, this caffe latte crap was stumping him. My first impression was that he was a cop, someone I hadn't crossed paths with before, but there was something different about the way he held his shoulders, his back wasn't military-straight and his black hair curled around his ears. He looked like one of my father's henchmen, but better looking, in that Frank Sinatra sort of way, Frank in the '50s, when he was still lean, when he was with Ava.

He saw me staring and actually had the

balls to wink. A real wink. I turned back to my new friends, who didn't seem to notice I'd gone away for a minute or so.

"There was a party," the pierced guy was saying. "We were all pretty trashed. David was there, but she didn't leave with him. I didn't see her leave with anyone."

"What time did she leave?"

He shrugged. "I wasn't paying too much attention."

I squirmed in my chair and glanced out of the corner of my eye back at the counter. He was gone.

None of them noticed what time Melissa left, although they all saw her consume quite a bit of beer. I finally took their names: Randy was the guy, Helen the pretty redhead, and Cynthia the blonde. They told me Melissa had lived at Davenport, one of Yale's residential colleges.

"You might want to talk to Sarah," Cynthia said quietly.

"Sarah?"

"Sarah Lewis. One of her roommates. I know David talked to her a lot."

I thanked my new friends after they told me how to get to Davenport College, left them each one of my cards, and said they could call me anytime if they thought of anything else.

Outside on the sidewalk again, I only felt worse when I saw the parking ticket tucked under my windshield wiper. The cop who left it there completely ignored the "Press" sign in my window.

I walked away, ignoring the ticket. Since I'd already gotten one, why not leave my car there?

Davenport College was just up the street, and I found it easily. A young woman was coming out as I reached the gate.

"I'm looking for Sarah Lewis," I said. "Do you know where I could find her?"

She looked me over and shrugged. "She's not here. I think she might be at the library."

I walked across the wide lawn of Cross Campus and approached Sterling Library. On the pavement in front of the building, students were reminded in pink sidewalk chalk of a party at Saybrook College the night before at 9:00 p.m. I neglected to ask the Atticus group where the party had been where they saw Melissa, but I was willing to bet it was the one at Saybrook.

I couldn't remember the last time I smelled musty books. My boot heels were loud as they hit the hard floor, and I went up to the desk.

"I'm looking for Sarah Lewis," I asked, hoping the librarian had a clue who she was.

She pointed her nose in the direction of the Starr Reading Room. I went through the thick, dark doors and looked left, then right, at tables of students studying. A lone brunette sat at a table to my right in the back, flipping through pages of a book, but she wasn't reading; her eyes were resting on the wall behind me, not seeing anything. I took a shot. I walked over to her. "Sarah?"

She tried to focus, but she seemed incapable.

"Sarah," I tried again, sitting down across from her. "My name is Anne Seymour. I'm a reporter from the *Herald*."

Now she saw me, and a flash of anger whipped across her face. "Can't anyone just leave me alone?"

Intruding on someone's grief is something I've never been able to do well, despite my reputation. "I'm sorry," I tried, but I did not get up.

"I thought no one would find me in here. The police finally let me leave, but they said I couldn't go back to my room until they were done." Her shoulders were hunched in that way tall people do to try to disguise their height, and her hair was matted, a little oily. She wore a big sweat-shirt that just accentuated how flat-chested she was. Her hands were free of jewelry, although there were small hoops in her earlobes. Her watch was a Swatch, oversized and colorful. Her face was drawn, pale, and two green eyes peered at me.

"Were you very close?" I asked.

Sarah managed a small smile. "That's the bitch of it all. I hated her."

"Did you see her last night?" I asked, hoping my face didn't reveal that she had succeeded in surprising me.

"Oh, sure. She was getting ready to go out. To that party."

"The one at Saybrook?"

She nodded.

"Weren't you going?"

Sarah bit her fingernail. "I don't like parties. I don't drink or smoke or do anything like that."

Sounded pretty boring, but the hangover was still occasionally crashing against my brain, reminding me that I should take it easy, too.

"Do you know how she ended up at University Towers if she was just going to that party?"

"She had a late date, after the party.

Maybe whoever it was took her there."

"How do you know that?"

"I took the message."

"What message?" I wanted to start writing this down, but was afraid the notebook would spook her.

"From the agency."

She was being far too cryptic. "What agency?"

Sarah's mouth curved into a small, sinister smile. "Everyone thought she was so wonderful, you know? Smart, pretty, but she did have a secret life no one knew about."

I waited.

She shrugged. "She worked for an escort service. Her parents thought she was spending too much money and stopped sending any except a monthly allowance. Melissa didn't think it was enough, so she answered one of those ads. You know, in the paper."

A million thoughts were running through my head, slamming against the hangover, pushing it out of the way. "Did you tell the cops this?"

Sarah smiled again, wider this time. "I told them she had a late date, but I said I didn't know who with. They didn't ask any more questions about that." She paused for a minute. "Are you going to put this in the newspaper?"

She was a sneaky one. She wanted this in the paper, wanted Melissa's name smeared publicly, to show everyone what her roommate was really like. I wasn't born yesterday.

Sarah's eyes were dancing. I could see she knew how much I wanted this story and that I wouldn't walk away until I had it.

"What agency was it?" I asked, taking the bait. Screw it. No need to pretend with this girl.

Sarah dug into the backpack slung over her chair and pulled out a business card, handing it to me: Come Together. Clever.

"She gave this to me, like a joke or something." I could see Sarah wasn't amused. "You know, she could've had anyone she wanted. She really was a bitch." Her voice was tight, the anger oozing into her words.

I'd had enough of her.

"If you think of anything else that might help, can you call me?" I handed her one of my cards.

She nodded. "Sure."

I got up.

"Have you talked to David Best, her ex-boyfriend?"

"No, not yet."

"He's a head case. After she dumped him, he found out about the escort thing and was really pissed. He started following her around, even once when she was so-called working."

"She told you that?"

Sarah laughed, a small sound from the bottom of her throat. "He told me. He thought I could talk her out of it. Yeah, right. Like anyone could ever talk Melissa out of anything."

Yalies fucking with their lives and the lives of those around them. This would become one helluva made-for-TV movie. I said goodbye and got out of there.

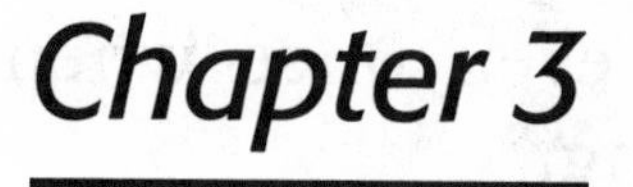

Chapter 3

The newsroom was quiet. Marty was sipping coffee at his desk, the other day editors savoring the calm before the storm.

Henry Owens didn't even notice me as he scanned eBay in his unending search for rare coins. Peter Martone briefly looked up from the *New York Post*, then resumed reading, and Jim Wingate was having a heated discussion with his wife on the phone.

Not a whole lot happened until stories started coming in about four in the afternoon, except if there was breaking news. The day editors did the brunt of their work in about three hours, spending the rest of their time in meetings and on the phone with the reporters in the bureaus, even though I wasn't sure anyone really talked to anyone about anything. Two reporters ended up doing the same stories on occasion because someone "forgot" to tell someone what he was working on.

Watergate and Woodward and Bernstein had lured me into this business. But the industry wasn't like that anymore, no one took the risks. Melissa Peabody was definitely a risk, a dead Yalie on the front page.

"Whatchagot?" Marty put his coffee down on top of the weekend rotation schedule. He was too tall for his desk and complained bitterly about neck pain, popping Advils all day. His glasses balanced precariously on the end of his nose. I always fought the urge to stick my finger on the center and push them up.

Marty Thompson came from the competition in Bridgeport about a year after I'd started at the paper. In those days, we stole their people and they stole ours, always for more money, and the people were always quality. From the first day he arrived, we had a good relationship. He respected me professionally, and after a required grace period, I respected him. His news judgment was solid, his editing good enough so I never knew where my words left off and his began. But it was starting to wear on him, too, the corporate mentality that profits were more important than anything, even the news. Unfortunately for him, he was just past that age where places would look at him as a viable candidate.

I ran through the interviews with the kids at Atticus, purposely leaving Sarah until the end. Marty's eyes grew wider when I told him about Come Together.

"Shiiiiiit," he drawled. "Can we confirm that?"

"The roommate told me."

"We're going to need more."

I hated it when he sat on stuff just because he didn't think the publisher would like it. "The roommate confirmed it," I tried again.

"No, we need another source."

"Why?"

His blue eyes got darker. "Think about it, Annie."

I hated this shit. "I'll get on the phone."

"Good. Dick's gone to the press conference."

"What press conference?"

"The one the cops are having as we speak."

I took a deep breath. "Why didn't you call me?"

"Because Dick was here and you weren't. I figured you had a good reason not to be."

I counted to ten. The editors all thought

we were out screwing around if we weren't in the office. I constantly argued that I couldn't get a story while sitting at my desk, but it fell on deaf ears. Dick somehow managed to be in more than he was out and still get stories. Dumb luck. I could see the byline now. "By Dick Whitfield and Anne Seymour." Was this worth the aggravation?

"Okay," I conceded and made my way to my desk. I booted up my computer and zoned out for the few minutes it took to log on. Clicking on the Internet icon, I waited again, until I got the page with the message that the server couldn't be found.

"What's up with the Internet?" I called over to Marty.

He shook his head. "Tech guys are working on it."

This wasn't new. I'd have to go the old-fashioned route to find Come Together.

A 1999 phone book was holding up my press release basket, and I pulled it out. No Come Together in 1999. I got up and wandered the newsroom, glancing at all of the outdated phone books. Finally I found one for 2002 under someone's computer monitor. It was the closest I could get. I just hoped Come Together had been in business then. I yanked it out, the monitor teetering, then steadying. If we had proper workstations, but don't get me started.

Come Together had a display ad in the Yellow Pages. "The Most Beautiful Girls in the World Good Conversation A Lot of Fun." No street address, just a phone number. Seemed harmless enough until you read between the lines. I picked up the phone.

"Come Together." The woman's voice was breathless, seductive. It was too much.

"I'd like to set up a date." Seemed like a good idea at the moment. How else was I going to infiltrate their world?

"Oh, well, okay." The breathless voice suddenly came up for air.

"Is there a problem?"

"Well, we only have female escorts."

Oh, great. Now I had to be a lesbian. There was no other way. "I prefer that."

A moment of silence, then, "We do have one girl who might fit your needs. What type of function will you be attending?"

I ignored the question and moved in for the kill. "Actually, I'd heard about someone from a friend. Is it possible to ask for someone specifically?" This was way too weird. I was giving myself the creeps.

"Who was that?"

"Melissa Peabody."

"She's not the one I was thinking of. Are you sure?"

"Yes. Perhaps there's someone in charge I can speak to." It was time to stop the charade, I had my answer.

"I'm sorry, but all appointments are made through me."

"Then are you in charge?"

A small, nervous laugh assured me she wasn't. "I don't know what the problem is."

"The problem is that Melissa Peabody is dead."

I thought I detected a silent scream, but I could be wrong. "Who is this?"

"My name is Anne Seymour, with the *Herald.* Is there someone I can talk to there about Melissa Peabody? I'm writing a story about her. She died early this morning. Apparently she had an appointment with one of your clients last night, and he may have been the last person to see her alive." I didn't say he could've pushed her off that balcony, but that was the general idea.

"I'll have to have someone call you back."

I gave her my number at the paper as well as my cell number. "You know, if no one calls me, I'll keep calling. You won't get rid of me." It was a good threat, and not an empty one.

"You'll hear from us," she promised before she hung up.

I glanced over at Marty and saw him looking at me. I gave him the thumbs-up. "I think we got it."

He nodded, a pained expression crossing his face. I was glad I didn't have his job.

The phone rang.

"Anne Seymour."

"Ms. Seymour, this is Hickey Watson of Come Together." The voice matched the name perfectly, a little twangy, a little whiny, a lot nervous.

"Thank you for getting back to me so quickly. I need some information about Melissa Peabody."

"I can't divulge clients' names, I'll say that right off."

"Even if it means it would screw up a police investigation?"

"Especially then."

It was worth a try. "Okay. But you can confirm that Miss Peabody had an appointment with one of your clients last night?"

"Uh, well, yes, I guess I can."

"What is your exact title at the company?"

"I run the place."

"So I can say you're the owner?"

"My name's going to be in the paper?" He was more nervous now, and I prayed he wouldn't say the words every reporter dreaded. "Can this be off the record?" He did it, he said them.

"I'm sorry, Mr. Watson, but what you said about Melissa Peabody being an employee was on the record. Anything you say now will be off the record, I assure you."

"You're certain of that?"

"I give you my word." I waited, hoping he'd say more, not sure if the conversation was over.

"The cops'll want that client's name, won't they?" he asked.

"When they find out she had a date last night, yes. They'll probably get a court order to make you tell them." I wanted to scare him into telling me first. "And it could be made public, so everyone would know. Especially if they make an arrest."

Dick waltzed past my desk with a big shit-eating grin on his face. I scowled at him, sensing I was losing Hickey Watson.

"They can just try," he spit in my ear and hung up, the dial tone reverberating through my brain. The good news was that it seemed my hangover was finally gone.

Dick was bending Marty's ear but good, and I couldn't pretend nonchalance. I strolled over to Marty's desk.

"The apartment is rented by the McGee Corporation," Dick was saying.

"What the hell is that?" I asked. Marty glared at me.

"I don't know," Dick said, "but I'm going to find out." He couldn't find his way out of a paper bag, but I held my tongue.

"Do the cops know anything more about what happened last night?" Even though I missed the press conference, I could answer that question myself. If they knew something, they certainly wouldn't tell anyone yet.

Dick was shaking his head. "They're still investigating."

The pat answer when the cops wanted to keep us at bay. I wondered if this mysterious client of Hickey Watson's was some muckety-muck at this mysterious McGee Corporation.

"What's our next step?" Dick was asking Marty, who looked from him to me and back again. I wasn't sure I liked what I saw in his eyes.

"Annie's found out that Melissa Peabody

worked for an escort service," he told Dick.

"No shit!"

"I think we need to find out as much as we can about this McGee company, since she fell from their balcony."

I held up a finger. "She had a late appointment last night."

"All the more reason to check out McGee." Marty looked at the floor, and I knew he was thinking. When he looked back up at me, his eyes were apologetic. "Dick should get on this McGee thing. Annie, we're going to need this stuff written up. Dick can type his notes into the system before he checks out McGee, and you can start putting this together."

My head was telling me that I got this particular assignment because I could actually write, unlike Dick, whose sentences were atrocities lamented every night by the copy editors. But my gut felt like I'd been hit with a brick. "Okay," I said quietly.

Dick bounced off to his desk like the puppy he was, and I sighed so loud Marty chuckled. "Don't be a prima donna, Annie. I know you're the better reporter, but you have to admit you can't be in two places at once and this is too big for just one reporter."

"I know." I did know it, I just didn't like it.

"You know, you might want to call Tom, touch base, see if you can find out anything, even off the record, we could work with."

I didn't like it that he suggested what I'd been thinking. We'd worked together too long, we could almost read each other's minds. Almost.

Dick typed his notes in pretty quickly, so I was able to throw something together in no time. I didn't want to call Tom: he wouldn't get the message or he wouldn't tell me anything over the phone. I had to go back to the scene. I knew I'd find him there.

The TV vans were gone, and the cops had dispersed, leaving bits of yellow tape on the street. Forensics had gotten all they could, and now passersby could come and go freely. Even with a high-profile crime, the cops had to clear out as soon as they could on a city street. As I pulled the door to the apartment building open, I saw movement out of the corner of my eye, something that made me turn.

It was the coffee guy, the one I'd seen in Atticus, the Frank Sinatra look-alike. He was coming toward me, his face unreadable. For a moment I thought he was going to stop and say something, but he sped up and moved past without a word, or a wink this time.

I made my way up in the elevator again; I didn't run into anyone I would have to mislead. The door to the apartment was ajar, and I pushed it open.

Tom was rubbing his forehead. He had a headache, on top of getting no sleep. I moved closer.

"You doing okay?" I asked quietly.

He jumped, his eyebrows coming together in a frown. "Dammit, Annie, you scared the shit out of me."

I shrugged. I had that effect on a lot of people.

"How's it going?"

He shook his head. "Who the hell knows. This one's got everyone stumped."

"I might have some information you'll be interested in," I said, not wanting to beat around the bush, hoping if I told him about Come Together and Hickey Watson that he'd reciprocate and tell me what wasn't said at the press conference.

When I was done, Tom sighed. "Oh, shit," he said quietly.

"My sentiments exactly," I said.

"You're not going to print that, are you?"

I stared at him. "Of course I am. Why wouldn't I?"

"It could really screw things up for us."

"It's a good story. And I got it without any effort."

"What about the ex-boyfriend? David what's-his-name, Best? Did you talk to him yet?"

I didn't even know how to find the guy, but I wasn't going to tell him that. "No. Not yet. He's next on my list." Something in Tom's face made me stop. "Hey, you did, didn't you?"

"He's been questioned, yes." I hated it when he got evasive.

"And?"

"And what?"

I should never have slept with a cop. Even though I consciously didn't do it to get information, as many of my colleagues believed, there may have been that tiny part of my brain that thought I would, maybe, get a tiny bit more information than the average reporter. But cops are always cops, on the street and in bed. This one did have a way with his hands that made me wild, made me forget momentarily we were on opposite sides of the story even though ultimately we both were after the truth.

"Is he a suspect?" I had to spell it out for him.

Tom's eyes narrowed, and I could see the wheels in his head churning: Do I tell her, do I not tell her? Finally, "He can be considered a suspect, yes, but this new information could change things."

"That's not off the record, is it?"

"Oh, Christ, Annie, do what you want with it. But I just hope that if you keep finding out stuff you'll let us know so we can put a lid on this one. There's way too much heat from the school, from the mayor's office. And now, with this escort service shit, well, let's just say you've made my job that much harder."

I wanted to put my arms around him, but he looked so damn sexy, his tie askew, his collar open enough to reveal a tiny tuft of chest hair, that I had to keep my distance. This certainly wasn't the time or the place.

"I thought you'd want to know before it was in the paper."

He sighed again. "Yeah, that would've been really embarrassing."

"The apartment is rented by the McGee Corporation. What's that?"

"I don't know. The address is a post office box in New York City. We can't seem to find a phone number."

He was tired, that's why he was telling me this. He wasn't on his toes, he wasn't up to playing the game. I had to get everything I could out of him before he stopped himself.

"A dummy corporation?" I suggested.

"Maybe. I don't know. They've rented the place for two years. Does it look lived in?"

I glanced around and saw the spare rooms again. "No."

Tom moved closer to me. "That's all I can give you. Really."

I nodded. "Sure. I understand. But if I have something, I have to tell you, right?"

"Give me a break." His voice was rough, and I backed off. It wasn't the time or the place for that, either.

I started to back out the door, then stopped. "Just one thing, though. Since her ex-boyfriend's a suspect, you think she was murdered and didn't just off herself?"

"Off the record?"

"The readers will draw their own conclusions."

"You can't use this," he said again, and I nodded.

"Okay."

"She was dead before she went over the balcony."

Chapter 4

Melissa Peabody died from a blunt force trauma to the back of the head. Tom said there was blood on the balcony, and the injury wasn't consistent with the fall.

"So whoever did this then dumped the body over the balcony?" I asked.

Tom shrugged. "There are a lot of sickos out there." But I could see he was stumped, too, as to why someone would do that.

It was irritating me that I couldn't include the cause of death in the story, but I'd promised Tom. As a reporter, I couldn't go back on my word or I'd never get anyone to tell me anything ever again.

Back at the office, I tried to get someone to tell me on the record, but no one returned my calls.

The streets were deserted when I finally climbed into my 1993 Honda Accord and made my way home in the dark. I parked near my brownstone on Wooster Square and instead of going right up, turned toward the smell of pizza. Sally's was still open, and I wanted a small white clam pie. It had been a long day, I'd missed lunch, Dick was getting top billing on the byline as I'd suspected, and Tom had disappeared.

The picture of Frank Sinatra on the wall at Sally's stared down at me as I moved toward the counter. Flo was bustling around but took the time to say hello as I gave my order to her son.

"Takeout?"

I nodded.

"Be a few minutes."

I was willing to wait for the best pizza anywhere. Most people did. Sally's opened at 5:00 p.m. every day, except Mondays, and it's rare not to have to stand in the long line that snakes down the sidewalk, people salivating for the crispy thin crust and savory sauce. Pepe's, just up the street, boasts similar lines, but I have to be honest. I've never eaten there. In New Haven, you ask, "Sally's or Pepe's?" and people always have an allegiance to one or the other.

We've got a lot of new reporters and copy editors who've moved here from other places and they don't want to wait in the lines, so they never experience either. I actually saw a Domino's delivery one night. New Haven was where pizza was born, or at least that's what they say, and some idiot's getting chain pizza.

Someone was peering through the front window as I sat sideways in the last booth waiting for my pizza, and when I squinted, I could make out familiar features. It was that guy again, the winking guy. He looked like he wanted to come in, but when he saw me looking, he turned and disappeared. I glanced at the kitchen. It would probably be a few minutes before my pie was ready. I went outside.

He was moving down the sidewalk at a fast clip and turned into Libby's, probably for cookies and a cappuccino if he had any sense. Flo knocked on the window. I went back inside.

"Thanks," I said as I took the box, glaring at the Sinatra portrait as if it had something to do with the mystery man.

He wasn't there. In Libby's, I mean. I risked getting my clam pizza cold so I could check it out. I shrugged and walked back to my building.

As I put my key in the lock, the phone began to ring. I rushed inside; it was probably a copy editor with a question about the story. I hadn't hung around while anyone read it, I was too tired and said I'd be home within a half hour.

"Hello."

"So you're home." It was my mother. No, oh, hello, dear, how are you doing? It was going to be a guilt trip about something, something I probably either didn't do or didn't remember. I brought the phone over to the refrigerator and reached in for a beer. Nothing like a beer with clam pizza topped with guilt. Maybe I should get caller ID.

"It's been a long day," I tried, knowing it wasn't going to work.

"I've been trying to reach you for days."

"I've been really busy at work. And it's going to be really busy for a while. You heard about the Yalie?" I took a bite of pizza, although I couldn't truly enjoy it as I'd hoped.

"Oh, the poor girl. Yes, of course I heard. It's all over the firm. Her parents called us, you know."

My mother went back to school after she divorced my father and became a lawyer. A good one. One of the best attorneys in the city, one who always managed to win her cases. And one who always managed to catch me off guard.

"What?"

"The family of that poor girl. They want to sue Yale. But you can't print that, it's just a mother telling a daughter something in confidence."

Bullshit. It was a savvy attorney giving her reporter daughter a big fucking tip that had to be off the record. It pissed me off.

"Don't get upset, dear. Nothing's in stone yet."

But just the fact that they called . . . I had no chance in hell of getting this until everyone else did. A useless cop for a boyfriend, a useless mother. What more did a girl need?

The pizza was growing cold. "What did you want?"

"When?" She was smart but could be fairly obtuse at times.

"Why were you trying to reach me?"

"Oh, yes, that. I'm having a dinner party Saturday night and would love it if you came."

One of my mother's dinner parties was the last thing I needed right now. "I'm going to be working on this story, probably all weekend."

"Which is why you need a break, something fun to get your mind off it for a few hours." She always had an answer.

I wanted to tell her I didn't want to go. But that would have been unacceptable. I thought about the black dress I'd worn the night before. Was it just last night? At least I had something to wear. "What time?" I was too tired to argue, too tired to try to come up with another excuse, even though I knew the evening would hardly be "fun."

"Eight o'clock." I could hear her smile, thrilled with yet another success. "Someone's going to be there I want you to meet."

Oh, God, it was another man. There had been many of them the last few years, lined up at these parties, dressed-up, good-looking men who were smart, funny, could make good conversation. I hated them all, plastic versions of each other, all run off the Ken assembly line. I wasn't Barbie, and I wasn't about to get sucked in by my mother's feeble matchmaking attempts.

"You know I'm seeing Tom." She had never met Tom and didn't consider him a viable catch. She kept telling me if he was going to marry me, he would have already asked. I didn't tell her I didn't need to get married. I enjoy living alone. I make my own hours, I don't have to think about anyone but myself; it's not a bad gig. I was old enough to be so set in my ways that if I did meet someone I wanted to cohabitate with, it would be more annoying than anything else.

"Do me this favor, please, Anne?" I knew she was serious when she didn't call me "Annie." "It will be a lovely evening, and you don't have enough of those."

How did she know? I fought back the urge to say something snide. Too bad I couldn't do that when I was talking to Marty about Dick.

"Okay, okay. I'll see you then."

I hung up and turned back to my pizza. It was only moderately cold and still damned good, with a lot of garlic. It was probably a good thing Tom wasn't coming over, he wouldn't be able to stand the smell of me.

The paper screamed death the next morning on the doorstep. I scanned the story, everything was in order, no editor had screwed anything up. I hate it when that happens. My eyes rested on Melissa's picture. I hadn't seen it, Dick had gotten it somehow, I hadn't even asked. She was pretty, very pretty. I could see how the girl at Atticus would have envied her. Long, sweeping dark hair pulled away from her face to accentuate bright eyes, straight nose, wide mouth that sported straight white teeth. Her neck was long, swanlike, like Audrey Hepburn in *Sabrina.*

I rubbed my own short neck absently as I put the paper down. Having a face to go with the name was important, but it made my job harder. I was going to have to ask the questions no one wanted to hear about a lovely young woman who had a secret life.

While I ate my bowl of Cheerios, I thought about what I needed to do to follow up. The McGee Corporation was first and foremost. I had to find out what that was, who the guy was Melissa saw that night, and what had gone so wrong. I also needed to get it on the record how she really died.

Tom's revelation about Melissa's death was only preliminary; the autopsy was scheduled for this afternoon and the cause of death would be made official in the medical examiner's report.

I shuddered, thinking about the autopsy. When I die, I don't want some doctor sawing into my body, taking me apart. I only hope I go naturally, when I'm very old and senile enough not to have any sense of what's happening.

I took another look at Melissa's picture. The indignity of what they were going to do to her body was second only to the indignity someone had already wrought. I could only hope that she fought, fought hard, and managed to break some skin.

Dick was sitting at my desk when I got in. I scowled at him. "What are you doing?"

"My terminal crashed."

"So reboot."

"No, it really crashed. The hard drive went."

Our computers were several years old, the software not much newer. We played musical chairs as keyboards, monitors, and hard drives were replaced. This was the first time someone landed in my space, and just my luck, it was Dickie Boy.

"Just because we're working on this story together doesn't mean you can sit at my desk," I snapped, maybe a little too harshly, but he didn't seem to notice.

"I talked to New York about the McGee Corporation."

When, I wanted to ask. I had barely had enough time for my cereal this morning, and we had both worked late last night. Maybe Dick had more hours in the day than the rest of us. Or maybe had less of a life. No, that couldn't be it. No one had less of a life than me.

"I have a friend in Albany," he continued, and that answered my question. Good to have friends in convenient places. Maybe Dick wasn't going to turn out to be so bad. Not.

"Anyway," he continued when I just stood there, staring at him, "it's on file with the state but very vague about what it actually is. But I did get an address that's not just a post office box. It's at Fifty-seventh and Lexington."

"Who's the CEO?" I tossed my bag on my desk, wondering if he'd ever get up.

"Listed as Mark Torrey."

Where had I heard that name before? Before I could access the recesses of my brain, I heard Dick's voice.

"Doesn't the city have an assistant corporation counsel by that name?" Dick's memory was obviously better than mine, but he didn't seem to see the implication in what he'd just said.

"But it can't be the same one," he said, still not getting it.

My brain was racing. Mark Torrey had been with the city for the past four years, if I was remembering right. I'd met him at one of my mother's dinners, maybe a year ago. The only reason it stuck in my head was because he wasn't hard to notice as he worked the room. He turned his charm on the people with power like my mother and her partners but ignored me and the obvious underlings. My mother thought he was a real up-and-comer.

"No address listed for him?" I asked, already knowing the answer.

"Just the corporation address."

"What was so vague about the company?"

Dick finally pulled out a notebook and thumbed through his notes. "It's some sort of financial investment company, I'm not really up on that kind of stuff."

"Like a Merrill Lynch, but smaller?"

"Much smaller."

"Do they have a board of directors listing?"

Dick shook his head. "I didn't get that. I didn't think to ask."

"Any phone number?"

"No."

How could a financial investment company not have a phone number? How would they make money that way?

I wanted to go to City Hall and see Mark Torrey. It would be the only way to nip this one in the bud. Maybe it wasn't the same guy. But I wanted to ask him face-to-face, see his reaction, before I made any speculation.

I grabbed my bag off the desk. "See you," I called as I left Dick sitting at my desk. He didn't try to come after me, which is what I would've done; he just sat there staring at me, which proved my point about him.

I couldn't find a parking spot. City Hall towers over the expansive Green, and it's crowded all day. After going around the block a couple of times, which took about ten minutes because of the lights, I finally found a spot on Elm Street and walked over to Church. The big thick doors opened into the lobby and I found my way to the corporation counsel's office.

"Mark Torrey?" I asked a young woman in an ill-fitting beige suit.

She cocked her head, pushed back a loose hair on her cheek. "Not here."

"When will he be back?"

"Not sure. He had a death in the family in California. He called yesterday morning from the airport. He'll probably be gone at least into next week."

Yeah, right. I had a feeling it might not be a coincidence.

"May I help you with something?" she asked.

"No thanks. It's personal."

She gave me a look that made me wonder whether I was too old for Mark Torrey. I decided to ignore it. "Thanks," I said again and turned around.

I walked to Willoughby's for a coffee, sorting it out in my head. I had a nagging feeling about this. Just as I was about to go into the café, I saw him again. The Frank Sinatra look-alike. He was across the street, leaning against the brick building on the corner, watching me. I deliberately stopped and stared at him. A smile broke across his face, he straightened up and waved. Waved. Like he knew me.

I started across the street, but there were too many cars, and as I was looking both ways, he disappeared.

Who the hell was he? This was getting way too creepy. Maybe he was a cop, but why would he be where I was instead of doing his job? No, he wasn't a cop. I knew that the first time I saw him in Atticus. I went into Willoughby's. He wasn't going to ruin a perfectly good coffee experience for me. But I kept looking over my shoulder, expecting to see him. He wasn't there.

"Did you see the *Times*?" Renee flung the paper at me when I got back to the office, knowing full well I hadn't seen it yet. Renee Chittenden has been at the *Herald* almost as long as I have. She's our only "general assignment" reporter. The social service agencies were always trying to get her to publicize their causes, and she could put a human face on any story. Her news judgment was solid.

I scanned the *New York Times*'s story about Melissa Peabody. Everything we had. What was the big deal?

"See the byline?"

Richard Wells. Another Dick. Okay, so he moved from the *Hartford Courant* to the *Times.* That wasn't any surprise, either. He'd covered a lot of big shit for the *Courant.* I'd never met him, but I heard a lot of stories. Not all of them good. He was rumored to be arrogant and sometimes his way of getting the story wasn't entirely kosher. I'd heard he slept with the mayor's assistant in Hartford to get a story once.

"He's an asshole." I put the paper down, determined not to get upset by this. Even though we had our share of TV reporters, I didn't consider them competition. Neither the Bridgeport nor the Hartford papers covered New Haven on a regular basis, if at all. I enjoyed a fairly competition-free zone, but if this *Times* reporter got a bee in his bonnet over Melissa Peabody, then it meant I had to be more on my toes than usual.

"What's going on with this McGee Corporation?" Marty was suddenly next to my desk, sneaking up on me again. Renee slid back to her own seat.

"Can't seem to get a handle on it, although Dick got an address."

"Yeah, he told me. What about Torrey?"

"In California, allegedly. A death in the family."

Marty scratched his chin in that way he does when he's not happy with how things were turning out. Another meeting with the publisher, another lambasting, another edict about what we could say in a headline or where it would have to be played. Another stake in the heart of journalism.

"We need to get a handle on this story. The cows are coming, and we're all going to have some extra stuff to do," he said.

My expression must have been as blank as my brain, because he added, "You know, the CowParade."

The memo about it was somewhere on my desk, but I hadn't read it yet. I didn't have time for cows anyway, I had to find out about McGee. I have a friend who works for the *Daily News.* She could check out McGee's address on her lunch break, I hoped. "I'll see what I can get on McGee," I told Marty, picking up the phone.

Priscilla Quinn was my best friend from high school, the only person worth keeping up with once we graduated. She was more of a workaholic than I was. I spend at least one weekend every couple of months in the city with her, and we stay up late drinking wine, dissecting the failed relationships we'd had. When we're thoroughly depressed, we sleep and then get up to go shopping. Sure, it's a cliché, but I always feel great when I get back.

"Quinn."

"Seymour," I said. "I need a favor."

"Shoot."

I could hear rapid typing in the background. "McGee Corporation. Fifty-seventh and Lexington. No phone, but I need to know what it is. Could you take a walk sometime in the next few hours and get back to me?"

"No phone?" I could hear the curiosity as the typing ceased. Few things can make her stop working.

"Some sort of small investment firm."

"No phone?" she repeated. This was a woman who had a phone in her bathroom. "What's up?"

"The Yalie who was found dead yesterday. May be some connection." She was my best friend, but I was unwilling to say more. She was a journalist, too.

"Right-o. I'll call you this afternoon." She hung up without saying goodbye. She never said goodbye.

I didn't know whether Tom was in the office, so I called him on his cell phone.

"Hello?" His voice was muffled.

"Anything new?"

"Annie, you know you shouldn't use this number." I could hear the unspoken words "when I'm working."

I didn't give a shit, and he knew it, but he wanted to give me a hard time anyway. That was the kind of relationship we'd nurtured.

"Anything new?" I asked again.

"Press conference at one. At City Hall." He hung up.

They must have pushed up the autopsy. The medical examiner's office wouldn't give me any information at all, referred me to the New Haven police department. I was making too many phone calls and not getting any real information.

I threw my bag over my shoulder and started walking out.

"Where are you going?" Dick caught up

to me in the hall.

"Tell Marty I'm going to the press conference. I have something I need to do now."

"But I thought I went to press conferences." He started whining, which did not endear him to me.

"You went to the one yesterday. Now it's my turn." That seemed to be a satisfactory answer for him, because he started walking away.

I got out of there before anyone could stop me.

Chapter 5

I found Sarah Lewis in the library again and sat down without being invited.

"Hey," I said.

She scowled at me. She might be pretty if she was more cheerful, but we can't ask too much of some people.

"David, Melissa's ex-boyfriend. How can I find him?"

"Oh, go bother someone else. I'm tired of you reporters."

That's right. Richard Wells had talked to her, too, I'd seen in the *Times*. "You also talked to that guy from the *New York Times*."

"At least he bought me a cup of tea."

I looked around. He must not have found her in the library.

I tried again. "I need to talk to David. Do you know where he is?"

Sarah sighed, a long-drawn-out sound that I thought only my mother had perfected. "His parents are here."

Great. And they probably had a good lawyer baby-sitting him, too, since the cops were looking at him. I didn't have a chance in hell, but I had to try. "So you don't know where they are?"

She shrugged. "You could try his college. He's at Saybrook."

I wasn't sure where it was, so she directed me, grudgingly. It wasn't too far, and the sky was bright, the air was comfortable, and I actually started to feel revitalized. Unfortunately, if I got too revitalized, I'd get frisky and I'd have to call Tom. At work.

As I got near the building, I saw a familiar figure in front, and I pulled back so he wouldn't see me. The winking guy, twice in one day, in the morning, no less. Maybe it was Richard Wells. Could be. He seemed to be hitting up all the major players and spots, too. But why would he watch me last night at Sally's? I wasn't the story, I was just an observer. Maybe it wasn't Richard Wells. Then who could it be?

I watched him turn the corner and he was gone. I quickly made my way across the street. A young man wearing chinos and a polo shirt was coming out of the gate as I pushed my way in, making eye contact to get his attention.

"David Best?"

He pointed across the courtyard at a stone building. "Second floor."

It wasn't hard finding the room. The door was wide open. The attorney, it had to be the attorney, was pacing in the small room. A fireplace was stuck to one wall, and two bedrooms shot off to the side. A couple a little older than me were perched on the edge of the couch across from the fireplace. I figured the young man with his back to me, looking out the window, was David.

I knocked on the door frame, and they all looked up as if they were expecting me.

The lawyer frowned. "Yes?"

"I'm Anne Seymour, with the *Herald.*" The lawyer ignored my outstretched hand, and I pulled it back. "I was wondering if you wanted to make a statement." I directed my question at the young man, who still had his back to his entourage.

"No comment," the lawyer said. "Now get out of here."

"But he must have a comment about Melissa. He was her boyfriend." I wondered how far I could push this before getting physically thrown out.

The young man turned then. He had circles under his eyes, and his hair was disheveled. It looked as if he hadn't slept in days, kind of the way I'd looked yesterday.

"I want to say something," he said, a low rumble coming from the back of his throat.

The lawyer shook his head. "David, you shouldn't say anything."

"For Christ's sake, I loved her," David said harshly. "I want everyone to know I couldn't hurt her, I loved her." I could hear the pain in his voice, but there was something in his eyes, something that didn't quite add up to this professed grief.

"David, honey," his mother started, but the lawyer held up his hand to silence her.

"Did you know she was working for the escort service?" I asked, knowing full well he did, but wanting to hear his response.

He rolled his shoulders back as if he had a crick in his neck. "Yeah, I knew."

"I'm advising you as your attorney not to say any more."

David and I both glared at him.

"Did you know who she was meeting that night?" I asked David as if we were the only two people in the room.

"Don't talk to her," his father advised, but lucky for me David wasn't listening.

"No. I saw her at the party, then she left.

I was pretty drunk, I stayed until about two-thirty, then came back here."

"I heard you had a fight."

Something crossed his face, but it came and went so fast I couldn't read it. "Yeah, we fought a lot. There's a lot of pressure, you know, it's tough sometimes."

The parents exchanged a look that wasn't hard to notice. "How are your grades?" I asked.

He shrugged again. "I dunno. Medium. I guess I could be doing better."

"How was Melissa doing in school?"

His face changed again, and the smile he was trying for didn't quite come off. "Oh, she was doing fine. She's, she was, I mean, one of those people who didn't have to study too much to get good grades."

"Why did she break up with you?" Throw him a curveball, see if he hits it.

His eyes grew dark. "She said she had to concentrate more on school, but that was a lot of bullshit. She was getting into that job, big-time."

"Now I have to ask you to leave. I won't allow him to talk to you anymore." The lawyer took my arm and started leading me out. "If you have any more questions, call my office." He handed me a card. I glanced at it. Bill Smythe, attorney at law.

"Thank you for your time, David," I said over my shoulder. When Smythe and I were in the hall, I asked, "There was a guy in here earlier, tall, dark hair, Italian-looking. Who was he?"

Smythe looked startled, then recovered. "I don't know what you're talking about."

He knew damned well who that guy was and he wasn't talking. If it was Richard Wells, he was making sure I didn't find out his angle. I was soon outside the building, wondering just exactly how I could get more information about David Best, when my cell phone rang. I dug in my bag until I found it. "Hello?"

"Hey, girl." Priscilla didn't waste any time. "I found that place."

"McGee?"

"It's a fucking Gap."

"What?"

"It's a Gap store. No kidding."

I stopped walking in the middle of the sidewalk and some guy crashed into me. He glared at me. "Sorry," I muttered. "What about upstairs? Anything upstairs?" I asked Priscilla.

"I checked it out. Lawyers, doctors. No McGee."

What the hell was going on? They had an apartment in New Haven but no office in New York, where they supposedly did business. "Jesus," I said softly.

"Gotta run. Let me know what's up, you've got me curious now."

I put the phone back in my purse and wandered aimlessly, trying to put the pieces together, but nothing fit. I found myself back at University Towers, staring up at the balcony.

"Come back to the scene of the crime?" Tom's voice pierced my thoughts and I stared at him.

"Do you know?" I asked.

"Know what?"

"About the McGee Corporation?"

"It's a Gap store." He knew and he didn't tell me. Figures. "How'd you find out?"

"Priscilla."

He chuckled. "It helps to have friends in convenient places."

"So what's the story?"

He shook his head. "Beats the hell out of me."

"What about rent checks?"

"They've got the post office box on them, and the rent's paid in full and on time every month. Landlord says Mark Torrey, representing McGee, checked out. Why would he double-check the checks when the guy renting the place works for the city?"

So it was the city's Mark Torrey after all.

"Have you talked to Torrey yet?" I asked.

Tom shook his head. "They say he's in California. We're checking that out."

These things usually were so damned neat. Maybe it really was the ex-boyfriend, but then what was this all about? A mysterious corporation, a missing city lawyer. This opened up a whole new can of worms regardless of the murder.

"Press conference in half an hour," Tom said. "I've got to be there. You going?"

I nodded. "Yeah. Medical examiner's report?"

"The whole case is going to break wide open once they find out how she died. Chief thinks if there's a big show, then Yale and the city won't freak as much."

"I talked to David Best."

He stared at me, his blue eyes dark. "How?"

"He wanted to talk. His lawyer said no, but he said some stuff."

"He loved her, right?" Tom was skeptical of everyone and everything.

"Maybe he did."

"That's the best reason to kill a girlfriend who's a hooker."

Point taken. Tom touched my arm, and it shook me out of my confusion. I touched his hand, and he winked. It reminded me of something.

"Hey, there's some guy wandering around who seems to be everywhere I am. Italian, good-looking, in that Frank Sinatra sort of way. Have you seen him?"

"He's following you?" Tom frowned.

"It's just that he always seems to be in the same places I am. I've seen him a lot the past couple of days."

Tom's forehead wrinkled in that way it does when he's worried about something or thinking. "Next time you see him, call me, okay?"

He seemed so concerned that I didn't have the heart to tell him this guy was here one minute, gone the next, so it probably wouldn't do any good.

"Time to get crucified," he said abruptly. "See you there."

I'd forgotten to ask him what he was doing at University Towers, and when I remembered, he was waving at me from the window of his car. He probably was here for the same reason I was: to get some sort of psychic message about who had done such a thing to this girl. I stared up at the balconies and shuddered.

* * *

It was a zoo. Reporters crammed into the conference room, TV cameras pointed at the empty podium, microphones were being hooked up. Like they were really covering the story. Next time I'd see all these guys would be at the funeral.

"You're here." Dick Whitfield always showed up in the wrong places at the wrong times.

"I said I'd be, didn't I?" I snapped, pissed that he would even think I wouldn't show up. "What're you doing here?"

"No one heard from you all morning."

"I've been working. I have to leave the office to do that."

Fortunately the police chief arrived at that moment, before I could say anything else. I had to get a grip on myself. I couldn't spend good energy arguing with Dick Whitfield. He wasn't worth it.

Tom walked in behind the chief as the primary investigator on the case. I think he saw me, but he didn't show it.

They ran through the information I already had, and when they came to the medical examiner's report, everyone froze. Until then, it had been fairly civilized. Everyone started shouting questions at the same time.

"Has anyone been charged yet?"

"What about David Best? Is he going to be charged?"

"Are there any other suspects?"

"Was she sexually assaulted?"

The last question was shouted from the back of the room, a deep baritone bouncing off the wall behind Tom. We all waited.

The chief shook his head. "No."

"But had she had sex before she died?"

It was the question we all wanted to know the answer to. I craned my neck to see who was asking the right things.

The chief took a deep breath. "Yes." He put his hand up. "I'm afraid that's all we have time for." He ducked out through a back door, Tom not far behind. They left a roomful of hungry reporters very unsatisfied.

"Who was that?" I whispered to the Channel 30 reporter next to me.

"The guy from the *Times*, Richard Wells. Asshole," he added before he turned back to his cameraman.

I wondered if I was as beloved as Richard Wells. I wanted to think I at least had the respect of my peers.

I pushed my way through the crowd and into the hall with Dick hot on my trail. "Where are you going now?" he asked.

I successfully suppressed an urge to say something really out of line. "Have you ever met Richard Wells?" I asked him instead.

"Sure. That's him over there." Dick pointed and I felt my mouth hang open down to my knees. This was the guy who bedded sources and wooed councilmen into telling him secrets?

Richard Wells was at least a head shorter than me, balding with a comb-over that seemed to tuck behind both ears. His gray eyes were small, his nose hooked, his cheeks chipmunk-like. He was heavyset and wore a red plaid sport jacket over brown pants. He spotted me looking at him and grinned. It was like a train wreck. I couldn't tear my eyes away from him. Unfortunately, it sent the wrong message.

"You're Anne Seymour, aren't you? I've seen your byline." He stuck his hand out and I felt compelled to take it. It was like shaking a dead fish. "I'm Richard Wells."

"Hi." I must have sounded and acted like a giddy schoolgirl, but I was merely in shock. He wasn't clever enough to see that.

"Want to get some coffee? Maybe we can help each other out on this."

Help each other? How? I didn't like the sound of that and it snapped me back into the moment. "Sorry, I don't collaborate with the competition," I said coldly.

"We could still get some coffee."

I searched his face, his person, trying to find the charm. If it was there, it was not obvious. "I'm sorry. I've got an appointment." I walked away.

Dick was laughing behind me. "Shut up," I said.

"He hit on you."

"Yeah. But I shot him down." Had I? I wasn't sure.

"He works at the *Times.* Maybe he could get you a job there."

"And maybe I could fuck a duck."

He was still laughing when we got out on the street.

Chapter 6

I had to call Hickey Watson again, but this time I didn't get a breathless "Come Together." I got an answering machine, would I please leave my name and a message, we're so sorry for the inconvenience. The cops got to them, and they were keeping a low profile, if not going out of business altogether. I left my name. It was the only option.

Within minutes my phone rang.

"I thought I gave you all the answers I could." Hickey Watson didn't waste any time. He was probably screening the calls.

"I need some more. Can we meet somewhere?" We weren't going to get anywhere on the phone, I knew that and he knew that, because I could hear him thinking, the wheels of his brain louder than a train whistle.

"Would it get you off my back?"

"Listen, I don't give a damn what you

do, but a girl is dead. You know, if you help out with this, the cops might look more kindly on you."

I must have pushed a button. We agreed to meet at the Twin Pines Diner in East Haven on Route 1, a little dive of a place, just out of the way enough so we would be left alone. It was his choice, so I wondered just where his "office" was located. "I meet all my girls there," he explained. I didn't tell him that even though I was thinking of a career change, it wouldn't include becoming one of "his girls."

"Early deadline tonight," Marty said as I passed his desk.

"Okay, okay. Why don't you have Dick write up the press conference?"

"Where are you off to?"

I told him about Hickey Watson. "I'm going to try to get more out of him about who Melissa met that night. I don't think he'd meet me if he wasn't going to tell me anything."

Marty sighed. "This whole thing is ballooning. Let's try to stick a pin in it."

A definitely murdered Yalie was worse than one who just jumped from a balcony. I wish I could say I felt his pain.

The diner was dark, darker since I'd left my sunglasses on.

"One?" the waitress was asking, pulling out a menu.

I shook my head. "I'm meeting someone."

She smiled. "Oh, yes, he's here." I was guided to a booth in the back, where Hickey was ignoring the ban on smoking in restaurants, but no one in any position of authority here seemed to care. I coughed on purpose.

"You're one of those reformed smokers, aren't you?"

It was the curse of quitting. After enough time without a cigarette, I felt any smoke that invaded my lungs was the enemy. I used to crave it, drink in second-hand smoke like baby's milk, but now it annoyed me. "You know, there's no smoking in restaurants anymore."

He took a long drag and purposely blew a smoke ring toward me. I still had my sunglasses on and I studied his face. Everything on it was wide: his cheeks, his nose, his eyes, his mouth. The crew cut just accentuated it. He was between thirty-five and fifty, I couldn't narrow it down more than that. He wore a sweatshirt with PENN STATE riding on top of a beer gut that barely fit behind the table. Between the smoke and the rank smell emanating from Hickey's person, it was too bad I was hungry and thought I'd be able to have lunch.

He was studying me as much as I was checking him out. He blew another smoke ring. "You know, a few years ago you would've made me a lot of money."

I think he meant it as a compliment.

"That hair is great, and a lot of guys might like those legs wrapped around them. But you must be over forty now, too old for me."

I kept reminding myself he was a source and I had to be nice to him. But I crossed my leg and whacked my boot into his shin.

"Shit!" he exclaimed, the cigarette falling out of his mouth. I took the butt and stamped it out.

"Let's get on with it," I said coldly.

"Hey, I didn't mean anything by that."

"I need to know about McGee." I didn't want to waste any more time, but the waitress suddenly was hovering over us. I shook my head, but Hickey picked up his menu.

"A cheeseburger platter with extra fries," he told her.

My stomach growled. What the hell. "A tuna melt with fries. And a Coke."

She disappeared.

"I told you I can't reveal anything about our clients," Hickey said.

I was going to have to do it. I had no choice. I needed a place to start and I was nowhere right now. "Off the record."

He paused, thinking about it.

"Whatever you tell me, I'll confirm with other sources. I won't use your name."

"The cops are coming down pretty heavy on me. They've already searched my place."

What place? An office? His apartment? A train station locker? I wasn't sure I really wanted to know, so I pressed on. "Did they find anything?"

Hickey's mouth moved into a grin. "Are you kidding? Nothing's on paper." He tapped his forehead. "It's all right here."

It was a scary thought. "McGee?" I said again.

Hickey sighed and leaned closer toward me. I tried to close my nostrils to the tobacco scent emanating from his mouth. "They're regulars. Three different guys, but they always want the same girls, young, smart, pretty. Melissa was hot, and they knew that."

"Do you have a regular contact?"

He nodded. "Same guy always set it up. But I'm not sure which one Melissa saw that night."

"Would it be possible to talk to one of the girls who saw these men?"

"I don't want to reveal my girls' identities."

"I don't care about them, I just want information about McGee."

The waitress reappeared with two plates. I took a bite of my tuna melt and savored it, despite the rank air around me.

Hickey nodded. "You know, I really liked Melissa. She was a good kid. So I'm going to hook you up with Allison. She's a Yale student, too. But you have to promise to keep her off the record."

I nodded. "Okay. When can I talk to her?"

"I'll call her when I get back and have her call you."

I finished my tuna melt in about three minutes and downed the Coke. I gave him my cell phone number again. "Have her call me on this. That way no one at the paper will intercept any calls."

He nodded, his mouth full of cheeseburger. I threw some bills on the table. "Thanks, Hickey, it's on me."

As I pushed my way out of the booth, he wiped his mouth. "You know, I think I was wrong about you. I've got some guys who'd really get off on you. Interested?"

I couldn't tell if he was kidding, so I just shook my head and walked away.

My cell phone rang when I got into the car. It couldn't be Allison this soon. It was Tom.

"Just thought you might like to know we're going to make an arrest."

"You're kidding."

"Why would I kid?"

"Who?"

"The ex-boyfriend, David Best."

"What have you got on him?"

"Fingerprints at the apartment. And we've got two witnesses who saw him, one outside as he was yelling up for her to come down, another who saw him in the hall."

"He was there? How did you ID his fingerprints?"

"He was arrested for drunk driving last year." So much for the clean-cut college boy. "We've got a warrant, his lawyer's going to get him to turn himself in in about an hour. Thought you might like to know." He hung up.

I stared at the phone. It was over. Sort of. I was still curious about McGee, but if they thought they had their man, then my job was to report that and get on with the business of the day. I'd had a nagging feeling about David Best from the start, when I talked to those kids and then when I talked to him. It was him. It was as simple as I'd first thought. But somehow I felt let down.

I didn't let myself think about it. I went back to the office and told Marty what was up. The furrows in his forehead grew. A Yalie killing another Yalie. I was glad I didn't have to tell the publisher about that one.

The police station was surrounded when I got there, cameras jockeying for position, waiting for the perp walk. Richard Wells caught my eye and winked. I was tired of the wrong men winking at me. Tom was nowhere to be seen.

But he was there, that guy, the other winker, the Frank Sinatra look-alike. He was off to the side, sandwiched between two television cameramen. At first I wasn't sure it was him, but when the guy next to him moved back a little, I saw him plain as day. This had gone on long enough. I squeezed my way around a couple of other reporters, but when I got to the spot where he'd been, he was gone. My brain kicked into overdrive. Maybe he was one of the McGee people; no, couldn't be, why would he be following me? Maybe he was another reporter. I let him slip away again as a dark car pulled up along the sidewalk, about six cops surrounded it, the doors opened and the show began.

David Best looked like hell. His face was pale, his hair slicked back. His lawyer stuck to his side, repeating "no comment" to anyone who even looked at him. In a second it was over, they were gone, and David would be under the gun all night. I'd caught a glimpse of Tom as he brought David in. The lines in his face were longer, deeper, and his eyes didn't reveal his thoughts.

"What do you think?" Richard Wells was at my side, his notebook closed, his pen secure in his shirt pocket.

"About what?" I just wanted to get back and get this story done.

"Do you think he really did it?"

I stopped and looked at him. "That's not really for me to say."

"Give me a break. You've got an opinion. We've all got one."

Yeah, and while reporters have a certain camaraderie that allows them to share a few beers and their own opinions away from the listening public, Richard Wells was hardly someone I would do that with. But that didn't mean I wouldn't take advantage of his willingness to talk to me. "So what do *you* think?"

He shook his head. "No way. The kid's not a killer. It's not in him."

"How do you know?"

Richard lowered his voice conspiratorially. "He's known about this life of Melissa's for a while now. Why now? Why would he suddenly snap? It doesn't make any sense. Sure, they had an argument that night, but would he really have the balls to kill her over this? I don't think so. He's just some snobby rich kid who couldn't get what he wanted."

"But anyone can snap at any time."

"True. But I think this is all bullshit."

"How did his fingerprints get in the apartment?" I wanted to trip him up, throw a wrench into his theory, but I was intrigued, being uncertain myself.

"He was there, but I don't think he has the balls to off anyone," he repeated.

I remembered my first impression of David Best, and I couldn't say without a doubt that I thought he did it or didn't do it. But even if he didn't, something had happened between him and Melissa that night.

"I've got to get back. Nice talking to you."

I left him with his mouth hanging open. I'm not sure what he'd expected.

Dick was already writing when I got back to the paper. He had canvassed the university and gotten reaction to the arrest.

"Memorial service tomorrow," he reminded me.

And my black dress still hadn't made it to the cleaners. Damn.

I quickly wrote up the main arrest story and dragged my ass out at a reasonable hour to an empty apartment with an empty refrigerator. I'd forgotten to get dinner. Abate's Pizza delivers. As I was dialing the number, my cell phone started chirping.

"Miss Seymour? This is Allison."

Hickey's Allison. I'd forgotten all about her. I could tell her the case was closed, but maybe I could get another story out of this, especially since Mark Torrey was the city's Mark Torrey. It was worth a shot.

"Hickey said I should talk to you." Her voice was tight. She didn't want to talk.

"Do you want to do this on the phone or do you want to meet somewhere?" I wanted to meet, I couldn't see her face this way, gauge her reactions, see if she was telling the truth.

"I don't like cell phones," she admitted.

"Where are you?" I didn't relish the idea of going out again, I wanted pizza to miraculously appear at my door, and then I wanted to go to sleep. But this could be my only shot to talk to this girl.

"I'll meet you wherever you say." I liked an agreeable girl.

I tried to think of a place where it was crowded enough to make her comfortable, but not crowded enough to keep us from talking. And a place that had food. "There's a Mexican restaurant on State Street, where the street forks. Do you know it?" It had fabulous food and was rarely overcrowded.

"Yeah. I can be there in twenty minutes."

My mouth was watering for a margarita, and I figured one wouldn't make a difference and might make Allison more comfortable. I was already sipping it and tapping my foot to the conjunto music when she arrived.

Allison could've been Melissa's twin, but blond. Her straight hair fell like silk around a perfect face and brought my eyes down to a perfect figure. She was about twenty, with intelligent eyes.

Since mine was the only table occupied by a single woman, Allison came over and slid into the chair across from me. "You must be Anne Seymour."

I nodded. "I'm having dinner. Would you like something?"

She picked up a chip and nibbled it without dipping it in the salsa. "No, I have plans for a little later."

I wanted to scream, what the fuck are you doing, but that would've been too much like her mother and not at all like an objective reporter. Shit, I was old enough to be her mother.

"I understand you and Melissa saw people from McGee Corporation."

Allison nodded. "They liked her better than me, but if she wasn't available, they asked for me."

"Hickey says it was three different guys."

"They were all pretty nice. They tipped well." She kept moving her eyes so she was looking behind me, probably embarrassed. I didn't blame her.

"Can you tell me anything about them? We're having a hard time tracking down anything about the company."

She picked up another chip. "They all thought they were pretty hot stuff."

"Can you describe them?"

For the first time she looked me straight in the eye. "I met all three guys at different times. They're all in their early thirties, very well dressed; one took me to the theater, the others to a couple of charity events. They seem to know everyone. I was surprised they didn't have wives or dates and that they had to go through the agency."

"The fast track?"

"Definitely."

My tacos arrived, three of them, wrapped up tightly in soft tortillas, the guacamole ready to be slathered all over them. I took a bite and washed it down with a slug of margarita. Nothing was better than this.

"Did you ever meet Mark Torrey?"

"Oh, yeah, I saw him a couple of times. He was the best."

I didn't want to ask what he was best in, and she continued without seeming to notice my cringe. "He is the youngest, but he bragged he was head of the company. Said he'd be a millionaire by the time he was thirty-five. Kept talking about some project involving some company with a Norwegian name."

"Lundgren?"

"Yes, that was it."

"Did he say anything else about it?" I put my taco down.

"You've heard of it?"

I nodded. "They're a big development firm, the city's pushing them for a redevelopment project. They've already done some studies. What does McGee have to do with it?"

Allison shrugged. "All Mark said was something about how his company was going to make it all possible."

I pondered that for a few seconds. I'd heard the city was trying to get some sort of grant for this project, which as of yet did not have a cute name attached to it. I didn't cover that part of the city and had only a peripheral knowledge of the project, but if Marty hadn't heard of McGee before, either, then maybe no one had.

"Did you ever go to the apartment?" I asked her abruptly.

She stared at the table and I saw a blush creep over her cheeks. "Yes," she said.

"Listen, Allison, it's not for me to judge what you do, but I guess I just don't understand how a pretty, smart girl like you would do something like that." I resumed eating my tacos, unwilling to let them get cold.

"It's good money," she said quietly.

"Is it that good?" When I wanted extra cash in college, I typed kids' English papers.

She smiled, the blush now gone. "Yes. You'd be surprised."

No, I probably wouldn't be.

"I don't come from a rich family. I'm on scholarship." Which made it even more sad, but I didn't say anything. "Melissa, well, I'm not sure why she did it, I think mostly because she knew if her parents ever found out they'd really hit the roof. They're loaded, she really doesn't, didn't, need the money."

"Are there drugs involved?"

Allison looked away again, and I could see the truth in her profile, but I waited to see if she'd tell me.

Finally she turned back to me. "Those guys, the McGee guys, they always had coke on them, and once they tried to get me to do heroin. But I'm not into all that. I'm not sure about Melissa. We didn't talk about the drugs. But I think maybe she got off on it. She got off on a lot of bad shit."

"Do you know David Best?"

"Sure. He was at that party that night, bugging her again."

"Bugging her about what?"

"Oh, she let it drop what she was doing later that night, and he was pissed. He didn't want her to see anyone else, even though they broke up. He was really possessive." No news there. "When she called me later, she said he'd followed her from the party."

"She called you?"

"She was out with Mark. He wanted a threesome."

I tried not to let my shock show. "So." I kept my voice even. "Did you go?"

Allison shook her head. "I couldn't. I had a test the next morning and had to study. But she was upset about David. Said she thought he was outside the building."

No shit. "I wonder how he got in," I mumbled to myself, and Allison frowned.

"What?"

"They arrested him tonight, David. Didn't you know? They found his fingerprints in the apartment, someone saw him in the hallway."

"But that's not possible." She seemed so sure.

"Why not?"

"She wouldn't have let him in. Neither would Mark." She had a point.

I needed to talk to Mark Torrey and the other McGee guys. I had a nagging feeling in my gut that something was very wrong with all this. "If you see Mark again, or any of the others, could you let me know? I want to talk to them."

Allison frowned. "I'm not sure I can do that."

Now she gets a conscience.

"Listen, I don't think these guys are on the up-and-up, I'm not sure what it is, but it could be dangerous for you." I needed to talk to them and I wasn't above scaring her.

She shrugged. "I'll see."

I handed her my business card. "I'd really appreciate it."

I finished my tacos and margarita after she left. I hoped she'd reconsider.

Chapter 7

I found a pair of black trousers in the back of my closet and put it together with a white short-sleeved blouse. It was too warm for a blazer, but I figured it looked solemn enough for the memorial service. As I ate a bowl of Rice Krispies, I remembered my mother said something about the Peabodys contacting her firm. Maybe I could try to find out something at this service. It would be crass to talk to the parents, but there was always a close friend or relative who might know something and would be willing to talk.

I tried to call the City Hall reporter before I left. I needed to ask him if he'd heard about McGee in all the discussions about Lundgren, but he wasn't home, even though it was a Saturday morning.

The newsroom was a wasteland of piles of paper, idle computer terminals, and a faint smell of Chinese food and popcorn. Dick Whitfield sat in my chair, typing furiously. I threw my purse down on the desk.

"A roomful of computers and you pick mine?"

"I didn't think you'd be in." But he didn't seem surprised to see me.

"Save that and get into the electronic library. Do a search on Lundgren and McGee."

He stared at me. "Are they connected? I mean, no one has made that connection."

At least he knew who Lundgren was. "Just do it."

No hits on both together. Only on Lundgren, nothing on McGee. We stared at the screen.

"What's going on?" Dick asked.

I shrugged. "Beats me. But my source says McGee is involved somehow in the project."

"No shit."

I skimmed the latest story about the city's redevelopment plans. Lundgren's design and engineering studies were completed a few months ago, and the city was trying to secure some grants for the project. Where would McGee come in? Maybe Torrey was just talking out his ass when he bragged to Allison. But I couldn't help but think there was something there. Call it weird intuition.

"There's got to be something here," I said.

I suddenly remembered Dick was supposed to be the enemy. But I just wasn't in the mood.

Dick was scrolling through the headlines, and something jumped out at me. "Stop, go back a couple."

"Torrey joins City Hall staff," I read. "Click on it."

Mark Torrey was appointed assistant corporation counsel. He formerly worked for developer Lundgren and Associates. Shit. If he was involved with the redevelopment plans on behalf of the city, this was a huge conflict of interest. Or a big fucking scandal.

"He's got to be a major player," I said, more to myself than to Dick. "Why did he leave Lundgren for the city? The city pays shit, he probably was rolling in dough before."

"He says here that he wanted to 'give something back' to the city he grew up in." Dick was getting into it, even though we didn't know what we were getting into.

"Bullshit. There's money for him in this, and probably for a lot of other people, too." I wondered if Torrey was really in California.

I thought about Allison and wondered if she saw Torrey or one of the other McGee guys last night after she saw me. It was possible. She was a little squirrelly. I wished I hadn't given her a carte blanche off the record and that I'd gotten her phone number. I'd have to go hunting her down at the school, and who knew if I'd have any luck.

The phone rang, startling both of us.

"Newsroom," I answered.

"I thought I'd find you there." I'm sure my mother has embedded some sort of radar tracking device on my person without me knowing about it. Either that or she really is the genius she likes everyone to think she is.

"What's up?" I was watching Dick scroll down through more headlines.

"Tonight, dear. I'm calling to make sure you haven't forgotten."

I sighed dramatically. "No, Mother, I haven't forgotten," although I almost had. But I wouldn't let her know that. "Eight o'clock?" I was guessing, I couldn't remember if she'd given me a time.

"That's right. Wear something flattering. Maybe you could have your hair done, it always looks like you've just come out from under a helicopter."

I bit back a smart retort that would get me nowhere. I had no intention of "having my hair done," but now I would be self-conscious about it all night.

"I'm a little busy," I tried.

"I'm serious, Anne. I want you to look your best tonight." She had an ulterior motive, and those usually involved a man.

"I don't want to get fixed up," I said, very aware of Dick's eyes on me and not on the computer. I didn't want him knowing my business.

"He's just someone I want you to get to know. Just be friendly." I heard the dial tone and hung up.

"Your mother found a man for you?" Dick's eyes were laughing, and he was trying not to smile. "What about that cop?"

"I don't want to discuss it." I stared at him, hoping looks really could kill, but he just continued to sit there. "We need to find out what's going on with this city project. I wonder where Kevin is." Kevin Prisley was the City Hall reporter.

"He's in Block Island for two weeks," Dick volunteered. "Left yesterday."

Why wasn't I in the loop anymore? Maybe I really should leave this business, if I couldn't even keep tabs on my colleagues and this boob could.

The boob was talking. "Maybe you could do this escort thing and you could meet these guys undercover."

I didn't think so. "Give me a break, Dick. Hickey Watson already told me I wasn't exactly what his clients are looking for." And after spending time with Allison, I knew I didn't want to be on the inside in that world.

"But they wouldn't have to know anything about you before, well, your date. And maybe you could ditch them after dinner or something, after you get your information."

I shook my head. "I can barely get through one of my mother's dinner parties without vomiting. It would be a disaster."

Dick was quiet for a moment. "You know, Annie, your mother is in the in-group. She knows everyone. Maybe she knows about Mark Torrey and McGee, and Lundgren."

I'd had the same thought, but it was too horrifying to think we were both on the same wavelength. I had seen Torrey at one of her parties, so this was not out of the realm of possibility.

"Maybe this dinner party won't be a wash, maybe you could ask some questions. Do you know who's going to be there?"

The usual players, I was sure of it. My mother's firm's partners, some politicians, some high rollers. I'd met them but paid them no mind, just like I ignored my father's friends. Sometimes I wished I were an orphan. I sighed, the last two days settling into my shoulders. I was tired. "I really don't want to work tonight."

"But you don't want to go to this party, either." He paused for a second, then, "Why don't I come as your date? Then your mother can't get on your back about men and we can both ask questions."

It came out of the blue, this proposition that I was turning down before he even finished speaking. Dick Whitfield at one of my mother's parties was about as ludicrous as my being at one of my mother's parties. He always wore green, green trousers or a green blazer, like he had some sort of Emerald City fetish. His ties were a mishmash of angles and circles, something that would freak out someone on acid. His hair was cropped short and spiked, and every once in a while he'd attempt to grow a mustache that managed to be only a couple of splotches on his upper lip. I noted that he was clean-shaven at the moment, but still not presentable.

"Not a good idea," I said simply, instead

of what I really wanted to say, which was "What the fuck are you thinking?" Maybe I was making progress after all.

"Oh, I'm not saying it would be a date."

I held my hand up. "No, Dick. I don't think so."

"We need a Deep Throat."

I had to agree, happy he even knew who Deep Throat was. Most of the kids coming into the business now thought Watergate was some sort of water treatment plant.

"We have to get to the memorial service." I didn't like it that he was coming with me, but Marty had made it clear we were to go together.

Battell Chapel was crammed with people: students, faculty, staff, the curious. The TV vans were parked along the street. I looked around for the winking guy, but I didn't see him. Maybe he finally gave up.

I hate memorial services and funerals. Dick pounced right up to the front and squeezed in somewhere between the family and my mother's law partners. My mother hadn't mentioned she'd be here when I talked to her, but then, she wouldn't. It was part of The Game.

Melissa Peabody was a Yale legacy. Her father and his father had gone before her into the Ivy League, paving the way for

Peabodys forever. She was a brilliant student, everyone loved her. But in the back of everyone's mind, the escort thing must have been swirling around, tarnishing their memories of her. I wondered if it didn't make her a little more human.

I stayed in the back, surveying the crowd. I saw Sarah Lewis dabbing her eyes a few rows up. Crocodile tears.

A guy around my age crept past me and out the door. Tired of hearing the same stuff over and over, I followed him.

He was lighting up just as I came down the steps. Another smoker. Great.

"Hey," I said. "Pretty awful, isn't it?"

He shook his head. "A shame. I've known her since she was a baby."

"Relative?"

"Uncle."

"I'm sorry."

He took a long drag on his cigarette. "These idiot cops don't know shit."

"Is that why your family's suing them?" It was a shot in the dark.

He was startled, the cigarette bobbed in his mouth. "They're not suing the cops. It's the school." He paused. "Hey, no one knows about that."

My brain started moving faster. "You'd be surprised what people know," I said mysteriously, or at least I hoped it was mysteriously. "They're pissed the school let this happen. That it didn't know about her, well, life."

His silence confirmed it. "Who are you?" he finally asked.

Truth-or-dare time. I held out my hand. "Anne Seymour. I'm with the *Herald.*"

"Oh, shit, you can't leave us alone, can you? You're all a bunch of unfeeling leeches." He stamped out his butt on the sidewalk and disappeared back inside the chapel.

I stood on the step, having gotten what I wanted. I didn't need any more from him. His words didn't sting me like they would've when I first started out. I didn't know Melissa Peabody, I'd only seen her body like I'd seen other bodies. I couldn't let my head get wrapped up with who she was, I just needed to report the facts. The first dead body I'd seen, well, it scared the shit out of me, and I found myself imagining who he'd been and the lives he'd touched. I couldn't report it the way it needed to be reported. I got too close. It was the first and last time I let that happen.

I dialed Marty on my cell phone and told him what I'd learned.

The sigh bounced off my ear. "Did you get his name?"

I sighed in response. "He stopped talking before I could get it."

"Then you need someone's name on the record before we can run it."

"Don't give me that, Marty. We've run stuff with less than this. Jesus, he said he was her uncle."

"Annie, you know where we're at on this one."

"I know." Everyone made my job hard. "Maybe I can get my mother to say something tonight. I'll give it a shot." I had my doubts, but it was my only hope.

The doors opened then and throngs of mourners poured out of the chapel. The uncle pushed past me with a glare. So much for trying to get his name. I spotted Dick talking to some students, taking notes. I jogged back to the car to wait for him so I wouldn't run into my mother. I'd deal with her later.

It took way too long to put the story together. Dick's notes were all over the place. I was more of an editor than a reporter. I didn't tell him about my discovery that the family was suing the school. He'd just have to find out when I was allowed to write it. It was mean, but I was in a mean mood.

* * *

I admit that while I put my makeup on for my mother's party, I thought about Dick's proposal that I impersonate one of those escort service girls to get inside. I wasn't sure that Hickey Watson would turn me down. I tried to ignore the lines around my eyes as I brushed on some mascara.

No, it was a stupid idea. I just needed Hickey or Allison to hook me up legitimately with Mark Torrey.

I pulled the little black dress out of the laundry basket, but even if it had been clean, I'd had too much pizza and Mexican food in the last couple of days to make it work for me, plus I was getting my period, which really made me bloated. I pulled dresses and skirts out of my closet, exasperated that nothing I owned was flattering. I finally settled on a longish charcoal knit skirt, A-line of course, and a simple brick-red shell and cardigan. It was understated, and I added my favorite strand of faux pearls and tiny pearl earrings. My hair would do nothing I wanted it to, so I finally just combed my fingers through the curls and let them drop down my back. Shoes were another issue altogether, and I finally found my black mules shoved under the couch in the living room.

I glanced in the full-length mirror (it was there when I moved in, no woman in her right mind would ever own one) and I was a fucking Talbot's ad without the short, straight blond bob. My mother would love it.

"What a gorgeous outfit!" she exclaimed when I walked into the den, and she handed me a snifter with some amber liquid that I quickly swallowed, savoring the burning sensation that followed.

She was wearing a little black dress I could never fit into. My mother is so tiny, she could wear my rings on her wrist as bracelets. It's disgusting.

She was pulling on my arm. "Dear, dear, come over here. There's someone I want you to meet."

I braced myself for another one of her geeks, and instead found myself staring into the eyes of the *New Haven Herald* publisher.

"Of course, you know William Bennett. William, this is my daughter, Anne, who works for your publication."

Bill Bennett is the guy who told Marty he couldn't put "Yale" in the headline when Melissa Peabody was found dead. I had about as much respect for him as I do the scum in my shower. The last person I wanted to hang with tonight was the guy who could make or break me, and my mother was, well, he had his arm around my mother's shoulders in a way that no one had had his arm around her in a long time. It took me a moment, but since I pride myself on being quick, it finally came to me.

My mother was fucking my boss.

At first I wouldn't let myself believe it, but it was the way they looked at each other. I couldn't ignore that, try as I might. I wanted to get the hell out of there before I said something really asinine, but all I could do was take another bourbon and down it more quickly than the first one. Great, now I'd get drunk in front of my mother *and* my boss. I was really glad Dick hadn't come with me. This would've been even worse if anyone caught wind of it.

"I've seen the stories you're doing," Bill Bennett was saying, trying to be a real human being. "You're doing good work."

He wouldn't know good journalism if it were a tractor-trailer coming right at him.

"Thank you," I managed to sputter. Not even here ten minutes and I was already a basket case. I couldn't deal with this.

And then I saw him. The winking guy. Out in the hall, over by the staircase. He had his back to me, but I could tell it was him. He wasn't going to get away from me now. "Excuse me," I muttered, "but there's someone over there I need to talk to." I left my mother with Bill Bennett, who was probably just as relieved I left as I was.

I touched the guy's arm lightly, and he turned around, his dark eyes smiling, his mouth twitching.

"Hello," I said. "You have me at a disadvantage. You know who I am, obviously, but I don't know who you are."

He smiled then, his whole face lighting up, and he took my hand. His was big, warm, calloused, and it sent tingles down my spine. Yeah, it's a cliché, but it really did. I was afraid my knees would give out; there was something incredibly sexy about this guy, in a different way than with Tom. Tom was Prince Charming, the blond German Protestant, the boy next door. This guy had something I couldn't put my finger on, but I wanted to put my fingers all over him.

"Vincent DeLucia."

Oh, Christ. Vinny? But this couldn't be Vinny. Vinny DeLucia was a tall, gangly kid, kind of like Dick, actually, who had buck teeth and never looked any girl in the eye. I'd heard he'd gone off to be some sort of scientist. This couldn't be him.

"You remember me, then?" he asked, and I nodded mutely. "I'm glad."

I wanted to scream: Who the hell wouldn't remember you? You were the biggest geek in the whole school.

"You didn't go to the reunion," he said, his voice caressing every word.

"Give me a break," I said, trying to pretend this wasn't a shock. "Why should I go see a bunch of people I haven't seen in twenty years?"

"Curiosity, maybe."

I had to ask. "How was it?"

"So you are curious." He was teasing me. Vinny DeLucia was teasing me, and, maybe, flirting with me. Which made me remember the wink.

I frowned. "What are you doing, following me around?"

"I'd like to say it's because I want to, but it's more business than pleasure."

Business? What sort of business? "I thought you were some sort of scientist," I said instead. What the hell was wrong with me?

"I did start out as a marine biologist."

I imagined a boat, wind whipping through my hair, and then I remembered my mother's helicopter comment and frowned. "But?"

"It didn't work out like I planned." I could see he was disappointed, truly disappointed about that.

"You miss it?"

"I was studying whales. They're the most magnificent creatures. Have you ever seen one up close?"

"I've been to Mystic."

He rolled his eyes. "I can take you sometime. You have to see them out there, where they really live."

A date? A date with Vinny DeLucia? Oh, I forgot, the business he was in now was what again?

"Funding got cut," he was saying, "and I lost my job. I ended up back here, living with my folks."

Who happened to own a pizza place on Wooster Street, I remembered now. That could explain why he was peering in Sally's window at me the other night. But it didn't explain the other times.

"So what is it you do exactly?" I pushed.

"Private investigation."

I stared at him. "You're a private detective?"

He nodded. "A few years with a friend of my father's, and I decided to go out on my own. It's fairly lucrative." He paused. "What about you? I heard you got married."

I didn't want to get into that. I'd gotten married right out of college, it was a huge mistake, we were way too young, and fortunately I got out of it before there was a house or, God forbid, kids. The only thing it did for me was give me a new last name that didn't link me to my mother or my father. In my job, that was a big plus.

I had to change the subject. "So you've been following me? Why?" I tried to keep my voice low, but I didn't like the idea of this guy hired to follow me by who knew who.

"I haven't actually been following you."

"You'd better explain that."

"You just happen to be in the places I've been lately." He moved closer to me, and I could feel his breath on my cheek. "I'm working on something for your mother's firm."

Which explained why he was at the party. My mother loved to invite her underlings to parties, to make them feel as if they were equals, even though they obviously weren't. But then it struck me. The lawsuit. It had to be why he was in all the same places I was, he was investigating the same thing.

"So you think you've figured it out," he was saying.

I blinked a couple of times. "What do you mean?"

"You've figured out what I'm working on."

"How am I supposed to know?"

"You're a reporter, you know a lot about your mother's client list. And I could see what you were thinking."

He was clairvoyant to boot. Go figure. But I was intrigued with this little game; it was far more interesting and diverting than having to make conversation with Bill Bennett.

"Do you think David Best killed her?" His question was simple, but loaded.

"The police think he did."

"I didn't ask you what the police think, although you obviously would know more than anyone else what they're thinking."

"I am sick and tired of people thinking I know more about this than I do just because of Tom." It came out more harshly than I intended, and I could see he was startled.

"Never mind about him," he said. "Do you think David Best did it?"

I wasn't sure why he was pushing me, but I thought for a minute.

"No, I didn't mean you should intellectually think about it," he said. "What does your gut tell you, without taking any time to think?"

"No, he didn't do it." I couldn't believe my ears. What the hell was I doing? I avoided telling Richard Wells what I thought, and he and I were on the same side, allegedly.

"I don't think so, either."

"Why not?"

He smiled, a slow smile that made me catch my breath. "I really can't discuss it with you."

I wanted to punch him in the stomach, but he was saved by my mother's announcement that dinner was served.

I barely ate a bite. My skirt was a little tight as it was, and I wasn't about to expand my stomach further. Fortunately, I didn't have to sit next to either Bill Bennett or Vinny DeLucia, although I kept my eye on both of them as some slick young lawyer tried to make time with me.

I wondered what Vinny had that made him feel so sure that David Best didn't kill Melissa. I remembered I was supposed to find out if anyone had any knowledge of McGee. I turned to the lawyer next to me.

"I don't suppose you know Mark Torrey." It was a shot in the dark.

His eyebrows rose about an inch. "You know Mark?"

"I haven't seen him in a while," I lied easily, trying not to show my surprise. "But I heard he's working for the city as well as for McGee."

"The city thing's just to tide him over until the money comes in from McGee."

"So he's really just getting started with McGee." I paused to pretend to eat. "Establishing a client base?"

"Yeah. Interested?"

I smiled, a genuine smile because he just made my job so much easier. "I've got some money I need to put somewhere. Do you think he could help?"

"Without a doubt."

"Do you happen to know how I can contact him? I tried the other day at City Hall, but they said he was out of town."

He laughed. "He's never there." He pulled a pen out of his breast pocket and grabbed the cocktail napkin under his glass. "Try this number. Leave a message and he'll get back to you," he said as he wrote.

Even though McGee had a phony New York address, this had the familiar Connecticut area code and New Haven exchange. "Thanks." I was now indebted to this man and found myself nibbling more and more as he told me about his yacht in Essex. No, I don't sail, I told him. No, I really don't have time. I work a lot of weekends. Practically every weekend. No, I get seasick sometimes. Dramamine really doesn't help.

Why didn't this guy get a clue?

I saw Vinny watching me from the other end of the table. He winked. I'm always attracted to men I shouldn't be attracted to. Vinny had everything going against him, except that he'd grown into an incredibly good-looking person. I didn't want to be reminded of St. Anthony's High School, it wasn't the best time of my life, and seeing Vinny brought back some embarrassing moments. Besides, I was seeing Tom, even though our "understanding" left the future wide open for both of us. I mentally slapped myself and took a sip of my wine. There was just no question that I would leave this party alone. Maybe I'd even stop at Tom's on my way home.

Chapter 8

You know what they say: best laid plans . . . yadda, yadda, yadda.

How was I supposed to know he'd follow me? After an excruciating three hours, I managed to squeeze my way out my mother's door, trying not to show my disgust at her taste in men and to slip out before Vinny saw me. But he is a private detective, and I am remarkably bad at being able to tell my mother I want to go home instead of just leaving. He was next to me on the sidewalk as I unlocked my car door.

"Would you like to go get a drink somewhere?"

He startled me, and I dropped my keys.

"I don't think that's a good idea."

"I want to pick your brain."

How romantic. "No, it's not a good idea. I'm tired, and I need to go home and get some sleep."

"But you're not going to sleep."

I picked up the keys and turned to him. Damn, if he really didn't look like Frank Sinatra. It was too tempting. I had to be strong. "How do you know?"

"Because you're going to be thinking about all of this. It's getting to you."

"What is?"

"Melissa Peabody. David Best's arrest. Mark Torrey and McGee. And you have to wait for Torrey to call you."

I feigned ignorance. "What?"

"I heard you talking to that lawyer about Torrey. I saw him give you a number. And I know you sneaked into the bathroom and left a message on his machine."

"Are you sure my mother didn't hire you to watch me?" He was pissing me off, despite the sexy smile. This was not attractive.

"I don't think you should do it," he said.

"Do what?"

"Meet Torrey."

"Why not?"

"He's not what you think. He's worse."

"How do you know?"

"Just take my word for it, okay?" Vinny rubbed the back of his neck. He looked tired. But I still didn't trust him.

After several seconds during which it became obvious I wasn't going to acquiesce, Vinny finally sighed. "Okay, okay. I'll leave you alone. But be careful." He started to walk up the driveway, but then stopped and turned. "Do you have a gun?" he asked quietly.

My father bought me the .22 that I kept in the drawer next to my bed. He'd taught me how to use it a long time ago. I'd never even told Tom I had it there, two feet from where he slept.

"Might not be a bad idea to keep it handy," Vinny said before he disappeared into the darkness.

How the hell did he know?

Vinny sufficiently scared me, even though I would never admit it to anyone. In the middle of the night, anything is creepy, and I kept thinking the cars behind me were following me. It was stupid, but I have a vivid imagination. I must have looked around me a million times, walking from my car to my apartment, my keys gripped between my fingers as I'd learned in a high school self-defense class, ready to stab into some perpetrator's jugular. Since I'd never had cause to use this strategy, I wasn't certain it would work, but it felt better to at least feel like I would try.

My apartment was dark, quiet as a cemetery, so to speak. The answering machine was blinking its red eye rapidly at me. I hit the button at the same time I turned on the light.

"Annie, it's Tom. Oh, yeah, you've got that thing at your mother's. I forgot. Thought you might like to get a drink somewhere." The case was closed, so he had a little time. I glanced at the clock. It was only a little before midnight. I was about to pick up the phone when the second message began.

"Anne Seymour, this is Mark Torrey." I'd left my cell phone number on his machine, not my home number, which was unlisted. A chill ran laps up and down my spine. "I would be happy to meet with you. I'm free at nine o'clock tomorrow night. Come to my office at 543 Orange Street, third floor." The machine clicked off and I sat down on the couch, still clutching my keys. How the hell had he gotten my phone number? And did I really want to meet him somewhere that wasn't public and at night? I had to shake this off. I'd let Vinny spook me too much.

I picked up the phone and dialed the familiar number.

"Could you come over?" I asked, trying to keep my voice level.

"Typical mother party?"

"Oh, God, it was worse than that. She's seeing Bill Bennett, the publisher. They seem to be very cozy. Which sucks, big-time, for me."

Tom chuckled. "Maybe she can get you a raise, a promotion."

"I doubt it." I thought for a minute. "Hey, do you know a private investigator named Vinny DeLucia?"

"I've run across him. Why?"

"He's the guy, the one who I thought was following me."

"Thought?"

"Yeah, seems he's just working on a case and happened to be in the same places as me at times. His parents own DeLucia's, you know, on Wooster Street."

"Really? They've got pretty good pies. I'm glad you're not really being followed, I was a little worried about you."

I smiled involuntarily. I would've hit anyone else who said that. "So are you coming over?"

"Give me twenty minutes."

Needless to say, I didn't need a few beers to enjoy myself as thoroughly as the last time we'd seen each other on our own time.

Because it was Sunday, we slept in, had

some coffee, lounged a little more in bed, then I made one of my famous ham and cheese omelets. I almost forgot about Mark Torrey as we sifted through the *Times.*

Tom's cell phone went off at the same time my phone rang.

"Annie, we got another one." Marty's voice was gruff, and I wondered if it hadn't been his turn to be out partying the night before.

Tom's mouth tightened as he listened to his caller, and he moved into the bedroom, out of view.

"Another one what?" I asked Marty.

"Another body."

I froze. "Where?"

"In a parking lot near Ninth Square. That's all I know. Turn on your scanner, that's where I'm hearing it from."

My scanner was somewhere in the pile of newspapers on the back seat of my car. "Is it a girl?"

"Yeah. But, like I said, that's all I know."

"Which parking lot?"

"The one across from that Chinese place, you know, Royal Palace."

I knew the place. They had a great crispy whole fish with spicy Hunan sauce and amazing sautéed green beans, not to mention delicious scallion pancakes. The owner talked me into trying jellyfish one night, but that was less than stellar.

"Okay, I'll call you when I know something."

I hung up just as Tom was emerging from the bedroom, fully dressed. He was one step ahead of me.

"I'm heading over there," he said. "I guess I'll see you." He slammed the door behind him without kissing me goodbye. I picked up a pair of jeans off the floor and pulled them on.

The street was blocked off, and I had to park near the Coliseum and walk over to the scene. A uniform held his arm out to keep me from ducking under the yellow police tape.

"I'm Annie Seymour, with the *Herald*," I tried.

"Sorry, I know who you are. I have orders to keep you as far away as possible."

That stopped me. Orders? "From who?"

"Detective in charge. Tom Behr."

The rage bubbled up into my chest and settled in my throat. I saw Tom on the other side of the parking lot, amid the crowd. Asshole. And I shared my last glass of orange juice with him. I made him an omelet. He couldn't do this to me. I walked around the edge of the chain-link fence and around to the back, to try to get a closer look. And maybe punch out the cop in charge.

He spotted me hovering.

"Get out of here, Annie."

It was then that I saw the blood. A lot of it, more blood than I had ever seen in one place.

"Is this all from her?" I asked.

"You can't come in here."

Suddenly I didn't want to. "Jesus, what happened?"

"Stabbed. More times than I can count at the moment."

"ID?"

"Not until next of kin." He walked away again, his shoulders sagging. But it didn't mean I wasn't still mad at him.

TV crews were arriving, and I thought I saw Richard Wells close behind. I maneuvered around a little and stooped down to see if I could see anything between the rows of legs.

Nothing. The cops had the whole place blocked off. I ran around to the other side of the parking lot, but still couldn't get a good look.

I looked up at the crowd across the way and saw no one was getting anywhere, I was glad I wasn't the only one. Uh-oh, there was Richard Wells turning the corner, waving a genial hello to the cops, making his way under the yellow tape . . . hey, wait a minute. Who gave him permission?

I skipped back to where I'd started, keeping an eye on Wells, who was talking to Tom. Maybe he could go home with Wells instead of me. This was way too much. I started to go under the tape, just as Wells had done, but a TV camera got in my way. I elbowed the reporter, who stuck her bony finger in my side.

"Move over," I growled. She moved close enough so my nose stuck into her fancy hairdo, and I almost fell over because of the noxious fumes from her hair spray. I caught Tom's eye as I got closer, and he shook his head, his forehead furrowed, his eyes meaning business.

Okay, so maybe I didn't really want to see the stabbing victim. Maybe the thought of all that blood made me sick to my stomach. But he let Richard Wells in, goddammit, and I was not about to be pushed away.

I've seen *Trauma: Life in the ER* on the Learning Channel. That's the show where they bring in the stabbing victims and proceed to stick their fingers into the wounds to see how deep they are. But this was worse. A hundred times worse.

Because it was Allison.

Whoever had done this had not touched her face, and I could still see it as I drank my margarita and wanted to yell at her like her mother.

I'd seen enough, and I backed off, nodding at Tom, turning toward the sidewalk to join the rest of the vultures. But I'd lost my appetite, even when Richard Wells smirked at me.

That's when I remembered I didn't even know her last name.

"Hey, Annie, wait up!" It was an all-too-familiar voice following me to my car. Seeing that girl like that and then hearing Dick Whitfield's voice made me stoop down and vomit onto the curb. So much for the omelet.

I managed to stand with as much dignity as I could, since Dick was still standing there like the moron he is.

"You okay?" he asked.

I snorted, not a pleasant sound. "Do I look okay, Dick? Give me a fucking break."

"Did you get anything?" He pointed toward the scene.

"Yeah." I got into my car. I had to go

home and change and brush my teeth. I couldn't think straight at the moment.

"What'd you get? Should I stick around?"

"Yeah, sure. Go ahead. Be my guest." I started to pull away.

"But what's going on? Can you at least fill me in?"

I stopped the car and stared at him. "There's a body. She's stabbed, many times. The cops aren't saying a fucking thing. Now I have to go home and put myself together and I'll be back." I tried to keep the exasperation out of my voice, but honestly. He's a reporter, too. It doesn't take a rocket scientist to do this job, even though so many have tried and failed. I really was getting too old for this crap. Not to mention I was extremely embarrassed at losing my breakfast all over the tires of my car.

I took a long, hot shower. They'd all still be there when I got back, although the body might be gone. But that would be a good thing. The body. Allison. Maybe it had nothing to do with anything except a serial killer was after girls who worked for Hickey. Maybe Melissa and Allison were going to break out on their own and Hickey was mad. Maybe he did it. It couldn't be David Best, not this time, since he was “being detained” as the lawyers put it.

I shut off the water and stepped out of the shower, wrapping a towel around me. The face in the mirror stared back at me, and I picked up the tweezers and started pulling out the hairs between my eyebrows. If I didn’t do that periodically, I would look like the Neanderthal man, which would be a complete turnoff to any man, with the possible exception of Dick Whitfield, who probably hadn’t gotten laid since, well, since ever. I tried to think of Dick with the layers of green peeled off and decided to stop thinking about it because I’d probably vomit again.

A clean pair of jeans and a flannel shirt over a long-sleeved T-shirt would have to suffice on a Sunday morning, since my laundry basket was overflowing and I didn’t know when I’d get a chance to do laundry. I picked up the pieces of the *Times* and piled them in the corner next to my desk as I dialed the all-too-familiar number.

“Come Together.”

“Hickey Watson, please.”

“I’m sorry, he’s unavailable.”

“Not to me, he isn’t,” I said. “Tell him it’s Anne Seymour. Tell him it’s about Allison.”

"Hold a minute, please." The words were pleasant, but the voice was cold. I started washing the coffee cups while I listened to a Muzak rendition of "Helter Skelter."

"Yeah? What's up with Allison?"

No hellos for Hickey. He's a busy man.

"She's dead." I shut the water off and put the mug in the dish drainer.

"What?"

"She's dead. She's in a parking lot near the Coliseum with a million holes in her beautiful body. Any idea who might have wanted to do that?"

Silence. I could hear Hickey's deep breathing. Then, finally, "Are you sure?"

"I saw her."

"This isn't good." I think he was talking more to himself than to me, but since I was on the other end of the line, I picked up his train of thought.

"No, it's not. Two girls in less than a week. Not very good for business, Hickey."

He hung up on me. And I didn't get a chance to ask him what Allison's last name was. I shouldn't have been so hard on him, but it was too late now.

I grabbed my purse and was about to go out the door when I stopped, remembering something. I went into the bedroom and pulled the drawer open. There it lay, the ray of sun slapping its steel, making it shine. I picked it up and put it in my bag. But again I stopped in the living room, opened the bag and stared at it. I didn't like the idea of carrying it around. What if it fell out of my purse in the middle of the newsroom? Some disgruntled reporter would inevitably pick it up and start shooting, and then the blood would be on my hands. No, a newsroom is definitely not the place for a handgun. I put it back in the drawer and slipped back outside.

I found Dick next to the TV reporter with the stiff hair. "I know who she is," I whispered.

"Who?" He was salivating. I'm not kidding.

"You stay here and get what you can. I'll see you back at the paper."

"You can't just leave."

"Whining is very unattractive." I let myself breathe again when I got out of the hair spray zone. No wonder the ozone layer is being depleted.

The campus was quiet, as any campus would be on a Sunday morning. I had no idea what Allison's last name was, much less where she lived. It was possible Sarah knew, so that's where I went, to Davenport College to find her. A friendly Asian coed directed me to Sarah's room, obviously unconcerned about who I was and why I was there.

Sarah was drinking a cup of coffee, the *Times* crossword puzzle neatly done in pen on her lap, when I came to the open door. I glanced quickly around the room, taking in the piles of folded clothes on the desk (she obviously had time to do laundry), rows of books on a makeshift shelf, a small refrigerator, and a hot pot with a mugful of tea bags next to it.

"Oh, Christ, it's you again."

She really needed to lighten up. "Yeah. Seems there's another girl who's been killed, and I wondered if you knew her last name. Allison. Blond, blue-eyed. Worked with Melissa at that service."

The more I talked, the wider Sarah's eyes got. "You're shitting me."

"No. Do you know her?"

Sarah shrugged. "Sure. She was over here a lot. They were good friends." She paused. "Was it like Melissa, you know, did she fall off a building, too?"

"No. She was stabbed."

Sarah's face went white, whiter than it was already. I hoped she wasn't going to ask me to describe it, because even though it was still plain as day to me, I didn't want to relive that moment. Even thinking about it for a second made my stomach churn. I forced myself to concentrate on the moment.

I walked over to the bookshelf and glanced at the titles. Biology and psychology textbooks were divided by *Tom Jones*, *Madame Bovary*, and *Crime and Punishment*. A bronze Buddha a little more than half a foot tall sat sentry and I picked it up, its heft reminding me that I should work out now and then.

"What's her last name?"

"Sanders. Allison Sanders." Sarah took a sip of her coffee, her eyes following me as I moved toward the window, still holding the Buddha. "This is really weird. What are the odds of two girls who knew each other being murdered within a few days of each other?"

My question exactly.

"Do you know where she lived? Anything about her background, anything that might help find out who did this?"

Sarah shrugged. She was good at that. "I really didn't know her that well. She hung with Melissa and her crowd." I'd hoped to get her while she was still in shock, people usually talked more then, but this girl was a stiff. Excuse the expression.

"Did you like her more than you liked Melissa?"

She shrugged again. "About the same. They were two peas in a pod." She got up. Her long legs seemed to go on forever. Sitting in the library, she'd seemed small, but she was taller than me, and I had to look up at her. Sarah came toward me and held out her hand. I glanced down at the Buddha, then gave it to her. She put it back next to the books.

I wasn't getting anywhere on this one, but I suspected Sarah knew more about Allison and Melissa than she let on. I had to push her buttons. She might not tell me anything anyway, so what was I going to lose?

"You must have heard them talking when they were in the room with you. You must have heard something that might help. Hell, I'd eavesdrop if I could, two beautiful girls working for an escort service. They must have intrigued someone like you." I could tell the "someone like you" was the key. I watched her eyes narrow and she studied me for a minute.

"What's that supposed to mean?"

"Their lifestyle was so not you. We can't

help but be curious about those who are different. And especially so beautiful."

"Why do you keep emphasizing the way they looked? It doesn't matter what people look like."

I chuckled. "Bullshit, Sarah. It does matter. First impressions are made on looks, not on personality."

She was quiet a minute, then, "Okay, suppose I did hear them talking once or twice. I usually just left when they were here, I went to the library. But I heard some stuff. It was pretty disgusting. I think they liked to talk about the sex while I was here, just to get me, you know."

"Did they talk about any man in particular?"

She thought a minute. "David, mostly. He was bugging Melissa all the time. She wanted Allison to get him off her back, but she didn't want to get involved."

"Was he interested in Allison at all?"

"I don't think so. Sounded like he did call her a lot, just to find out stuff about Melissa. You know, like when she was going out, who was she going with."

Typical guy. Go to the friends, not to the woman herself to find out what was up. "Anyone else?"

"The last couple of weeks they kept

talking about this one guy. He called here a few times. Sounded kind of snobby. I think they were both seeing him."

"Do you remember his name?"

She shrugged and turned away, but not before I saw her face go flush. "Mark, I think."

It always seemed to come back to Torrey. And I had my clandestine meeting with him tonight. After seeing Allison's mutilated body, I was even less inclined to keep the date. I still had all day to decide.

"Did you ever talk to him at length?"

The flush was gone and she shook her head. "No, not really."

I wasn't sure I believed her, but she'd plopped back down on the bed and resumed her crossword puzzle. I was being dismissed.

I made my way toward the door. "Thanks, Sarah. I appreciate your help. Do you still have my card?"

"Yeah, sure." She didn't look up.

"If you can think of anything else . . ."

"Yeah, sure."

I let myself out.

Chapter 9

He was sitting at my desk again, and this time I slammed my purse into the back of his head.

"What — ?" Dick turned around, rubbing his head, a Jim Carrey expression on his face, which pissed me off even more, since I hate Jim Carrey.

"Get the fuck out of my chair," I hissed.

He really does listen to me when I talk like that, because he jumped up faster than I could say "moron."

Marty was hovering. "You guys really need to start getting along."

It would do me no good to tell him that I'd tried, that we'd actually had moments, but in the long run it would be completely useless for us to be a team. The odds were stacked against us, I was too curmudgeonly and old to change my ways, he was too young and stupid to ever live up to my expectations.

It made me feel better to sort that out in my head, even if I didn't tell Marty.

"I don't think she's cracked up for this," Dick was saying, and I tuned back in real quick.

"What?" I could hear my voice pounding in my ears, and the few people in the newsroom at this hour on a Sunday looked up.

"She upchucked all over the crime scene."

Marty was laughing. I could feel my face grow hot, but it didn't keep me from glaring at Dick. Now he was a tattletale, too.

"You really have to try to get along," Marty said again.

"She won't tell me who it is," Dick complained.

"Who who is?" Marty took his glasses off and started cleaning them on his shirttail.

"The stabbing victim. Annie says she knows who it is, but she won't tell me."

Marty's myopic eyes turned to me. "Who is she, Annie?"

"It's Allison Sanders. She was a friend of Melissa Peabody, they worked together at that escort service."

I thought I saw tears fill Marty's eyes, but maybe it was that he was trying to see me clearly and finally put on his glasses. "You're kidding."

"I wish I were."

"Another Yalie?"

I nodded.

He sighed. "Fuck," he said quietly.

"I still need to track down some information on her. I was lucky to get her last name."

"This was the girl you met at the restaurant, right?"

I nodded again. "Yeah. She was going to alert me about Torrey." I wondered if I should tell him about my appointment with the elusive Mark Torrey later that night, but opted to leave that out at the moment. He was still having trouble digesting this new information.

"Do you think they're connected?"

I knew he was asking if the murders were linked to Torrey, but Dick wasn't getting a clear signal.

"Connected to who?" he asked.

The look Marty gave him at that moment verified what I'd thought all along: Marty thought he was an idiot, too, and had to get on my case only because he was the boss. It was a small victory, and one that I could never voice, but I would always know it in my heart of hearts and it could comfort me. Maybe.

Marty's eyes came back to me.

I nodded. "Yeah. How could they not be? The coincidence would be too much."

"Do you think the key is Torrey?"

"Maybe. David Best didn't have the opportunity to kill Allison, and anyway, why would he kill her? There's no motive. In fact, David was trying to get Allison to help him with Melissa."

"Do you think he killed Melissa?"

I thought about what I'd told Vinny. "I don't think so." Vinny also made me think of something else. "You know, my mother's law firm is investigating this, too. They've got a private detective working on it."

"Didn't you get anything out of your mother last night?"

I was so distracted by the man on her arm that I'd forgotten to ask her about the lawsuit and Torrey. Anyway, Marty didn't know what he was asking. Getting that sort of information out of my mother is like trying to take a big hunk of meat away from a hungry lion. "No," I said simply.

He sighed again. "What about Tom Behr? Can you get anything out of him on this one?"

Probably not, but I had to appease him with something. "Maybe."

"Do the cops know about Allison's connection to Melissa?"

"I don't think so. I didn't tell Tom about my meeting with her. It didn't seem relevant because they'd already arrested David Best."

At that moment, the scanner started going crazy, dispatchers' voices in and out, loud and soft. There was an accident. A bad one. Marty looked at me.

Sure, I'm the police reporter. But I had a fatal stabbing and didn't think I had to check out an accident. "Come on, Marty, send someone else. Who's on today?" I hoped by reminding him subtly that I wasn't scheduled to work that he'd get the message I didn't want to go.

"Robin's the only one here, but she's heading out in a few minutes to cover the Polish-American parade in the Valley."

"What about Dick?"

Marty looked from me to Dick and back to me. "Okay." Back to Dick. "Can you get out there?"

"What about this stabbing?" Usually he was the first one to ride on the back of the ambulance, but he was getting a taste of what was a good story and what was routine. This could not bode well for me in the future.

"Annie can handle it for now. Get out there, see if there's a photographer in the lab to bring along. Might be a good time to get a picture."

We watched Dick lope to the other side of the newsroom and disappear into the lab.

"You owe me," Marty was saying.

I nodded. "Yeah, sure. Thanks."

"I want something on this today. Talk to that escort service guy again, see if you can track down anything on Allison that can connect her to McGee and Torrey so we can put these two together."

"Will they want that?" I asked, thinking of the suits upstairs and the sacred cows grazing in our backyard.

"Fuck them," Marty said, then clenched his teeth. "Forget I said that."

I chuckled. "Come on, Marty, it just means you're like the rest of us."

"I am not like you, and if it gets back to me that I said that, I'll have your ass."

I didn't have the heart to tell him that my mother was fucking the publisher and I might now have some temporary clout.

My phone rang, keeping me from saying something I shouldn't, and he wandered back to his desk.

"Newsroom," I answered. I usually don't

like to identify myself, just in case it's some nutcase who wants to complain about why he didn't get his newspaper or that the paper was left in a puddle or we somehow forgot to put in his listing about the chicken dinner at the local VFW.

"I saw you with Vinny DeLucia last night." My mother has impeccable timing: When I don't have time to talk to her, she calls me, wanting a heart-to-heart.

"It's nothing, Mother. We went to high school together. That's all."

"He didn't, um, tell you anything, did he?"

"Like what? Like he's working on a big investigation for you, something that has to do with Melissa Peabody?"

That got her, because she didn't say anything for a couple of seconds. "Did he tell you?"

I sighed. "No, Mother. But why don't you tell me about it?"

"It's privileged," she said, and I knew I wouldn't get shit out of her right now. Direct confrontation would never work; passive aggressiveness was the way to go, and I'd blown it.

"You know, Mom, I have to get going. A friend of Melissa's was killed, and I have to get back on it."

"Killed?" The curiosity seeped through the receiver into my ear. I smiled. Two could play this game.

"Sorry, Mom, gotta go."

Under normal circumstances, I would have to wait for her permission to hang up. It almost gave me an ulcer while I was in college, before I realized I could just zone her out while I waited. But it was time to change the rules.

I hung up.

I began writing the top of the story. I'd fill in the blanks later, if we had anything to fill them with. I was doubtful. This murder would tie up Tom all day. Even if I paged him he wouldn't call me back. Sarah had been little help. I'd have to hoof it around campus and try to get more of a description of Allison, other than what I already knew, and maybe even a picture if I got lucky.

On my way back to the campus, I stopped by the crime scene again. There were still some officers milling about, the yellow tape giving me a sense of déjà vu. I spotted Tom and pulled into a parking space.

"Anything?" I asked when I got closer to him.

He jumped, startled at the sound of my

voice. "Oh, shit, Annie."

"Sorry. Did you find the murder weapon?"

He shook his head. "If it wasn't for all the blood, I'd think she was killed somewhere else and moved here. It's the cleanest fucking scene I've ever seen."

He was pointing, and I noticed what he meant: There was no litter. Nothing. It looked like it had been swept up. A shiver ran down my spine and pinched me on the ass.

"Do you think there's some serial killer after Yalies?" I tried.

He stared at me. "She's a Yalie?"

I'd forgotten that he didn't know who she was and I hadn't enlightened him earlier.

"You know who she is," he growled.

I took a deep breath. "Yeah. She's a friend of Melissa's."

He started walking in circles. "I can't believe you didn't tell me. You were here earlier, you saw her."

"And I proceeded to lose my breakfast on the curb over there. I wasn't exactly in a state of mind to help the police at the moment. I'm here now." I hadn't come here to tell him about Allison, I wanted him to tell me what he knew about her death so I could write about it.

"What's her name?"

"Allison Sanders. She works for that escort service, too. I met with her the other night. She and Melissa were Mark Torrey's regulars."

"Jesus Christ."

My thoughts exactly.

"What else do you know about her?" he asked.

"Nothing. Really. I was heading over to the school now to try to find someone to tell me about her."

"You can't write about this," he said.

"Say what?"

"If you write about this, people will think there's some serial killer after Yalies. That wouldn't be good."

"But you've got David Best for Melissa's death. And Allison was killed so differently. They were both involved in a business that's shady anyway, why would people think it's a serial killer?" But even as I asked him that, I knew I was wrong. No one would care about the MO. They would only see "Yale" and "murder" and jump to their own conclusions, excuse the pun.

"I have to write it, Tom. It's my job." That was the truth. Marty knew about it, we couldn't sit on this. I couldn't do it, not even for him. "Anyway, all those other reporters, do you really think Richard Wells doesn't know who she is yet?"

I almost felt sorry for him. His shoulders sagged even lower, his eyes glazing over. "I shouldn't have asked you that."

"No, you shouldn't have." I can't keep my mouth shut.

He glared at me. "I have nothing else to say to you. Please leave the crime scene. We'll notify you if there's anything official to report."

I was dismissed. It felt only slightly less demeaning than when my mother dismissed me. When I was in my car, I remembered I forgot to tell him about my meeting with Torrey. But I was pissed at him and I knew he'd be pissed about that, too, so I just kept going.

Dick was three steps ahead of me. I ran into him in Atticus. Okay, I wanted a cup of coffee and thought maybe I could recreate my uncanny luck of finding people who knew the victim while I was there. All I found was Dick, waiting in line for a cappuccino.

"I thought you were at the accident."

"No biggie. A couple of graphs. But I got a picture of Allison Sanders." He pulled a wallet-sized picture out of his breast pocket. It was Allison, all right. But how?

"Her roommate was really nice." Dick kept talking while I ordered my coffee. "Allison was from Michigan. Detroit. She was here on a scholarship."

I was too stunned that he'd actually gotten something to be upset about his stepping on my toes. God knows I hadn't even gotten the girl's last name when I'd met her. I figured just this once, I'd give Dick a pass.

Dick and I actually managed to come up with a pretty damned good story in the end. The cops weren't having a press conference until the next day, which meant they knew nothing, had nothing to tell. Didn't bode well.

It was getting late and I needed to meet Torrey. I hadn't had time to go home, and I'd eaten half a small pizza with Dick at my desk. All the pizza I was eating lately was sitting on my thighs. When I stepped outside, it was dark and the air was calm. I could smell the harbor, not a nice smell, a little fishy, a little rotten. I thought of the gun in my bedside table drawer and wished I'd brought it with me. The pepper spray in my purse would have to do.

I maneuvered my car into a spot near the building, and as I approached, I wondered if Torrey had tried to reach me to cancel. The windows were dark, and I almost turned back to my car when I saw a light go on on the third floor. A silhouette of a man paced around the room, and I watched it for a minute, debating whether to go face him or run like hell.

I pulled my cell phone out of my purse and dialed Tom's number. Voice mail. I left a message, telling him where I was and who I was meeting. Just in case.

And before my head could talk me out of this, my feet were up the stairs and I was pushing the heavy door open.

"Miss Seymour?" The disembodied voice echoed through the stairwell.

"Yes. Mark Torrey?"

"Right up here."

I reached the top of the stairs and turned toward the light. "In here," the voice directed.

He sat behind a big mahogany desk, a small desk lamp emanating an orange glow. I had the feeling I was in some sort of Surrealist painting. He stared at me without saying anything. I recognized him from that party at my mother's. He had curly brown hair and a very high forehead. His shoulders were broad, his neck thick, and I was willing to bet he'd played football in high school. He wasn't what I considered good-looking, but he had the rich-boy arrogance oozing from every pore that some women find attractive.

"I don't think you're here to talk finance," he began.

I sat in one of the big leather chairs in front of the desk without being asked. I don't believe in protocol at clandestine meetings. "No, Mr. Torrey, I'd like to talk about Melissa Peabody."

He folded his hands in front of him, his elbows on the desk. "What can I tell you? She was a lovely girl. It was the most unfortunate accident."

I stifled a chuckle. "It was no accident. She was murdered. And you were there."

"For a while, I admit. But she was very much alive when I left." He smiled then, a hypnotizing smile that caught me off guard, and I found myself leaning toward him, as if he had some sort of gravitational pull on me. In that second, I saw his charm, almost felt like I could trust the guy, it seemed so genuine, even though I knew he was a fraud. I took a deep breath, fighting it, sitting back in my chair again, farther away.

Jesus, he was like that goddamned wormhole on *Star Trek* that sucked in everything that came into its path.

"Why haven't you come forward to tell the police what you know if you weren't involved?" I was back in the game.

The smile disappeared, and he bit his lip. I don't think he knew I could see that well in the dark. "I haven't been ready to talk about it. I was very close to Melissa, as you probably have figured out by now."

Close in the biblical sense, sure. Any other way, well, I doubted it. "Why did you agree to speak with me tonight?"

He stared straight into my eyes. I guess he was going to try to tell me what he perceived was the truth and try to get me to believe it because he was being "honest." By doing that, he was proving to me that he was going to drop a big fat lie on me and expect me not to feel it.

"My conscience was bothering me."

What an asshole this guy was. He could fool some Yale students who thought he was Mr. Wonderful, but he certainly wasn't going to fool me, not now. My X-ray vision was seeing the rat underneath the nice suit.

"Why not talk to the cops? Why to a reporter?"

"You have connections. You'll tell them."

Oh, Christ, even this guy knew about me and Tom. "What about Allison Sanders?"

He frowned, and I could see he was genuinely puzzled. "What about her? Yes, I know her, but besides being a friend of Melissa's, I see no reason why she should be involved in this."

Could he be that good an actor? The skeptic in me said yes. But I encouraged his charade and played along.

"She's dead, Mr. Torrey. Didn't you hear? Someone stabbed her to death in a parking lot. She was found this morning."

I saw something cross his face that I couldn't read. It pissed me off. "Why are girls you knew and had recent contact with dying?" I demanded. The sentence structure left something to be desired, but it got the point across.

"I really don't know about that." But he was a little flustered. I could see that, even in the dim light.

"Maybe you should come with me and talk to the cops." I didn't really want to spend that much time with him, but I couldn't shake the feeling that he was planning to disappear for good.

"Maybe I should." He was staring into my eyes again. Bad sign.

I pulled my notebook out of my bag. This was probably the only chance I'd get to talk to this guy, and it was time to make it official. "Can you tell me everything that happened the night Melissa was killed?"

"I met her at the apartment, we weren't going anywhere that night. We'd done that before, it was mutual."

"But you paid for it."

"I never paid for it," he said firmly, like it was true.

But before I could press further, he continued, "When we were done, I had to get back to my place to get some sleep because I had an early meeting. She was getting dressed and said she'd lock up on her way out."

"Did you see David Best that night?"

"The boyfriend? Oh, yes. He was yelling from the street for her to come out. We closed the sliding doors so we couldn't hear him."

"Why did you call in to work the next day saying you were in California because of a death in the family?"

"But I *was* in California. I did have a death in the family. There was a message on my machine when I got home. I just wasn't there as long as I let on."

I wasn't buying any of his shit, but I was

writing it down. "Why is the address for McGee Corporation a Gap store?" While I was here, I figured I might as well go for the whole kit and kaboodle, as my grandmother used to say.

"It was a typo."

"A typo?"

"It was a mistake. We're actually on the next block, but there was a screwup."

This guy was lying like a rug, but I had to admit he was smooth. He had a fucking answer for everything. "What's the correct address?"

"I don't think that's relevant to Melissa."

It was, but I figured I'd get back to that. I tried another tack. "Are you working on the redevelopment plans with Lundgren?"

I could see the puzzlement in his face, but he answered me. "Some of the legal issues involved, yes. That's part of my job as assistant corporation counsel."

"Legal issues like what?"

"We may have to take some property over by eminent domain, and that's always difficult."

Difficult because people didn't want the city to take over their properties and homes and force them to move elsewhere just in the name of progress, but that wasn't what I was here for.

"But isn't the fact that you used to work for Lundgren a conflict?"

Torrey sat up a little straighter. "I'm just part of a team, doing routine legwork."

"How about funding? Is McGee helping with that?"

He frowned. "McGee is separate from the city."

"What is it, then?"

He sighed in that exasperated way people do when their knowledge isn't common knowledge and they want people to feel stupid. "McGee is an investment firm I started three years ago when I got my stockbroker license. With my connections at City Hall, I have been able to establish a good client base."

"Who invests?"

"Anyone who wants to make money."

"Like who, specifically?"

"Private citizens who make private investments." In other words, he wasn't going to give up names to me.

"If McGee is an investment firm, why don't you have a public phone number, an office, something?"

Again with the sigh. "We have a very private clientele."

"Why did Allison Sanders tell me you were expecting to make a lot of money because of the redevelopment project?"

He paused for a moment, then laughed. "Haven't you ever embellished on something to impress someone?"

"But why would you mention Lundgren?"

"I made some money working for them before my city job."

"Is Lundgren somehow involved with your investment company?" I asked.

He straightened his back and sucked in some air. "I'm not going to reveal private business, Ms. Seymour. I thought I made that clear."

I was pissing him off, which probably wasn't a good idea. I wondered where Tom was.

"I'm not sure how we got from Melissa's unfortunate death to this. I'm afraid I have another appointment and will have to end this interview." He stood up, the momentary anger gone, and I didn't sense any urgency in his voice. I had to admit that I admired Mark Torrey for his control, which was probably why he was as successful as he was. "My business with McGee and Melissa have nothing in common. I hope you'll keep that in mind when you're writing your story." He seemed so sure they didn't, and I was so sure they did.

"Fine." I could lie along with the best of them. I was a reporter, after all. "How did you get my phone number?"

He smiled. It was a patronizing smile, with something in it that I didn't quite understand. "Have a nice evening."

"If I have more questions, can I call you?"

The smile was back, and again I steeled myself against it. What the hell was it about this guy?

"No. This is the end of our interview. You'll get nothing else from me."

I shrugged. Maybe not from him, but I'd find someone else who wanted to talk. There's always someone at the bottom who's getting screwed who wants to spill the beans. And I was certain there were a lot of beans teetering on the edge of this one.

Chapter 10

It wasn't too late to write a story telling Torrey's account of the night Melissa died, along with the scant stuff about McGee, since it was only 9:30 and deadline was at 10:15. I still hadn't heard from Tom. I called the department and left a message with the dispatcher that Tom should get in touch with me as soon as possible.

I knocked the story out in about twenty minutes, then headed for home, stopping for some takeout at Boston Market. I hunkered down in front of the television while I ate my chicken and mashed potatoes.

I woke up a couple of times in the middle of the night with Allison's image in front of my eyes. I moved my bathroom night-light to the bedroom, which served only to scare me more when I awoke to see odd shadows across the ceiling.

I was happy when the sun poked its rays through my mini-blinds, but not happy when the phone rang during my coffee and toast.

"You couldn't call me?" Tom was pissed, more pissed than I expected.

"I did. Didn't you get my message? I left two, one on your cell phone and the other at the department."

I heard him fumbling with his phone. "Shit. Where is he?"

I gave him the address. "I met him there last night."

"Alone?"

"He's not a suspect. You've arrested someone. Or am I mistaken?"

"You're going to get yourself into big trouble one of these days, pulling that kind of shit."

I already had a mother and was about to tell him that when I spotted something under my door. I walked over to it, ignoring Tom's voice, and picked up a piece of paper: "Stop asking questions or else."

It was one of those notes that you always see in the movies, the ones that have all the letters cut out of magazines so handwriting analysts can't be brought in to solve the crime.

"Tom." He was going on about how I should make sure my pepper spray was in working order. "Tom."

I think my voice was wavering just enough for him to stop. "What?"

"I've gotten some sort of threat." I described the note.

"See? This is what I mean. I'll be right there."

I didn't like it that someone had gotten into my building and stuffed this under my door while I was home, unaware. A key to the front door was necessary to gain access to any of the three apartments in the brownstone.

I don't know my neighbors. I'm embarrassed to admit that, since I've lived here for five years. I like to keep to myself, and if I ever commit a heinous crime, my neighbors will be quoted as saying, "She was a quiet girl, kept to herself." It was mostly that I enjoy being antisocial, and I felt if I knew my neighbors enough to become friends with them, all chance for privacy would be out the window. It would be like having a roommate, and after five roommates in three years of college, I knew I wasn't exactly the roommate type. I could have blamed them for the trouble, but since I kept moving from room to room, it seemed I was developing a pattern that wasn't conducive to living harmoniously with another human being. I didn't even have a pet.

But here I was, going upstairs to actually face one of my neighbors.

"How did you get in the building? Never mind, I don't want to buy whatever you're selling." His round face was scowling at me, and I felt I was face-to-face with a pit bull on two legs. Before I could say anything, he growled, "I bet it was that weirdo on the second floor who let you in. She has all sorts of riffraff coming in all the time."

Could he mean me? I'd never laid eyes on this guy before, so chances were good he'd never seen me, either. But riffraff? Could a member of the New Haven police department be riffraff? Tom would get a kick out of that.

"I'm sorry to bother you, sir." I put on my reporter attitude, which wasn't much but it was the best I could do at this hour. "But I'm the woman who lives on the second floor. I was just wondering if you'd seen anyone wandering the stairwell."

He narrowed his eyes at me, obviously not believing me. "Who are you?"

I held out my hand, although I was afraid he'd take a bite out of it. "Anne Seymour. I really do live downstairs."

"Why do you want to know if someone's been in the stairwell?" He didn't take my hand. I must really have gotten some sort of reputation around here I didn't know about. It was a little disconcerting, because although I didn't really give a shit, I still thought unless someone got to know me, he might think I was okay.

"Someone pushed a note under my door, and I'm trying to find out who it was," I explained.

"Well, it wasn't me." He slammed the door in my face before I could say anything more.

One down, one to go.

I'd seen the woman who lived below me. By her mode of dress, I figured her for a New Age type, with the flowing print skirts and big and plentiful bangle jewelry. Sometimes I could smell incense as I went up the stairs, which made me nostalgic for simpler days.

"Yes?" I could see her eyes from behind the chain lock.

"I'm Anne Seymour, I live upstairs. I was wondering if you'd seen anyone just now in the stairwell."

"He said he knew you."

"Who 'he'? Can you describe him?"

"So you didn't know him?"

I shook my head. "No, but he pushed a note under my door."

The door opened a little farther, but the chain remained. I could now see fuzzy brown hair and a square chin. "What sort of note?"

"Let's just say he's not my biggest fan."

"Really?"

I wouldn't say it if it wasn't true, I felt like saying, but I didn't want to push it, so I kept my mouth shut. Although I was getting a little information about the mysterious note, meeting my neighbors was all I'd expected and more. "What did he look like?" I tried again.

"Oh, about average."

I suppressed the urge to scream. "Average what?" My voice was rising with my frustration.

"Oh, brown hair, medium build. I didn't really pay attention."

Why the hell not? I wanted to ask. She wouldn't open her door for me and I lived upstairs. Instead, she lets in a complete stranger who might possibly be a murderer. "Was he young, old?" I prompted.

"Oh, maybe about twenty or so. Maybe younger, maybe older."

This was getting me nowhere.

"Did you ask Walter about this? Maybe he saw him."

"Walter?"

"He lives upstairs."

Oh, yeah, him. Mr. Pit Bull. "I was up there already. I don't think he saw anyone."

"That's all I can tell you."

I smelled that incense again and heard some sort of weird Yanni-like music in the background. "Thanks," I said as I started back up the stairs.

When I was almost to my apartment, I heard footsteps behind me, and when I turned, she was standing there in an Indian sarong. "He had a mole on his chin. It was about the size of a dime."

I stared at her. She really was very pretty, in that breathless sort of way. I guessed she was in her mid- to late twenties.

"My name is Amber Pfeiffer. It's nice to finally meet you. You're the reporter for the newspaper, aren't you?"

Oh, Christ, my reputation was preceding me. "Yeah. A mole?"

"I don't know if that helps you or not."

"It might."

"I'm sorry I let him in. But like I said, he said he knew you."

Just then, Walter the Pit Bull came down the stairs and the three of us stood there, staring at each other. Walter was the first to break the ice, which seemed only appropriate.

"What the hell's going on here? Amber,

you're talking to this woman?"

"I let that guy in, the one she's asking about."

They were talking as if I wasn't there, and I wondered how many times they'd talked about me behind my back. Then I remembered I didn't care.

Walter turned to me. "Just go back into your own world and let us be."

So much for the Welcome Wagon. But just as I was about to open my door, Tom came bounding up the stairs and froze just below us, his eyes asking me what was going on.

I pointed to Amber. "She saw a guy in here. Probably the guy who left the note. He got in by telling her he knew me."

"You really shouldn't let strangers in the building," he told Amber. "And who left the door unlocked downstairs?"

"I didn't realize she didn't know him, Tom." How did she know his name? And she was batting her eyes at him. Really. I could see his eyes soften. It pissed me off.

"You two know each other?"

They looked at me at the same time, but Tom spoke first. "I usually run into Amber in the mornings when I'm leaving and she's coming in from her run."

A beatnik who runs? I guess nowadays

anyone can do anything. I still didn't like it that they seemed to have some sort of relationship, peripheral as it might be.

"Did you see anyone, Walter?"

Oh, Christ, he knew the Pit Bull, too.

"No, Tom. I just got up and was making my coffee when she," he tossed his head in my direction, "interrupted me."

"He had a mole on his chin," Amber repeated.

Tom started writing this shit down. I just stood there like an idiot.

"What else did he look like?"

"Brown hair, brown eyes, average height —"

"Jesus, Tom, that could be anyone," I interrupted.

Tom frowned at me. "Anything can help."

I rolled my eyes and went into my apartment and slammed the door. I could hear the voices just outside, murmuring, but I couldn't make out what they were saying. I poured myself another cup of coffee and was stirring a spoonful of sugar into it when Tom came in.

"You really shouldn't be so rude," he scolded.

"I was perfectly happy not knowing my neighbors."

"They're really quite nice. Why do you

have to be so mean?"

I don't know what happened at that moment, but I burst into tears. I never burst into tears. I am one of those people who can see *Terms of Endearment* and laugh at the end. Maybe it was the stress. Maybe it was the thought that my life would never be the same now that I knew who my neighbors were. I would have to say hello on the stairs, let them into the building if they forgot their keys, help them with grocery bags. Oh, God, I might have to move.

And it might have had something to do with that note, the one Tom was inspecting carefully, not even paying attention to my waterworks.

"David Best's roommate has a mole on his chin," he said quietly.

"What?" I blew my nose.

"You heard me."

"You're kidding, right? I'm certain it's Mark Torrey, it has to be. Especially after my interview with him last night. He really didn't like me asking anything about McGee."

"But he didn't have to talk to you. He knew you were going to ask questions, that's your job. He expected it. But whoever sent you this wants you to stop doing your job." He stared at it a little longer, and I drank some of my coffee. "No," he said, sitting on the sofa, "this is someone else."

"But I haven't talked to David Best since before his arrest. And he was in custody when Allison was killed."

"No, he wasn't."

"What do you mean?"

"Posted bond. I didn't even know about it until I got back to headquarters."

"His bail was a million dollars." I couldn't believe they'd let him out.

"And he comes from a very rich and influential family." Tom had a point.

I remembered something. "Allison said she saw David the night Melissa was killed."

"Do you think David Best knew you were asking Allison questions?"

I saw where he was going with this. "But wouldn't it be stupid to get your roommate to deliver a threat? Especially someone with a distinguishing mark on his face?"

"Criminals are the stupidest people I've ever met."

He was right. I did a story about two burglars who were caught because the cops followed their footprints in the snow to their house. That was about the mentality of the average criminal.

"But wouldn't a murderer be more careful?" I asked.

"Maybe not," Tom said. "Maybe it was a crime of passion, it wasn't planned, it just happened, and he found himself in the middle of it without really expecting it. And David Best is really young, he grew up in a sheltered environment. He could afford to be sloppy because he'd be bailed out no matter what."

All points well taken. But it still left me with a threatening note and a feeling that Mark Torrey was just around the corner.

"I can't shake the feeling that Torrey's somehow involved."

Tom shrugged. "Maybe he is, maybe not. But I can't say one way or the other until I can interrogate him, and we can't find him."

"He said he'd go to the police."

"And you believed him?"

Okay, I was batting a thousand today. And it wasn't even 10:00 a.m. "If it's David Best, then I can move forward with checking into this McGee thing, right?"

"Sure, sure. But if Torrey calls you again, I want to talk to him about Melissa Peabody. He was one of the last people to see her alive, and he saw David Best that night, too. Do you have a Baggie?"

I pulled a Ziploc bag out of a drawer. It had some bread crumbs in it.

"Do you have a clean one?"

I shook my head. "Sorry. All out."

He emptied the crumbs in the sink and put the note in the bag. "I need this for evidence."

"In case I'm murdered, too, and you can say, oh, she was threatened?" I was trying to make a joke out of it, but it didn't make me feel any better.

He didn't say anything, which made me really start worrying.

"Do you have any leads on Allison's murder?" It was my feeble attempt to change the subject, but I couldn't stay away from death completely.

Tom shook his head. "Nothing. Crime scene was so goddamned clean. It just doesn't make any sense." He absently kissed me on the cheek. "I'm going to go talk to David Best's roommate."

"What's his name?" I asked, innocently, I hoped.

"No, you're not getting that out of me."

"Like I wouldn't be able to find out."

"But by the time you find out, I'll already have talked to him, and that's the way it should be." He closed the door behind him and left me with a half cup of cold coffee.

Chapter 11

Vinny DeLucia was leaning against my car when I left my building. So much for thinking my day could turn around.

"What are you doing here?"

He grinned. "Do you know you have very nosy neighbors?" He pointed up, and Amber's curtain fell back just as I looked. I could see Walter's silhouette behind his mini-blinds.

"Ignore them. I'm looking for another place anyway."

"Why? This is a great location."

I had to agree. I loved this place, but my anonymity was one of the things I loved about it, and now that was gone. I sighed.

"Why was the cop here?"

I rolled my eyes, but didn't say anything.

"I know he didn't spend the night, so why would he show up in the morning when he was already at work?"

"How did you know he was at work already?" I ignored his reference to Tom's not spending the night. I didn't want to get into how he knew that.

"Because I was at the police station earlier and found out David Best was released on bail."

I wasn't even going to ask him what he was doing. I didn't really want to know, and I didn't really care.

"So why did he come here?" he tried again.

"It's none of your business."

"I can find out from one of your neighbors."

And he probably would, too. They'd be more than happy to tell him.

"Okay, I got a note under my door. Said I should stop asking questions."

"Will you?"

"Will I what?"

"Stop asking questions."

"Of course not."

"Do you think it's a real threat?"

I stared at him. "What are you doing here? Why are you leaning against my car?"

"You met Mark Torrey last night."

"What about it, and how do you know?"

He chuckled. "I'm a private dick, remember?"

He was a dick, all right.

"Don't even say it."

How did he know everything I was thinking? This guy was nuts. "I'm in one piece, okay? It wasn't a big deal."

"But you got a threatening note this morning. You don't think they're connected?"

I did, but I wasn't about to tell him that. "Tom thinks David Best is involved."

Vinny bit his lower lip thoughtfully. "I guess so. Could be. But my bets are on Torrey."

"What's your interest in all this, Vinny? What's my mother got you working on?"

He smiled, a slow, seductive smile that made my toes start to curl; then I reminded myself he was the geek from high school. He couldn't have that effect on me.

"Wouldn't you like to know," he teased.

"Is it about Melissa Peabody's family suing the school?"

"You have to ask your mother. I'm not at liberty to say."

"All right then, why were you following me to Torrey and why are you here now? I don't have anything to do with Melissa Peabody's death."

"But you did have contact with Allison Sanders, who is now dead. And you've talked to Mark Torrey, who until then and since has spoken to no one else. You seem to be some sort of key."

To what? The door to nowhere? "I have no key. I just get phone calls and I talk to people." We stared each other down. "Hey, wait a minute. It's Torrey, isn't it? It's not Melissa. It's Torrey. What's he done? Why is my mother so interested in him?"

"Give the girl a gold star. But I still can't say."

"Maybe I could help. He did talk to me. Maybe he'll contact me again."

Vinny smiled.

I was slow on the uptake, but once I started to figure things out, there was no stopping me. "So why didn't you get to him last night, after I left him?"

"Who says I didn't?"

Something else dawned on me. "That's why you're watching me. To see if he contacts me again."

He still didn't say anything. It was infuriating.

"What did he do, Vinny?"

He shook his head. "You'll have to figure it out for yourself." He pulled himself away from my car and started down the street.

"You're a real asshole, you know that?" I yelled after him.

He turned and laughed. "You're such a charmer. I'll see you around."

I slammed the car door and cranked up the radio, as if the Rolling Stones could erase Vinny DeLucia's voice from my head. But he'd gotten me thinking despite myself. Mark Torrey was into something that my mother knew about. I was going to have to see her, continuing the day's unfortunate course.

I had to drive around the Green more than once before I found a parking space near my mother's office building. I refuse to pay to park in one of the garages or lots. Luckily, someone was pulling out just a block away from the building when I came around the corner for the fourth time. I slipped my parking pass on the dashboard so I wouldn't have to feed the meter and hoped this wouldn't take too long.

I could feel my heart quicken in that panic-attack sort of way I get when I smell fresh paint and clean carpets. I remember the smell of the hot wax in the composing room where we pasted up the stories in the old days, before computers, before everything went straight to the pressroom, rendering the waxers useless. They were idle for a while, until one day they were gone. It would be like that in the newsroom, too.

One day we'd come in and we'd all have cubicles instead of being out in the open where phone conversations could be heard five desks away and we all knew when our society reporter arrived because we could smell her perfume before we saw her.

I had a theory that the only thing that kept the company from dividing us up now was its fear that we'd somehow misuse our time if we weren't able to be watched constantly.

"Hello, Angie. Is my mother in?" My mother's secretary was about my mother's age, but without my mother's style. She was intelligent, and I have the utmost respect for secretaries, who usually know more than anyone and are invaluable sources, but she lacked that certain something that made other women her age go back to school and become hotshot lawyers.

"She has a meeting in a few minutes." Angie's eyes flickered with the lie, but I played along.

"It'll only take a couple of minutes," I said as I pushed open the door to my mother's office.

It's never ceased to amaze me that my mother, who once spent her days creating floral baskets and ironing underwear à la

Martha Stewart, now had a corner office with a huge window overlooking Church Street. The mahogany desk shone with its polish, and I couldn't help but wonder if my mother stayed after hours to give it her own elbow grease. She certainly had never trusted anyone else to clean her belongings before, but times had changed.

"Oh, Annie, yes, what is it?" Her eyes were wide, she looked like a rabbit about to flee. But I closed the door.

"I need to talk to you."

"I have a meeting in a few minutes." She pushed some papers around on her desk to make it look good. But the full cup of coffee gave her away. My mother would never get a cup of coffee if she was going into a meeting, for fear of dribbling in front of those she felt should be in awe of her.

I plopped down on the leather chair in front of her desk. "Mark Torrey. I know you're after him. What for?"

She stared at me over the top of her glasses, trying to figure out how much I knew. "I can't tell you," she finally said.

"Bullshit. Off the record then. I'll find out from someone else officially."

She laughed. "Oh, Annie, I'm your mother, but I'm also a lawyer. And you're a reporter. You can't take advantage of the fact that you're my daughter."

"Bullshit," I said again, for lack of anything else. "I met with Torrey last night."

"I know. I read the paper." She probably read it in bed with Bill Bennett, the thought of which made my stomach turn.

"Vinny DeLucia wants to talk to him. So do the cops. But I'm the only one he's contacted. Want in on the action? I can make a deal."

"How do you know he'll contact you again?"

"He already has," I bluffed, hoping I wouldn't give myself away. She was my mother, after all.

That did pique her interest, because her back stiffened and she took the glasses off. "When?"

"Tell me first what your interest in him is."

"Now, Annie," she started, and I knew I was in trouble. She had that preachy voice, the one she used when she was going to "teach me a lesson." "I told you I can't tell you. The only thing I can say is that if you continue to talk to him, you could be charged with obstruction of justice."

Christ, he really was hot. "Does it have to do with the city redevelopment project?"

She shook her head condescendingly, and I knew I wouldn't get it out of her. I wondered if Bill Bennett could. No, I really didn't want to go there.

"You should tell me where he is, Annie."

I got up and grabbed my bag off the floor where I'd dropped it. "No. Forget it. I'll find out somehow."

I started to leave, but I heard her say, "Wait." I turned.

"Two girls are dead, and they both had contact with Mr. Torrey." She paused, and I could see she was struggling between mom and lawyer. Mom was winning, and I waited. "He's made some people very unhappy, some very rich people. That's all I can say. Watch yourself. Do you still have that gun your father insisted on giving you?"

The gun again. First Vinny and now my mother. "Yeah. I've got it."

"Keep it handy, Annie, especially if you meet him again. But I hope you'll be smart and call the police if you hear from him. It's terribly important."

Despite my mother's warning, I left the building with a lighter step than when I'd gone in. Mark Torrey was ripping someone off. But who? Lundgren? I hated to stereotype developers, but I couldn't help myself. If they were mobbed up, it wouldn't be too much of a stretch. Norwegian mobsters? Why not? Maybe they weren't even really Norwegian. My brain picked through all sorts of scenarios on my way to the paper.

Dick wasn't in my chair for the first time in a few days. In fact, he wasn't even in the newsroom. Neither was Marty. The message light on my phone was winking at me, and in seconds I was hearing Mark Torrey's voice.

"A good story, Ms. Seymour, but you should've left out the references to McGee and my work with Lundgren." I'd used them at the end, as a sort of background, with the intention of following up on them in my next story. "I also thought you'd be smart enough to leave the private investigator out of it, even though he's obviously not as good as his reputation." So Vinny had tried to get to Torrey last night and failed. That made me smile.

The message continued: "I'd hoped we could've formed a relationship, but I don't think that's possible now." Damn. "It was lovely meeting you."

So I really didn't lie to my mother. Torrey had contacted me again. But it was to say goodbye. I pulled my address book out and dialed the number that the lawyer at my mother's party had given me. "The number you have dialed is out of service."

The guy was good. So good that I didn't have a clue how to move ahead with this. Except . . .

"Come Together."

I was getting so used to hearing it that it didn't even make me chuckle anymore. "Hickey Watson, please. Anne Seymour calling."

He made me wait just long enough to hear the Aerosmith version of the Beatles' "Come Together." It isn't a bad version, but I don't like remakes of something that's perfectly fine just the way it is.

"I'm getting a little tired of this, Miss Seymour. It's bordering on harassment."

"No, it's not, Hickey. I'm just trying to get to the bottom of all this, and you cared about those girls, so I know you'll want to help me." It was worth a shot. "I need to know the names of those other two guys who were in with Torrey."

"You're crazy if you think I'm going to give you that information."

"Okay, I'm crazy. But it could help."

"Sure it could help. And I could lose all my business if my clients find out I'm naming names."

"But one of them could be the killer."

"They've got the killer. That kid."

"Maybe he is, maybe he isn't. I know you want to help find whoever did this. If you didn't, you wouldn't have a heart." I wondered if a heart really did lurk behind that big belly of his. "And if you help now, maybe the cops won't come down heavy on you. Melissa would never have met Torrey if it weren't for you."

Silence. Then, "Two o'clock. Entrance to the Peabody Museum." He hung up.

The clock read ten to twelve. Seemed like as good a time as any for lunch, but then I spotted Dick and Marty coming around the corner into the newsroom, Dick's face solemn, Marty's mouth moving. What was that all about?

Marty saw me watching them and gestured for me to come over. I wasn't sure I was going to like this.

"We've just come from a meeting with Bill Bennett about the Melissa-Allison story." Marty's face was flushed. Uh-oh.

"Why didn't anyone tell me about this? I'm the main reporter on this, not him." I indicated Dick, who was still uncharacteristically quiet.

Marty steered us into one of the empty conference rooms near the circulation department and closed the door. He turned to me.

"He didn't like your story about Mark Torrey. Said Torrey's not involved. David Best was charged, we need to concentrate on him."

I was speechless.

"Apparently he's getting some heat from somewhere, and he said unless we have cold, hard facts we're not to write any more about Torrey or McGee. The Yale murders are moving inside, off the front page."

I finally found my tongue. "This place is fucking unbelievable."

Marty sighed. "Listen, for what it's worth, I agree with you. I think there's something dirty with Torrey. I got a call from someone I know at City Hall who said we should keep digging, because if it comes out, the shit could hit the fan."

"What could come out?"

He shook his head. "I don't know. She wouldn't say. But she said we're on the right track."

"Kind of like Deep Throat." So Dick wasn't unconscious.

"I talked to my mother. She said if I kept talking to Torrey, I could be charged with obstruction of justice."

Marty's eyes grew wide. "Is there a complaint or a warrant for his arrest that we don't know about?"

Dick and I looked at each other. We'd been so wrapped up in these murders that we had let some things slide. Like routine cop checks, where we actually go to the police station because they won't tell anyone anything over the telephone.

"I'll take that as a 'we don't know,' " Marty said. "Get over there and find out."

"Which one?" Dick asked.

"Which one what?" I could hear Marty's exasperation.

"Which one of us do you want to go over there?"

Marty rolled his eyes. "Annie. It's her beat, those guys will talk to her." I could hear what he didn't say. Dick's attitude with the cops had gotten him a reputation no reporter should ever have with a source. They thought he was an annoying asshole and cut him off cold. Although I could be the most abrasive person I'd ever met, and sometimes I'm even bothered by my own abrasiveness, somehow the cops seem to like that in a woman. I think Tom first got turned on when I was working the night beat and I made a smart-aleck comment about his handcuffs.

So it wasn't subtle. But I got what I wanted.

Chapter 12

Speak of the devil, Tom was coming in just as I arrived at the station.

"Did you get anything on that note?" I asked, hoping he'd gotten nothing. I wasn't sure I wanted to find out who my stalker was.

"No. Not yet. But they're working on it."

"Is there a warrant for Mark Torrey's arrest?" I didn't have enough time to beat around the bush, since I was supposed to meet Hickey.

Tom's eyes narrowed, and I knew he was going to lie.

"Don't give me any bullshit, Tom. Is there or isn't there?"

"I'm not working on that," he answered, skirting the question.

So there was some sort of investigation. "Who is?"

He shrugged. "It doesn't have anything to do with this department."

"But there is something going on?"

Tom took my arm and led me over to the corner. "You have to get information from someone else," he hissed in my ear. "I'm getting all sorts of shit, and it's because of you."

I wanted to remind him of the handcuffs, but it would only piss him off even more. We were swimming over our heads in the pool of conflict of interest, and I was pretty certain one of us was going to go down. Right then it seemed like it would be Tom, but we would both lose in the end.

"Then just tell me who I should ask about this and I'll leave you alone," I whispered.

He pulled back a little, and I could see the circles under his eyes. He'd been working overtime and not getting much sleep. "It's out of our jurisdiction. Talk to the feds." He started to walk away.

"The FBI?" I asked, too loud because the desk sergeant looked up.

Tom sighed. "See ya."

My watch said 1:45 and I had to get going to meet Hickey, but I wanted to call my source at the FBI. I walked across the street to the train station and dialed the familiar number on my cell phone.

I'd met Paula Conrad at one of my mother's dinner parties. She'd been dating an up-and-coming lawyer and I could see she was suffering as much as I was. We'd locked ourselves in the upstairs bathroom, which is as big as my apartment, and smoked cigarettes until my mother knocked on the door, asking if we planned to burn the house down or if we were trying to kill ourselves by asphyxiation. Since Paula had a mother who was exactly like mine, we became immediate friends.

I didn't like to call her at work. While I didn't mind risking my reputation by sleeping with Tom and trying to get information from him at the same time, I always felt that if I needed something from the feds, I could try to get it from the public information guys and leave Paula out of it.

But desperate times call for desperate measures. I never got anything out of the PR guys except the most basic information, and I might be able to get something from Paula that I could actually use.

"Hey, what's up? I haven't seen you in a while." Paula was always in a good mood. In most people that would annoy the hell out of me.

"I'm working on these murders."

"Oh, yeah. I've read about it. What a

shame." And she was really sorry about it, too. There was no bullshit.

"I hate to cut to the chase, since it's been ages, but I need some information. I know I don't ordinarily ask you, but I'm hitting a lot of closed doors on this."

"Mark Torrey."

"Yeah, that's right."

"I saw his connection to that dead girl. I figured someone would come around asking questions."

"What's up with him? Why is he so hot?"

I heard her ruffle some papers on her desk. "We got tipped off a couple of months ago that he might be ripping off a lot of people."

"Ripping off how?" I was acutely aware of the time. I didn't want to push her, but I didn't want to be late for my appointment with Hickey, either.

"He says he's a financial adviser, but he doesn't have a stockbroker's license, even though he's telling people he's got one. He takes people's money and says he's investing it in all sorts of things, mutual funds, CDs, stocks. But the money's disappearing. He's been submitting false statements to his investors."

"Whose money is he taking?"

Paula chuckled. "Your mother's, for one."

I almost dropped the phone. "What?"

"And a bunch of people in her circle."

"Why isn't it local? Why are you guys investigating?"

"His company, McGee, is based in New York, and he's doing business here, too, so he's crossing state lines. We also think he's stashing the money in the Channel Islands. It's a pretty sophisticated scam. We're not the only ones who want him. The Securities and Exchange folks are pretty pissed, too, as well as the IRS. He hasn't paid his taxes." She paused. "By the way, you talked to him, didn't you?"

I could tell it wasn't a casual question. She really wanted to know, and for professional reasons. Okay, I'd crossed the line of our friendship by trying to get information out of her, so I owed it to her.

"Yeah. Met him in an office on Orange Street, but I don't know where he is now. The phone number I had is now out of service."

"Shit. I was hoping he'd stay in touch with you. He hasn't been to City Hall or his house in a week."

"Didn't you know about the apartment at University Towers?"

"Not until I saw your story. We checked it out, but it was clean." I heard her sigh.

"Goddamned local cops don't tell us shit."

I knew that worked both ways, though, so I kept my mouth shut.

"We've been wondering where he's been running his business from," Paula continued. "I'll need that Orange Street address."

I gave it to her.

"Torrey did call me this morning, but he said he wasn't happy with the story and our 'relationship' was over."

"That's too bad."

A thought crossed my mind. "Was my mother the one who tipped you off?"

She was quiet, too quiet. Then, finally, "I really can't say." But she told me without telling me.

I was going to push her for more, but my watch hands were precariously close to two o'clock. "Listen, Paula, I have to meet someone. Can I call you back?"

"Sure. But if Torrey does call you again, please let me know right away."

I promised her I would and hung up.

Hickey wasn't in front of the museum, so I'd rushed Paula for nothing. I paced up and down on the sidewalk, mulling over what she'd said to me, when a white Toyota sedan with a dent in the rear passenger's-side door pulled up beside me.

The rear passenger window was rolled down, but I couldn't see inside, there were too many shadows and the angle was all wrong.

"Get in," a male voice echoed.

I looked around and pointed a finger at my chest. "Who, me?"

The door opened, and my reflexes made me step backward, away from the car.

"Get in the car!"

I kept walking backward, praying I wouldn't be gunned down like a dog, when Vinny appeared out of nowhere beside me and the car door slammed shut and the Toyota sped off.

"You don't have your gun," he said quietly.

"What's going on?"

"I keep trying to tell you you shouldn't get involved in all this."

"Are you following me?"

Vinny grinned. "Sue me. I want to make sure you're okay."

"You just want to see if I lead you to Mark Torrey, who was probably in that car. Why didn't you go after it if you're such a hotshot private eye?"

He shrugged. "Why do you think it was Torrey in that car?"

"Who else would it be?"

"You think he wants to talk to you?"

I sighed. I was tired of this cat-and-mouse shit. It was turning out to be the longest day I'd ever had, and it was barely half over. "I know about Torrey. I know he ripped off my mother and a bunch of other people."

"You have good sources."

"I'm a good reporter."

"I'm not saying you aren't. Don't get so defensive."

"Just leave me alone, okay? I'm tired of seeing you all over the place. I'm supposed to meet someone here, and I don't want you to scare him away."

"Does your meeting have anything to do with Mark Torrey?"

"It's none of your fucking business."

"I like it when you sweet-talk me." His eyes were dancing, and his resemblance at this moment to Frank Sinatra was even stronger than usual. My eyes settled on his lips, and for a second I wondered what would happen if I leaned over and kissed him.

"Don't think I haven't thought about it, too," he whispered, moving so close he brushed his arm against mine. The connection startled me, pushed me out of the moment. I backed up.

"I don't even want to go there," I said.
"Might be fun."
"Yeah, in another lifetime."
"I don't think he's going to show."
His change of topic threw me. "Who?"
"Your appointment."
"He'll be here."
Vinny shook his head. "I don't think so. Want to go in?"
I had no clue what he was talking about, but then he indicated the museum. I had fond memories of the Peabody Museum, the reconstructed dinosaur bones, the bird room, getting kicked out of Girl Scouts because I was caught smoking in the back during a field trip. I wasn't up to a trip down memory lane, though. I shook my head. "I have stuff to do." Although I wasn't really sure what my next move would be.
"You'll tell your mother I didn't say anything to you about Torrey?"
It had crossed my mind that I would let my mother think Vinny told me, just to get him back, but then she'd get pissed at him and he'd have to bear her wrath and I didn't want to do that to anyone.
"No, I won't say anything."
"Thanks." He started to walk away.
"Are you going to keep following me?" I asked loudly.

He turned, cocking his head in a very Sinatra way, and I was attracted to him again for about a nanosecond. “Maybe I will, maybe I won’t.”

I was about to say something, but I heard my name being called behind me. It was Hickey.

“Sorry I’m late.”

I turned back to try to finish up with Vinny, but he’d disappeared in that really annoying way he had. I concentrated on Hickey. “That’s okay.”

“Let’s go inside.”

It was starting to drizzle, and while an afternoon at the museum with Vinny had been out of the question, I could more easily talk to Hickey while warm and dry. We bought a couple of tickets and moved into the dinosaur room, as if there were no other room to see. The bones climbed high over our heads, and we stared at them for a few minutes to give them the respect they deserved.

Hickey sat down on one of the benches, and I sat next to him. There was only one other person in the room, across from us, hovering near the prehistoric turtle skeleton.

“So what do you want to know?” he asked. His eyes skirted around the room, as if someone was going to pounce on us.

"I found out Torrey's into some pretty big-time scam. There's a lot of money involved. Did either Allison or Melissa ever say anything to you?"

Hickey shook his head. "No, should they have?"

"I guess not. Did they ever say that anything was unusual about Torrey or the others?"

"No. Except that sometimes they liked threesomes. I don't like to encourage kinky stuff, it could get me a bad rep, but the girls didn't seem to mind."

I tried not to visualize anything. "Can you get me the names of the other McGee guys?" I whispered.

His foot started tapping, but he didn't seem aware of it. "I never told you any of this."

I nodded. "Okay. Fine."

"Albert Webber and Nicholas Curtin."

Albert Webber was the lawyer I'd gotten Torrey's number from at my mother's party. My mother must not have known he was in tight with Torrey, or she wouldn't have invited him. It hadn't dawned on me that he would be involved directly, especially since he obviously knew who I was. He'd gone along with my innocent ploy to get the number, all the while knowing I wanted Torrey for my story. It was a way for Torrey to speak without talking to the cops. It got his side of the story: how he'd left Melissa very much alive in that apartment, how much he liked her, how tragic this was.

Nicholas Curtin, however, I didn't recognize.

I winked, or at least gave it my best effort, since it's not my best talent. "It's funny, but you said something just now, but I can't remember what it was."

"I appreciate that," he said, his eyes straying to my thigh. I pulled my jacket closer. "I'm serious," he added. "I think you could have a good career as an escort."

While I *was* getting used to him, his career choice still made my skin crawl. "Why don't you find another line of work, Hickey? Something that wouldn't put young girls in any danger."

"I know it may not last forever," he conceded. "I've thought about other options. I've thought I could eventually write a book or something."

It would probably end up on the bestseller list. "You need some celebrities first."

"Who says I don't have them now?"

I couldn't help myself. He piqued my interest and I wanted to know which celebrities. As the question reached my tongue and I was about to ask, the guy looking at the turtle suddenly turned around and asked loudly, "Do you have the time?"

My heart jumped into my throat, and Hickey looked like he was going to have a stroke on the spot.

"Two-thirty," I offered.

"Thanks." He turned and as he moved out of the room, something struck me.

"Did that guy have a mole on his chin?" I asked Hickey, getting up without waiting for an answer.

He shrugged. "Beats me."

I can move pretty fast when I want to and I was in the museum lobby in seconds.

"Did you see a guy walk through here with a mole on his chin?" I asked the woman selling tickets.

She shook her head. "I'm sorry, dear, I didn't notice."

I went to the stairs and paused, trying to hear footsteps. It was him, David Best's roommate. It had to be. It was too much of a coincidence.

Hickey was panting behind me, his big belly a sign that he should start working out and stop eating crap.

"Who was it?"

"Maybe he *is* somehow involved in all

this," I thought out loud.

"Who?" Hickey repeated.

"I think it's David Best's roommate."

"The ex-boyfriend?"

"Yeah."

"This isn't making any sense."

I couldn't tell him that I didn't have a clue either, so I kept my mouth shut, thereby insinuating that I perhaps could make sense of this and just chose not to say anything.

He wasn't outside when we got there. I looked up and down the sidewalk, but he had disappeared just as Vinny had. Shit. And I didn't even know this kid's name. I thought about Sarah, not sure if I could impose on her again. She certainly wasn't welcoming me with open arms. Those kids I met at Atticus the day Melissa died might help. I was so busy thinking about my next move that I almost took off without saying goodbye to Hickey.

"You won't say anything?" he asked, and I pulled myself back to the moment so I could answer.

"Don't worry, Hickey. I really appreciate it."

That was all I could give him — he was lucky he got that — and I got into my car and barreled off.

Chapter 13

I ran into Sarah on York Street near David Best's college. At first I wasn't sure it was her: She was wearing a baseball cap and sunglasses.

"Hey," I said loudly.

She almost fell over, and her eyes grew wide. "Oh, shit, it's you."

"Don't be so happy to see me."

"What're you doing here?"

"I need to find David Best's roommate. What's his name?"

She cocked her head, and I wished I could see her eyes through those damned glasses. "Why?"

"Just tell me." This girl was testing my patience. God knows I had precious little of it under even the best of circumstances.

"You know, I may remember something about Melissa that night."

Okay, so it wasn't what I'd asked, but it got my attention. "What?"

"She said there was something going on that she didn't want to have anything to do with."

"Did she say anything specific?"

Sarah shrugged. "Not really. But it sounded like something."

A couple of murders and everyone was Miss Marple. "Thanks. I'll keep that in mind. Why didn't you tell me this before?"

"She wanted out."

She still didn't answer my question, but I was intrigued. "Out of what?"

"I figured it was that escort service stuff. She'd had enough, but she said she couldn't get her boss to leave her alone."

Hickey? Had he been holding back on me? "How do you know?"

"She was my roommate. I heard her with Allison."

"Did Allison want out, too?" It was a test. Allison liked the money, she told me that, so if this kid was trying to pull a fast one, she'd try to tell me otherwise.

"No." It seemed like she wanted to tell me something else.

"Listen, Sarah, are you sure you don't know more about this than you're saying?"

Her face changed slightly, I couldn't put my finger on just how, but she bit her lip and she shrugged. "No, um, well, maybe." Sarah glanced at her watch. "Gotta go." And she scurried off, leaving me wondering just what the fuck was going on over here in the Ivy League and pissed that she hadn't told me about David Best's roommate.

I walked a block to the college, hoping for some good luck. An Asian kid was coming through the gate out onto the sidewalk.

"Hold up," I said, sprinting toward him. Thank God chivalry is still on a respirator; he held the gate for me and I stepped into the courtyard. A tall, pimply kid with shocking red hair lounged against a wall to my right, smoking a cigarette.

"Hi. I'm with the *Herald.* I was wondering if you know David Best's roommate."

His smile was long and slow, his eyes a little glazed, and I looked at the cigarette to make sure it was tobacco. It was, but I had a strong suspicion the one before this wasn't. "Oh, you're looking for Matt. He's not here."

"What's his last name?"

"Minneo."

"Do you know him well?"

He shrugged in that way teenagers do

when they know more than they want to say. "Little bit."

"You wouldn't know where he went?"

Another shrug. This guy was way too stoned for me to get much out of him. "If you see him, can you call me?" I scribbled my cell number on the back of one of my cards and handed it to him. He was still staring at it like it was some sort of mysterious secret code when I walked away.

I wasn't going to find Matt Minneo unless I staked out the dorm, and I really wasn't in the mood to do that. I could've gotten Dick to come down and do it for me, but I wasn't sure how I could explain that without telling him and ultimately the entire newsroom about the threatening note. I didn't want anyone to know about it.

So I pushed the facts around in my head as I walked back to my car, trying to sift through the shit and come up with my next move. Which had to be Torrey and his scam. Which meant yet more contact with my mother in a very short period of time. I would need a shrink after all this.

I left a message with her secretary. Either she really wasn't in or she didn't want to talk to me.

Marty was hovering when I got back to

the newsroom. I briefed him on what Paula had told me about Torrey.

"We need confirmation."

"Yeah, yeah. I'm trying to get it." How could I explain that my mother would call me back when she felt like it? It could be ten minutes, it could be a week.

"Do you know any of the other people he's scammed?"

I shook my head.

Marty eyeballed me. "Can you find out?"

It was not really a question, it just sounded like one. I wanted to go home and have a beer and watch some stupid television and go to bed early.

"We're not even on the front page anymore," I tried, my voice as tired as I felt.

"And we won't be for a while. The cows are coming tomorrow."

I stared. "What?"

"The cows. Remember?"

It was coming back to me. "That's tomorrow? I thought it wasn't until Thanksgiving." I had managed to skim the memo while waiting for callbacks.

"That's when it's over."

The powers that be in the city of New Haven had seen something on the Internet about the CowParade in Chicago and then a similar event in New York City. It was a big economic boon. Three hundred fiberglass cows decked out in everything from mirrors to rhinestones, all over the city, luring the suburbanites who never left their malls and playgrounds. New Haven actually thought it could cash in on the cows. I was disappointed the city couldn't come up with another idea, dinosaurs maybe, to give it its own unique flavor. But the cows came cheap from some factory in Switzerland if they were bought in bulk. Local artists had the job of taking the nude cows and creating their visions on them.

It worried me, those naked cows, just placidly standing there while those artists did what they would to them.

After a reasonable time on display throughout the city, the cows would be auctioned off, the tourists' money tucked firmly in City Hall's pocket. City officials decided to combine the cows with the annual influx of leaf peepers.

I didn't want to be the one to write the stories when someone shot them full of holes during a late-night drug raid. Vandalism was inevitable. Those poor cows had two months with us. The graffiti artists should've been given first shot; they'd get the last say anyway.

My pessimism was even getting to me. I

needed a drink, it was late in the day, I had no story to write.

"Fuck the cows," I said quietly.

Marty shook his head. "Go home, Annie. You're burned out. Get a good night's sleep."

He was right. A good night's sleep would do me a world of good. But I couldn't resist. I had to ask.

"They're writing some stupid slogan that's going to run on the front page every day until the cows leave, aren't they? Something dumb like If You Moove Them, They Will Come?"

I saw the corners of Marty's mouth curl up as if he was going to smile. But he still couldn't even look me in the eye. "The cows aren't a bad idea, Annie. I think it's one of the better ideas the city's come up with. People are already calling, asking about the cows and if they're on display yet."

Oh, Christ. They're going to take all the parking spots. They're going to clog up the streets and crowd the coffeehouses. I needed some air.

"Fuck the cows," I said again as I walked out.

I didn't notice the car at first. But then it

kept turning everywhere I turned. I kept my eyes on its headlights in the rearview mirror, turning off Mick Jagger so I could concentrate on my jitters. It slowed down when I got to Wooster Square; it seemed sure I would stop, but it had gotten me going, so I went around the square a couple of times. It kept with me.

I tried to shake the ominous feeling. But then I remembered Vinny. He'd been following me all over the city. It had to be Vinny.

I finally stopped in front of my building. The car moved past, my headlights illuminating it briefly. It was white, but that's all I could make out about it before it turned right, out of sight. I sighed with relief, probably just someone who was lost. I was getting way too paranoid. I saw Amber's curtain move a little, the pink glow from her lights splashed against the window. I fumbled with my keys, dropping them, and as I bent over to pick them up, I could hear heavy footsteps approaching. I straightened up, expecting to see Vinny, but before I could focus on who it was, I felt a sharp pain scream through my head and something pushed over my eyes.

"She's heavy," I thought I heard, and it pissed me off. I tried to ignore the pounding across my skull and attempted to struggle.

"You should've hit her harder." The voice was familiar, but I couldn't place it.

"So hit her again if you think you can do it better."

Maybe they'd hit each other and leave me alone. But no such luck. I jerked my head back and felt something land on my shoulder, sending waves of pain to my fingertips. I shouldn't have given up those tae kwon do classes so quickly three years ago. Maybe I would've been able to actually defend myself.

"Oh, shit," one of them said.

"Oh, shit" was right. Someone was dragging me by the back of my shirt along the sidewalk. Just when I needed a nosy neighbor, they seemed to be busy concentrating on their own lives. Wouldn't you know.

My face scraped against the rough concrete, and I think I finally made a sound something like "eeeooowww."

"Christ, can't you hit her again?"

A car door opened and a blast of warm air slapped against my face.

"Just get her in."

Where had I heard that voice before? I felt myself levitating, but then I heard screeching tires and I fell with a thump, my back slamming against the curb. Car doors slammed, a car moved past me with enough force that I could feel my hair blow back.

A cold hand touched the scrape on my cheek and I finally screamed.

"Ssshhh. It's okay."

Vinny. I felt him struggling with whatever was over my eyes, and in a second I was looking at him.

"You've been following me for days, but when I really need you, where the fuck are you?"

"I should leave you right here in the gutter for that."

"Could your conscience do that?"

"Do I have a conscience?"

He helped me to my feet, the pain in my back moving quickly through my legs. I stumbled.

"Do you know who they were?"

I shook my head, the waves of pain spinning behind my eyes. Bad idea. Keep the head still. Don't move. But his arm was around me, and we were getting closer to my door.

"Where are your keys?"

I shrugged, which was also a bad idea, considering the state of my shoulder. "Fuck," I said quietly.

"Did I ever tell you you have an amazing vocabulary?"

I didn't have the energy to keep it going. "I dropped my keys. Near my car."

He propped me up against the railing and fetched them, then unlocked the door. Amber's door opened a crack as we ascended the stairs.

"What's the matter with her?" she asked Vinny.

"You didn't by chance see anything outside, did you?"

"I don't think so." The door closed.

"She probably thinks I'm drunk," I managed to say.

"Probably."

My apartment was dark and warm. Vinny put me on the couch. I heard him rummaging in my bathroom, and when he came back, he washed the cut on my face with a soapy cloth.

"We should call the police," Vinny said.

I knew that. But something made me hold back. Maybe it was because I felt like a train had run over me and the last thing I wanted was a cop asking me to remember specific things about something I just wanted to put out of my mind at the moment.

"Do you have any idea who they were?" Vinny asked again when I didn't respond.

I shrugged, sending little slivers of pain up and down my back and arm. I winced, and Vinny's face grew dark. "If you have any idea, you need to let the cops know. That boyfriend of yours . . ."

I shook my head. "Oh, Christ, Tom will tell me I should've stopped asking questions, especially after that note."

My eyes rested on the bottle I keep on top of my refrigerator. "I'd love a brandy right now."

The transition startled him, but Vinny got up and found two snifters in my cupboard. "I hope you don't mind if I join you," he said when he sat back down and handed me my glass.

"No."

"So tell me more about the note."

"Yeah. Okay. My neighbor saw a guy with a mole on his face, and Tom said David Best's roommate has a mole on his face, too, so I went over to find him and he wasn't there, so that was that."

It seemed like a million years ago.

"Do you think it was the same guy who attacked you tonight?"

"I think Mark Torrey's involved somehow."

"Why?"

I couldn't explain it, but I was careful

not to shrug again. I took a sip of the brandy and savored its warmth as it moved down my throat.

"You're right. I probably should call the cops." I meant I should call Tom. If I kept this from him, he'd kill me before whoever wanted to got another chance.

"Do you want me to stay?" Vinny was sitting close to me, so close I could feel the heat from his body. It was too bad for him I felt like shit or the night might have taken a very different turn. But the last thing I wanted at the moment was for anyone to actually touch me.

"They might want to question you, too, see if you saw anything. Did you?" It hadn't occurred to me to ask until then, I was too preoccupied with my pain.

Vinny shook his head. "Sorry. I saw shadows. One was tall, the other a little shorter, not too much, though. I didn't see faces, I couldn't even tell what sex they were."

"One man and one woman." I could hear their voices back in my head, but I still couldn't place them. "But that's all I know. I didn't see them, either."

"Your neighbor downstairs, she said she didn't think she saw anything, but maybe she did."

I remembered Amber's curtain moving when I'd pulled up. "Maybe." But I didn't want to talk to her. It was getting too cozy, and if she had seen something, I'd owe her.

"Why don't you call the cops and I'll go talk to her again." Vinny was up and out the door before I could say anything.

I dialed Tom's cell phone number, and he answered on the first ring.

"There's been a little incident," I started.

"What sort of incident?" he asked warily.

"I sort of got mugged."

I could hear his breath get quicker. "What do you mean, sort of?"

"I guess I got mugged."

"Are you hurt?"

"A little beat up."

"Did he get your purse?"

"No. I don't think that's what they were after."

A very pregnant pause, and then, "They? What were they after?"

I took another sip of my brandy. Maybe I should get drunk before he got here. I knew where this was going. "I think it was the people who sent me that note." And before he could say anything more, I added, "Vinny DeLucia showed up. He scared them off and brought me up to my apartment."

"So they were in front of your apartment? Lying in wait?"

I thought about the car following me. "Actually, no. I think they followed me from work." Getting drunk was sounding better and better. I drank some more brandy.

"I'll be right over." I heard the dial tone, and I put the phone down. Any natural curiosity I possessed as a reporter seemed to be absent in this situation.

Vinny came back in while I was finishing my brandy.

"Shadows. That's all she saw. Shadows, just like me." He saw my empty glass. "Is he coming?"

I nodded. "Sure. And he'll do what you just did. I think I want to take a bath."

He helped me to the bathroom and filled the tub for me. Tom came in and their voices were quiet as they talked about me. I couldn't hear exactly what they were saying, but I heard the door close and then a while later it opened again and more voices. Finally Tom stuck his head into the bathroom.

"You okay?"

I managed to open my eyes. The water had gotten tepid, and I started to shiver. Without a word, he brought me a towel and held me.

"I really don't want to talk about it right now," I whispered. "I feel like shit."

He nodded. "Okay, but I'm staying tonight, and there's no discussion."

I would've been pretty pissed if he didn't spend the night, so I wasn't going to say anything.

"And in the morning, we'll go over everything that happened. Vinny filled me in on what he could."

"He doesn't know any more than me."

Vinny was standing awkwardly in the hall when we emerged from the bathroom, me wrapped in my fleece bathrobe with Tom's arm still around me.

"I guess I'll be going. If you need any more from me, you know where to reach me." He was talking to Tom, and he wouldn't let himself look at me. I was sure I looked like hell, but I hadn't looked in the mirror. I'd had too many shocks for one night.

I think I said good night and the next thing I knew I was snuggled under my comforter and fell fast asleep.

Chapter 14

The first thing I saw when I looked out the window was a cow grazing in Wooster Square. But it was no ordinary cow. This cow had fucking pizzas painted all over it. Pepperoni pizzas.

They had arrived.

"What do you think of those stupid cows?" I asked Tom as he poured me a cup of coffee.

He shrugged. "I haven't really seen any yet."

"Well, look out there, there's one."

He peered through the blinds and started to laugh. "Oh, Christ."

"My sentiments exactly."

I gingerly fingered the scrape on my chin. I also had bruises on my face, arms, back, and legs. I didn't want to remember what happened, but every time I moved, it brought everything back. The cows, while idiotic, were a convenient distraction.

"I came up with a slogan: 'If You Moove Them, They Will Come.' What do you think?"

Tom chuckled. "Not bad. I guess the paper's going to go over the top on this one."

"You bet. This is a tourist thing, they want people to come to the city. I personally don't think anyone will come. They're still too afraid of being shot to risk coming to look at fake cows. They could go to Durham and see the real things."

"But they smell. These cows don't shit."

He had a point. But I still didn't think anyone would come. Even though New Haven offered great theater, restaurants, nightlife, and shopping, there was still a large contingent out there in the suburbs who thought they'd become crime victims if they crossed the city line. Back in the '70s, a girl got murdered in a parking garage downtown, which was pretty much the kiss of death for the Chapel Square Mall. It was still struggling but managing to come back slowly. And sure, there were neighborhoods that I wouldn't visit after a certain hour if I didn't have to, but overall, the city was a lot safer than the suburbanites thought it was.

"They're here till Thanksgiving?" Tom was still talking about the cows.

I nodded. "And they're going to be a pain in my ass until they're gone."

"Why can't you lighten up? They're funny. Admit it."

His expression was so earnest, but I just couldn't do what he asked. "Maybe you don't remember, but I got pretty beat up last night, Tom. Somehow the cows aren't making me feel much better."

"I'm going to bring in David Best."

"Why?"

"I'm going to ask him where he was last night."

"You think it was him?"

"We don't have any other suspects. I couldn't track down his roommate yesterday, but I think Best is behind the note you got."

"I couldn't find him either," I mused. "What about Mark Torrey?"

Tom smiled. "What do you have against that guy?"

"The feds are after him."

"Yeah, I know. But they're being pretty closemouthed about it, won't tell us shit."

I remembered Paula saying the same thing about the city cops and suppressed a smile. "So you don't know any details?"

"I was hoping you'd tell me."

"Apparently he's been taking people's

money, claiming he's going to invest it, and then the money disappears."

He shook his head. "What an asshole."

"He apparently ripped off my mother."

"No shit."

"She hasn't called me back so I can't confirm that she got the feds after him. I can't write the story until I can get someone on the record."

He didn't ask me who I'd gotten this from. He knew Paula, but they were always careful to keep business out of any conversation if we were socializing. It was mutual respect for each other's profession. I never bothered to remind them that I was the Evil Media.

The phone rang. I reached for the receiver.

"Are you never at work on time?" It was my mother.

"It's only nine o'clock, Mother. I don't have to punch a clock." I tried to keep my voice light — I did need her, after all.

"So you wanted to talk to me? I hope you're not going to lecture me about Bill."

"No. I don't care who you go out with." That was a lie, but if I said it, maybe she'd be more amenable to talking about Mark Torrey. "Paula tells me you were one of the people Mark Torrey embezzled from." I don't like to beat around the bush.

"Have you seen any of those cows yet?" She doesn't like to answer anything she doesn't want to answer.

"Please tell me, Mother. Don't change the subject."

"You want a story. I don't want to give you one."

"But I'll find out, with or without you, and at least this way you can make a statement."

She loves to make statements. I knew I had her on that one.

"How close are you?" I knew she meant to having the story.

"Pretty close." I paused. "He's got your money." Then I took a stab in the dark: "And Bill Bennett's."

"You have to keep him out of it."

"Who? Bill Bennett? But he's a victim, too."

"But it wasn't just his personal money."

Something very evil was dawning on me. "He didn't invest the pension money, did he?" There were rumors that something was going on with our pension money. But this would be pretty bad. And it would never see print. I wasn't that naive to think that I could write this story and it wouldn't get held. Until at least the year 3000.

"I'm not sure whose it was. This is off the record, dear." Her voice was firm and not very endearing.

"Can you give me anything?" I would have to deal with the Bill Bennett angle later. "You're not the only victim, and he could be swindling innocent people as we speak. We have a responsibility to tell the public about him." It was my crusading journalist speech, and it almost always worked.

"I'll think about it." She sighed, and I could tell she was very tired. For a moment, I wasn't a reporter trying to get a story.

"Did you invest a lot with him? Are you okay?"

"It's been a bit difficult. I took quite a bit of my divorce settlement money and invested it. It's all gone now."

"But you're successful. You'll get it back." I knew she would. She worked eighty hours a week and charged her clients more than should be legal.

"I'll have something drafted for you. You can pick it up after lunch."

I hung up and watched Tom finish his coffee. "It's too easy."

"What?"

"She's giving me something. It's too

easy. There's got to be a catch."

Tom reached over and touched my cheek. "Can't you trust someone for once? Stop being so cynical?"

I pulled my face away and winced when my head swirled with pain. "You should talk," I said, trying to ignore it. "You're a cop. Cops are the most cynical people I know."

He was shaking his head. "You have us all beat."

"When are you going to bring in David Best?"

"Are you going to work?" Tom asked.

I suppose it was a fair question. I was feeling rather under the weather, and I knew I must look like hell. It would raise some eyebrows and I'm sure more than one person would make a comment about my appearance and express curiosity how I got into such a state. Because even for me this was bad.

"I haven't decided yet."

"It's getting late." So he and my mother were co-conspirators. "I think you better call in."

"I look that bad?"

"Yes."

I picked up the phone. This was a man who thought I looked good anytime, anyplace. If he was telling me I looked awful, I must really look like shit.

Marty picked up on the first ring.

"Where are you?"

"I'm not feeling well."

"So?"

I never call in sick. I'm one of those annoying people co-workers curse because I'll just bring a big box of tissues and suffer through my day.

"I can't come in." Not to mention that I didn't sound sick.

"Oh." He hesitated, uncertain about this curious turn of events.

The hell with it. "Okay, Marty, this is the scoop. I got mugged last night. Someone threatened me and then someone beat me up and tried to abduct me."

"Sure, Annie. Fine. I believe you're sick. You don't have to make up stuff."

"I'm not making it up."

He actually laughed. "Give me a break. What time will you come in?"

I sighed. "I'm not coming in, Marty. I got mugged. Tom's here. He's going to try to find out if it's connected to Melissa Peabody."

Silence. I could hear him thinking. Then finally, "You're serious."

"Damned straight I'm serious. Would I

joke around about something like this?"

"Yes."

Okay, so I probably would.

"Today's the cow inaugural," he said.

"Then it's a good day to be sick."

"We've got a team working on that. You're really not coming in? I need some stuff for the police blotter, and no one else can get the cops to give them anything."

He knew how to make me feel guilty. "Listen, I could make some cop calls, send a couple of things over by e-mail."

"It would be a big help." I could tell the cows were going to weigh heavily on Marty until they were gone.

"I've got a cow covered in pepperonis outside my window."

He laughed. "That's the Mooster Street cow."

It was going to be a long two months.

Tom was getting his coat on. "I'll give you a call later."

"Will you tell me if you find the guy who did this?"

He walked over to me and took my face in his hands. "I'll kill him, I swear." Then he kissed me and left.

I'm not quite sure what to do with myself when I'm not working. I like to read, but my attention span is short unless I've got something really riveting. I looked over my bookshelves and found nothing that fell into that category. At least nothing I hadn't already read. I turned on the TV and channel-surfed while I finished my coffee. I spent a few minutes with Ellen, then less time with Dr. Phil. I skipped over Elmo and the Sesame Street gang and some crafty shit on the Home & Garden network. It was a wasteland. I was sorry it wasn't later in the day. I admit to being secretly hooked on *General Hospital.* My mother used to watch it before she became Super Lawyer and through osmosis I got stuck on it.

I called a couple of police stations and got the runaround. I wanted to call Bill Bennett and ask him if my pension money was in Mark Torrey's Channel Islands account, but toasted a bagel instead. When the phone rang, I jumped on it, eager for any human contact.

"I'm on my way over." It was Vinny.

"What for?"

"I think I've got something."

But before I could ask what, he'd hung up. Within minutes, my doorbell rang. I buzzed him in.

"Your friend Hickey knows more than he's saying." Vinny bounded over to the window in my living room and turned around to see my reaction.

Which was, pissed off.

"Can't you even say hello?"

"Hello. Hickey knows something. I'm sure of it."

"Do you want a cup of coffee?"

"Black. Don't you want to know what I think?"

I'd spent the last twenty years not even aware that Vinny DeLucia was alive, so to wonder what he was thinking seemed a little out there. I went into the kitchen and poured him some coffee. My silence was annoying him. For the first time that day I was enjoying myself.

When I came out of the kitchen, Vinny made a face. "Oh, Christ, you look awful."

I handed Vinny the cup and sat down. "Thanks a lot."

"Sorry. But you usually look so much, well, better than that."

It didn't exactly sound like a compliment, but I decided to take it as one. "Okay, tell me what Hickey knows."

"Hickey's got a secret bank account."

"Like he wouldn't. Listen, he's a fucking pimp. Wouldn't you have a secret account?" I sounded more cocky than I felt. I admit I was intrigued.

"But one that gets money dumped in it regularly from the McGee Corporation, via the Channel Islands?"

I straightened up, ignoring the pain in my shoulder. "How much money?"

"Thousands at a time."

"No shit. How do you know?"

Vinny smiled. "I have my ways."

"You're a computer geek, aren't you? You hacked into some secret place and found it, didn't you?" I always wanted to hack into an important place like a bank or the federal government, just to see how it was done, just to see what I could find out. But my computer skills are minimal at best.

Vinny continued to smile and sip his coffee.

"So it's for more than the girls?"

"It's too much to be just for the girls."

I thought for a minute. "You know, I think he was really trying to help me."

"Then why didn't he tell you about this? He wasn't up front about his relationship with Torrey."

"Maybe he didn't know what Torrey was up to."

"Oh, come on. He had to know something. And maybe Melissa found out and that's what got her killed."

"Tom thinks it was David Best."

"Yeah, and there's a cow on every corner."

"There *is* a cow on every corner. Haven't you seen them?"

"Right. I bumped into one outside City Hall. It was covered in mirrors."

I didn't want to talk about the cows. They gave me the creeps. "I think Melissa was asking questions. I think Torrey killed her. So how do we prove that? Torrey's nowhere to be found. He's got people's money that he's not supposed to have. Since you're a computer genius, can you find out about that?"

Vinny shook his head. "Torrey's covered his tracks so well even I can't trace him. It's too bad you pissed him off."

"Right. Blame me."

"You did piss him off."

"Don't remind me. What's our next step?"

"We have to find out what Hickey knows."

"What if it was Hickey who did this to me last night?" I pointed to the scrape on my chin.

"Amateurs."

"What?"

"I don't know who did that to you, but

I'm sure that if it was someone who meant business, you'd be dead already."

"Oh, that makes me feel better." I was just about to call him an asshole when the phone rang. I picked it up.

"I have been advised not to give you a statement."

"Hello, Mother. Who advised you?"

"My lawyer. And you'll be getting a phone call from Bill."

Great. "Why are you covering this up?"

"I'm not. I'm just not going on the record with it."

"Who else got scammed?"

"I'm not at liberty to say."

"You know, though, don't you?"

Vinny was looking out my front window, drinking his coffee, his back to me.

"I can't believe you're stonewalling me. This is my job."

"And it's my money and my life and I'd like a little privacy." She paused. "Oh, by the way, I think Vinny DeLucia's got a crush on you."

I felt my face turn hot even though I knew he couldn't hear what she was saying.

"Why do you think that?" I tried to keep my voice light.

"He's been asking a lot of questions

about you. What do you like to do in your spare time, have you been dating this police officer for a long time, is it serious, that sort of thing. I think he's rather cute, don't you?"

Okay, so I had a dream about him that I didn't want to mention because it might indicate I had some deep-seated sexual feelings for the guy. But I certainly wasn't going to tell my mother. "No. No, I don't," I said coldly, coldly enough for Vinny to turn around, his eyebrows arched, questioning my conversation.

"Methinks she doth protest too much."

Sometimes I really hated my mother.

"Can't you give me another name, someone I can talk to about Mark Torrey's scam?"

"You don't seem to understand, Annie. These are people who would rather not see their names splashed all over the newspaper proving they were stupid enough to get scammed."

No shit. And what didn't I understand? "Fine. I could keep names out of it. I just want someone on the record to tell me the feds are after Torrey and what the reason is."

"I've got another call. Sorry, dear." The dial tone pounded into my ear.

"No luck, huh?" Vinny asked when I hung up.

I shook my head. "You know, don't you? You know who these people are. You're working for my mother. Why can't you tell me?"

"I'm looking for Mark Torrey. That's my job. I get paid when I find him."

"But why are you still hanging around me?"

"Because I think he's going to contact you again."

"I pissed him off, you even said it yourself."

"I think he likes the idea of talking to a reporter. I think he wants to see his name in the paper. If it goes long enough without any news about himself, he'll call. He wants to show off, let everyone know that he can be invisible. But no one's that clever. He'll slip up. And I think it'll be because he craves attention. That's why I'm hanging around."

"What will you do with him once you find him?"

Vinny grinned. "I turn him over to the police and I'm a goddamned hero."

He took a long drink from his cup and I studied his face. I lied. I did find him attractive. But I'd never admit it.

"My mother tells me you have a crush on me."

I saw the splash of coffee come out of his nose as he sputtered, "Where'd she get that idea?"

"She says you're asking all sorts of personal questions about me."

He wiped his nose with a handkerchief he pulled from his pocket. He was stalling. "It's for the case," he tried.

I smiled condescendingly. "Don't think it's going to make any difference."

"Don't flatter yourself."

We scowled at each other for a few seconds, but it got boring. "I'm going to call Hickey," I said. "Maybe I can get something more out of him." I picked up the phone.

He put his hand over mine. "Don't let on we know about the bank account. See if he tells you first."

I could feel the heat from his hand move up my arm and down my spine. The images from the dream came back to me, and I pulled my hand away. "What do you think I am, stupid?" I barked.

His lips parted in a slow smile, and this time I could feel it between my legs. "I love it when you talk dirty," he whispered, and I turned my back on him, dialing and praying they'd pick up on the first ring.

Chapter 15

I didn't have anything. Hickey didn't return my call. My mother wouldn't give me anything. Paula wouldn't give me anything on the record; she said she was only part of the investigating team and would get into deep shit if her bosses found out she was talking to me. Sometimes my job really sucked.

And then the publisher called me. At home. He said he was sorry I wasn't feeling well, but could I try to make it in that afternoon? He had something pressing he wanted to discuss with me. I couldn't say no: My face looks like a truck ran over me, I haven't done laundry in more than a week, and I have no clean underwear. I was stuck like a pig. Shit.

I finally found a clean pair of slacks in the back of my closet, but when I pulled them on, they were so tight I was afraid they'd split. I remembered why they were in the back of the closet. I found a skirt, but it was in the same shape. Maybe I should try working out or something. Or maybe not. I usually just bought several items in several sizes, knowing I'd fit into them at one point or another. Aha! A knit skirt with an elastic waist tucked behind my pile of sweaters. If I pulled a shirt out of the laundry basket, who would be the wiser? I squirted a little perfume on myself and doubled up on the deodorant.

The makeup job wasn't going to be easy. I surveyed my face in the mirror, the scrape looking like the Grand Canyon with a bloody Colorado River running through it. I touched it and winced, but fearlessly pushed ahead and smeared some foundation over it. When I was done, I still looked like hell, but it was better than before.

Walter met me in the hallway when I was locking up.

"Christ. What happened to you?"

I shrugged. "Another tough night on the wrestling circuit."

I think he thought I was serious.

I went into the building through the executive side. I didn't want to run into Marty or, God forbid, Dick. My investigation was stymied, and I didn't want to have to admit that. And now Bill Bennett was going to tell me to stop where I was and not go any further.

He was leaning back in his big leather chair and motioned for me to sit in the uncomfortable straight-backed chair on the other side of his desk. I'd been in this office only once before, a long time ago, when there was still a Christmas party every year. I vaguely remember making out with someone.

"I suppose you know why you're here," he said. Maybe he thought I walked around all the time looking like this, because he didn't even raise an eyebrow when I walked in.

"Mark Torrey."

"I would prefer it if you let this one go." It was nice the way he pretended to make it my choice.

"When they catch him . . ."

"When they catch him, we'll assess the situation."

He was smooth, but I wouldn't have expected less from any man who dated my mother.

"The private investigator on the case seems to think Torrey will contact me again."

"Then you call the police."

It seemed easy enough, as far as he was concerned. But I couldn't stop myself.

"Between you and me, I've heard you invested some of the paper's money." It wasn't the stupidest thing I've ever said, but it was close. His eyes narrowed and I could see them grow dark.

"I don't know where you heard that, but if I ever see it in print, in our paper or another publication, you're fired."

He couldn't get more direct than that.

"And what happened to your face?"

I sighed. "Someone decided to use me as a punching bag last night."

"Did you call the police?"

"Sure."

"Does your mother know?"

I snorted. "Yeah, right. Like I'm going to tell her this. I would appreciate some discretion on your part, too."

He straightened up and put his elbows on his desk. "Is this connected in some way to the story?"

I told him about the note.

"That does it. You're not to write another word about this."

I bit my lip to keep my mouth from opening. He was pushing me toward updating my résumé. "The community should know if a city lawyer is embezzling money from people. This is our job, isn't it?"

Bill Bennett nodded, but he was no Ben Bradlee, that was for sure. "I can't have my reporters being threatened, being beat up because of a story."

"It means I'm getting close."

"But I just told you to stop. Now." He stood up. "Considering what's happened, too, I think you should have a lighter load for a while. With your connections, I think you'd do a fine job covering the cows. I talked to Marty Thompson about this earlier."

I froze, even though he was walking next to me, trying to get me out his door so he could move on to whatever else it was he did during the day. He frowned when I stopped.

"Is that a problem?"

I should've said no. But I heard myself before I could think about it. "I don't exactly believe in the cows, Mr. Bennett."

Incredulity moved across his face. Not believe in the cows? What sort of New Havener was I? Didn't I want the economy to prosper from a bunch of silly fiberglass bovines? He shook his head. "Your mother told me you could be difficult. I'm going to ignore that. If you want to continue working here, you'll do as I say."

The door shut behind me.

I didn't care anymore who saw me. I strolled into the newsroom and ignored the shocked faces staring at me. Marty dropped his pen when he saw me.

"Christ, you look awful."

"Thanks. We need to talk."

Dick's eyes followed us to the conference room and I shut the door on him, turning to Marty.

"Bennett wants me to cover the fucking cows. I have to stop work on the Torrey story. I know why, too. I think he invested pension money and he doesn't want anyone to find out."

"Where did you get that one from?"

"Something I deduced from something someone told me off the record."

"We're not the story here."

"Maybe we are. Maybe Bennett really fucked up and lost a lot of our money."

"You're not exactly in a position to be making statements like that."

It was his tone that made me sink into one of the chairs. "I'm in deep shit and all I did was my job."

He pulled a chair up next to me. "I understand. It pisses me off, too. But there's nothing I can do. It's out of my hands."

"Stupid cows."

"I need a story about the cow hospital."

He said it so matter-of-factly and without a trace of a smile.

"What?"

"The place the cows will go when they're vandalized."

"So I'm not the only one anticipating major graffiti and demolition."

"It's in an old warehouse off Hamilton Street."

"You're serious. I have to cover the cows."

He nodded. "Just for a week or so."

"What if Torrey contacts me again?"

"Call the police." Everyone had the same answer.

"What about Dick? Isn't he going to be the slightest bit curious as to why we're not covering this anymore?"

"I'll have him make the daily phone calls and get him on something else."

"That might work for a while, but in the long run . . ."

"Let me worry about that."

For the first time I wanted Dick Whitfield to put up a stink, to be his obnoxious self so everyone in the newsroom would know what was going on. I couldn't tell anyone else; Bennett would know it came from me or Marty and I couldn't risk that. But Dick, well, I could risk Dick's job with absolutely no conscience.

"Like I said, the cow hospital is off Hamilton. I understand there's already a couple of casualties."

"Graffiti?" I hoped.

He shook his head. "One artist was a little ambitious. Tried to attach the cow to the side of the Yale Rep and it fell right into that restaurant, you know the one I'm talking about, the one with the outside tables."

I nodded. Marty's senior moments were only a tad worse than mine these days. "So is there some sort of cow doctor at this place?" I knew my tone was more than sarcastic, and I didn't even try to disguise it.

He ignored me and handed me a card. "The guy's name and number are on that. You'll have to make an appointment."

So I'd even have to schedule this, organize my day around the cows. This was too much. "I'm going home, Marty. I called in sick. I'm tired and I feel like crap. I'll set something up for tomorrow, maybe the next day. I don't get the impression this is something that's breaking news."

"We already covered the incident with the falling cow. Dick's on top of that. Minor damage. No one was eating outside at the time."

He said it all with a straight face, like it

was real news. I walked out without another word.

Dick caught up with me in the parking lot.

"What happened to you?"

"I had a little accident."

"Does it have anything to do with Torrey?"

I shrugged. "Maybe. But we may never know. Bennett put the kibosh on the story. And you didn't hear that from me. I'm not even officially here."

"What?"

"You heard me." I opened my car door, but Dick put out his hand to keep me from getting inside.

"The story's off? Why?"

I shook my head. "You're a reporter, Dick. Find out. But if I hear you used my name in vain I'll send the same guys who did this to me after you."

His mouth was still hanging open when I drove off.

I knew it would be all over the newsroom in less than half an hour. But I didn't expect to have three messages from my colleagues on my answering machine by the time I got home. Yeah, I stopped off for a loaf of bread and some tunafish, but it didn't take *that* long.

"Heard what happened with the story, Annie. That sucks."

"Maybe we should just cover the story and when it breaks, give it to the *SunDial.*"

I liked that one. The *SunDial* scared the shit out of the *Herald* editors, God knows why. It was your basic alternative, go-against-Corporate-America little rag that had great restaurant reviews and very unique personal ads. Every once in a while, the *SunDial* got a good story, something we should've had but didn't for a gazillion reasons, some of which having to do with the fact that most of our reporting staff was inexperienced and underpaid.

The third message was simple, straight to the point:

"U-N-I-O-N." It was whispered, probably from the pay phone in the cafeteria. It could've been anyone, but I suspected it was Fred Wheeler, who'd been at the paper longer than I had and who was even more cynical. Whoever it was, he made me smile.

I stripped off my clothes and pulled on my fleece bathrobe. I liked the way it felt on my skin, and I wondered how I could be horny after being beaten up, but I was. I thought about calling Tom but opted against it, it was late in the day and he'd be working. Instead, I pulled a beer out of the refrigerator to have with my tunafish sandwich. It wasn't much of a supper, but I didn't have much of an appetite.

I dialed the number on the card Marty gave me but it just rang and rang. I guess there weren't any sick cows today. I'd try again in the morning.

I plugged my cell phone into its charger and started channel-surfing. I fell asleep watching Donald Trump belittle a group of wannabe Donald Trumps. It was pathetic.

I was having a dream that a cow was in my living room and I couldn't get it to leave. Just as I opened the door to push it out, I heard the doorbell. And then I heard it again. I struggled to wake up, realizing the doorbell wasn't in the dream but it really was ringing. I glanced at the clock. Midnight.

"Yeah?" I asked the door, vaguely aware I was wearing nothing under my robe.

"Let me in." It was Vinny. I pulled my robe closer, checking to make sure there weren't any cheap thrills, and opened the door.

"How'd you get in downstairs?"

He ignored me and went right to the refrigerator and pulled out a beer. "I've been trying to reach you for hours."

"Make yourself at home," I said sarcastically and slumped down on to the couch. The phone was off the hook at my feet. "So I didn't want to talk to anyone, sue me. Anyway, I'm off the story. I'm on to a better one. I get to cover the cows."

Vinny was frowning at me, uncertain whether I was joking.

"I'm off the story," I said again. "Even if Torrey contacts me, I can't do a fucking thing about it."

"I have copies of legal affidavits filed by Torrey's victims, along with some other damning evidence."

I was fiddling with the collar on my robe and stopped. "What?"

"Do you want it or not?"

I took a deep breath as I struggled with myself. Of course I wanted it, but what could I do with it? Give it to the *SunDial*, like my colleague had suggested? Give it to the *Courant*? Give it to Richard Wells? Or write it myself and sell it somewhere else, thus quitting my job and going freelance? But first there was a more important question.

"Why?"

"Why what?"

"Why do you want to give it to me now? I know you've had this all along, and you didn't offer it. Now, when I'm off the story and I've been forbidden to write another word about it, you suddenly become very generous. Why?"

"You've been forbidden to write about it?" He seemed amused with my choice of words, but they were accurate.

"Damned straight. I could lose my job, straight from the horse's ass himself, my mother's boyfriend."

"He's not officially one of the victims named in the complaints, but I do know he invested."

"Why?" I asked again.

"He wanted to make money."

"No kidding. Why do you want to give me this stuff now?"

"It needs to be made public. Torrey needs to be forced out."

"Wouldn't that just push him underground even further?"

"It would make everyone aware of what's going on. So if someone sees him, or if he contacts someone, he could be traced."

It made sense. It also told me Vinny was having no luck in finding Torrey himself.

"How much is my mother paying you to find him?"

Vinny smiled. "That's none of your business."

"But if I help you find him, then I should get a cut, right?"

"It's your job."

"Not anymore." The words hung in the air between us like a smelly fart.

After a couple of minutes, I finally gave in. "Okay, let me see it."

"You think I have it with me? It's at my office. Come by in the morning and I'll show it to you."

"And your etchings, too, will you show me those?" I felt like an idiot.

"No, really, Annie. It's safe at the office. But you'll have to come early, I have to be at Bradley at ten a.m."

The airport. "You do know where he is."

"I'm not sure."

"But you have an idea."

"Maybe."

"Then why do you need me?" We were going in circles.

He stood up. "I'll be in my office at seven."

"Seven a.m.?"

He didn't even turn around as he let himself out. I locked the door behind him and put the chain on. It wouldn't hurt just to look at it, I told myself as I went into the bathroom and brushed my teeth. If Bill Bennett wasn't named specifically, maybe he'd let me write something. Maybe pigs fly, too. I took off my robe and slid between the sheets, cold against my skin. Just before I fell asleep, I realized I hadn't heard from Tom all day.

Chapter 16

As I blinked into the mirror in the morning, I thought my face looked a little better. Or maybe it was just the goop in my eyes. I was getting too old to go to bed that late and get up this early. I rummaged a pair of jeans and T-shirt out of my laundry basket. Maybe later I'd get a little time and drop my dirty clothes off at the laundry. I paid extra to have the little old lady behind the counter take care of them. It was worth it. I'm certainly not going to spend my time listening to my clothes in a washing machine while I watch bad TV. Someday I'd actually purchase a washer and dryer. I'd been told there was a spot for them in the basement, but since I'd never been in the basement of my building, I couldn't say for sure. Just another place to run into my neighbors.

Speak of the devils, they were early risers, just my luck.

"You look better today," Walter mused. He actually looked good in a suit.

Amber peered into my face and I suppressed the urge to slap her. "What happened?"

"You were looking out the window when I got mugged," I said.

She shrugged. "Is that what was going on? I just thought you'd met up with friends."

I hung back and let them move past me on the sidewalk, turning to their cars. It was hard for me to believe that she'd seen me on the ground with two thugs trying to shove me into a car and thought they were my "friends." It strengthened my resolve to stay out of the way of my neighbors.

Vinny's office was in a brownstone on Trumbull Street. Besides "Private Investigations," the sign out front also boasted "Madame Shara: I'll Read Your Palm and Tell You Your Future for the Right Price," and "Cobb Doyle, Attorney-at-Law." I walked up to the door and let myself into one of those fake foyers. The inside door was locked, and I found Vinny's bell and pushed it.

There was no answer. No buzz letting me in. I rang the bell a few more times, but there was no sign of life behind the door. I peered through the glass at a dark hallway. It puzzled me, since he'd been adamant about the time and I didn't think he was the type to stand me up. I pulled my cell phone out of my bag, found his card in my wallet, and punched his number.

"This is the voice mail for Vincent DeLucia, Private Investigations. I am unable to take your call, so please leave your name, number, and a detailed message and I will get back to you as soon as possible."

"Where the fuck are you?" I said into the phone and hung up. Still no response.

I saw Vinny had scribbled his home number on the back of the card. Maybe he overslept.

"I can't come to the phone right now. Please leave a message and I'll get back to you."

"Vinny? Are you there? It's me, Annie. I'm at your office and you're not here."

He didn't pick up.

Footsteps behind me made me freeze, memories of being jumped from behind still too fresh.

"Hello?" The man had a narrow, long face, like a horse, with big teeth, also like a horse. He carried an armful of manila envelopes.

"I'm looking for Vinny."

He shook his head. "Too early for Vinny. I'm Cobb Doyle."

"He said I should meet him here."

Cobb Doyle frowned and stuck his keys in the door. "You can come in if you want, but Vinny never comes in early. Sometimes he never comes in at all."

An interesting tidbit to sometime throw back in his face, but at the moment I was actually getting worried.

"Hmm, that's funny," Cobb Doyle murmured as I followed him into the dark hall.

I saw an open door farther down the hall.

"That's Vinny's office," Cobb Doyle said, two steps ahead of me.

The office was in a shambles, papers strewn on the floor, file cabinet drawers open; the computer was on, but the monitor was blank. I stepped over the mess and moved the mouse. A photo of Humphrey Bogart in *The Maltese Falcon* popped up as his screen saver. How unoriginal, I thought.

"Don't touch that!" Cobb Doyle barked.

"What?"

"This obviously is a crime scene. Look at this place. We have to call the police." As he moved out of the room, he suddenly stopped. "By the way, who are you?"

"I'm Annie Seymour, with the *Herald.* Vinny wanted me to meet him here, he said he had a flight out of Bradley at ten."

Cobb Doyle nodded, his head bobbing like one of those stupid dogs in the back of some vintage vehicles. "He said something about the airport."

"Where was he going? I didn't get a chance to ask him. Do you know?"

"He said he was working on something. That's all. Maybe all this" — he swept his arm around to indicate the paper trail — "is somehow connected."

Okay, so he went to law school. He wasn't stupid.

"How could someone get in here if the door's locked?" I asked.

Cobb Doyle ran his hand through his hair. "Maybe he came through the back."

I followed him farther down the hall and into a little alcove that looked out over the back parking lot. The door was ajar and one of the windowpanes was broken.

"Don't you have a security system or something?" I asked.

Cobb looked decidedly uncomfortable. "We've been trying to get the landlord to do something about that."

We started back toward Vinny's office, and Cobb veered off to the left into another office. He unlocked the door and turned the lights on. It was sparse, with a big desk that could've come from any of those office stores. Several file cabinets lined the back wall; a tall bookshelf stood sentry across from the desk. A pile of old law journals spilled along the floor in the corner, but that must have been the way he left it because he sighed deeply. "Thank God no one got in here."

I didn't think whoever had broken in was looking for Cobb Doyle's files. But I didn't want to burst his bubble.

I went back down the hall to Vinny's office, pulling my phone out of my purse again and dialing a familiar number.

"Hello?" My mother is always up at the crack of dawn, first her exercises, then a cup of coffee and a bagel to start her day.

"Where was Vinny DeLucia going this morning?"

"And hello to you, too, dear."

"Listen, Mother, I think Vinny's in trouble. His office is trashed and I don't know where he is. I was supposed to meet him here."

"Oh, my, you are getting close to him, aren't you?"

I wasn't in the mood for her this early. "Do you know where he was going today or not?" I couldn't keep the edge of out my voice.

She must have heard it. "He said he had a lead, but he didn't say what it was. Do you really think he's in trouble? I think he seems fairly capable."

"I don't know. All I know is, something's up and I could try him at the airport if I knew which airline he was flying."

"You've got me there. I didn't know he was flying. Did you call the police?"

"Not yet." I could hear Cobb Doyle talking in his office and I assumed he was taking over that job. Too bad Madame Shara wasn't here yet, maybe she could channel herself into some other world and locate Vinny for us. Maybe a cow had fallen on him somewhere in the city and he was the first human victim of this silly parade.

But that wouldn't explain the mess.

My mother was saying something as I checked out Vinny's desk. Whoever had done this probably found what he or she was looking for, but you never know. I took a pencil off the floor and pushed some of the folders around.

"So you don't know what he was up to?" I asked again.

"You haven't listened to a word I've said."

No shit. "The cops'll be here soon. I'm going to call the airport and just ask them to page him. Maybe he's there. It's worth a shot." I hung up. She was useless again. Why did I keep trying?

I heard the police arrive. Cobb was greeting them.

"Who are you? You have to get out of here," the uniformed officer growled at me. I stepped aside, my eyes still scanning the room. But there wasn't anything that caught my attention. It was just a big mess. I didn't have a clue.

"I'm Annie Seymour. I was supposed to meet Mr. DeLucia here. We had an appointment this morning. I tried his home number, but he doesn't seem to be there, either."

"You're that reporter." It was an accusation.

I nodded, trying to ignore the tone of his voice. "But I'm not here as a reporter. As I said, I had an appointment . . ."

"You'd better wait outside."

I was used to being shunned, pushed out of crime scenes. It was all part of the job. But this time it was different. I was part of this story. *I'd* discovered this. *I* was a witness, for Christ's sake. It felt very odd.

It dawned on me that the cops might be

able to track Vinny down better than I could. I went back into the office, and I could tell by the scowls that I wasn't welcome. But I didn't really give a shit.

"I was supposed to meet Mr. DeLucia here," I said for what felt like the umpteenth time. "I know he had a flight out of Bradley at ten. I was hoping maybe you guys could track him down and let him know what's gone on here."

More scowls. Okay, so it's not good form to tell the cops how to do their job. But if they didn't know about the flight, they should know, so I told them. So there.

"You have to leave," they said again. It was getting old.

"Could you at least let me know if you find him? I'm a little worried," I said, handing my card to the tall cop with the bad teeth. He took it, much to my surprise.

"Okay, but do you want me to tell the detective about this?"

His question caught me off guard. I thought they all knew me just because I worked for the *Herald.* But it was Tom.

I frowned. "You can tell him whatever you want," I said curtly and finally left. But once on the sidewalk, I realized Tom might wonder what I was doing at Vinny's office at 7:00 a.m. I shrugged the thought away. I wasn't at Vinny's apartment. Which led to my next thought: Where did Vinny live and was his apartment trashed, too?

I drove to the paper, which was pretty empty because no one in his right mind would come to work this early. I located a recent phone book and looked up DeLucia. I found his parents on Wooster Street. But no Vincent DeLucia, which figured. A private investigator wouldn't exactly advertise in the phone book where he lived. I glanced at the clock. It was almost eight. Parents were always up early. Or so I told myself.

The voice was a little groggy, or maybe she just hadn't had her coffee yet.

"Hello, Mrs. DeLucia. I'm Anne Seymour, an old friend of Vinny's. It's very important that I find him and was wondering if you could give me his address."

As I spoke, I realized I sounded like a complete nut. I wouldn't give me his address, and she agreed with me.

"How do I know you're a friend of my son's? If you were a friend, you would know where to find him yourself."

The dial tone rang in my ear. He probably was at the airport, waiting for his flight, maybe I'd misunderstood when I was supposed to meet him.

No. I didn't. Vinny obviously was on to something, and something had happened to him because of what he knew. I dialed again. She must have had some coffee since I'd talked to her a minute ago.

"I really hate to bother you, Mrs. DeLucia, but I'm afraid something has happened. Vinny's office was ransacked, and I haven't been able to get him on his phone. That's why I was wondering if you could help me out here." I put a little pleading into my voice, but not too much so she would think I was a whiner. I also didn't want to emphasize that I thought something bad happened. But I guess I did anyway.

"Ransacked?" The panic rose in her voice.

"I was supposed to meet him at his office an hour ago, but he wasn't there and his office had been trashed. I'm sure he's fine, but I just want to make sure."

"Come to the restaurant and I'll go with you."

"The restaurant?"

"DeLucia's Pizzeria."

It was on Wooster Street, right around the corner from my apartment. "I'll be right over."

She was a tiny woman with big eyes.

Vinny must look like his father. She jangled some keys at her side. "It's not too far," she said, and I had a hard time keeping up with her as she moved down the street. Much to my surprise, she brought me to a brownstone just catty-corner to my own building on Wooster Square. Vinny was my neighbor. Go figure. No wonder he'd been around so much, especially the night I got jumped.

"What happened to your face?" Mrs. DeLucia asked as we moved up the stairwell.

"I had a little accident." I didn't want to tell her any more, but she turned around and glared at me. Since my father's Italian, I recognized my grandmother in Mrs. DeLucia's eyes. She knew I'd been up to no good, and it was no use lying to her. But I kept mum. She could think what she wanted for the moment.

"You're Joey Giametti's daughter," she said matter-of-factly.

I nodded, hoping that was a good thing.

Mrs. DeLucia nodded back, but didn't say anything else. She stopped at a door and knocked. "He might be home," she explained, as if I was leading her on a wild goose chase. But when we waited a little too long, she finally put the key in the lock and swung the door open.

It was neat. Really neat. Obsessively neat. Not a thing out of place, not a dust bunny to be seen. It was creepy.

"There doesn't seem to be a problem here," Mrs. DeLucia said accusingly. Okay, okay, so I'd gotten her worried for no reason. I was a troublemaker. I was the first to admit it. But Vinny was still missing.

"I'd like to just take a quick look around, just in case," I said apologetically. I started moving around the apartment, which was set up kind of like mine. I peered around the kitchen and went down the hall and looked in the bedroom. The bed was neatly made. Either he'd made it up this morning or he hadn't gone to bed last night. A picture of a very pretty brunette sat on the night table next to the bed, and I admit I had to look. I was holding the picture, studying the woman's face, when Mrs. DeLucia caught me.

"I thought you were looking for Vinny, not snooping around his private things."

"Who is this?" I asked.

"That's Vinny's fiancée, Rosie."

Fiancée? Did I hear that right? And I thought he was coming on to me all this time. Was I so wrong? Were my antennae that out of whack? Couldn't be. Could it?

"When is the wedding?" I tried to keep the curiosity from leaping from my throat.

"May twenty-second."

Next spring. A springtime wedding. This was really bothering me for some reason. I had to snap out of it.

"He never mentioned her," I explained.

Mrs. DeLucia frowned. "They've been together five years." She paused. "Have you seen what you need to see?"

I put the picture down and glanced around the room. Nothing. Not a paper out of place. The red light was flashing on his answering machine. I pushed the button, even though I was getting the evil eye from his mother. "I've got something you might want. Come to Edgerton Park, the entrance off Whitney, at seven a.m." I couldn't make out the voice, but it sounded vaguely familiar.

Seven a.m. That's when I was supposed to meet him. He was probably at the park when I showed up at his door. It wasn't too far from his office. He could be back at his office right now.

And then I heard my own voice asking if he was home, and I was glad I swore on his office phone and not on this one.

I dialed the number at Vinny's office, ignoring Mrs. DeLucia's raised eyebrows.

The cops answered.

"This is Anne Seymour. I've discovered that Mr. DeLucia had a meeting at Edgerton Park this morning."

"How did you find that out?"

"Listen, he might still be there. At the park. You might want to send someone over there." Here I was, telling them what to do again.

"Yeah, right, thanks." A dial tone. I was getting hung up on a lot and it was pissing me off.

"I'm going over there," I told Mrs. DeLucia.

"Where?"

"The park. To see if he's there." I followed her out of the apartment and back down to the street. Then the lightbulb went off in my head. I turned to Mrs. DeLucia. "Could he be with his fiancée?"

She smiled, a smile that said, I know why you're asking, and it's not just that you're worried about him. Okay, so maybe she was right. But I didn't want to think about it at the moment. "No. Rosie is in California on business for a few days."

At least I was covering all my bases. The park was next on my list.

My gut told me I wouldn't find him.

And he wasn't there. But one of those cows was. It had daisies painted all over it and its plaque informed me that it was "Please Don't Eat the Daisies," designed by an artist named Zak. I shrugged off an urge to kick it, as if it and the rest of the herd were responsible for everything that was happening to me.

Without any new ideas, I found myself parking in front of Vinny's office building again. Where there had been two cop cars earlier, now there were none. I went back into the building. Vinny's office was roped off with yellow crime scene tape, and I went down the hall, to Cobb Doyle's office.

He was hunched over his computer.

"That was quick," I said.

He must have jumped five feet into the air. I chuckled, because it looked pretty funny. "Sorry. I didn't mean to startle you."

He struggled to compose himself. "What was quick?" he finally asked.

"The cops. They're gone already."

"They got a call and left."

"Concerning Vinny?"

Cobb frowned. "What's your interest in all this? Vinny's got a fiancée, you know."

I nodded. "I know." Of course he didn't

have to know I just found out. "We were working on something together. It's pretty important."

Cobb got up and went over to his file cabinet. He rummaged around for a few minutes, then handed me a big yellow envelope with "Annie" written on the front.

"What's this?"

"Vinny gave it to me last night, before I left. He asked me to hold on to it. When you told me your name, I remembered it, but I didn't get a chance to ask you earlier. Does it have anything to do with what happened to his office?"

So Cobb Doyle did have a secret file in his office after all.

I opened the envelope and saw the copies of the affidavits Vinny had mentioned and more than a handful of tiny cassette tapes. Underneath were copies of checks, all made out to McGee Corporation. I recognized my mother's handwriting, and saw Bill Bennett's name on some. There were also checks from some of the biggest movers and shakers in the city. They weren't your average checks for $200 or $300, either. The zeros just kept going on and on and on. At the back of the folder were what looked like three or four bank statements. I gasped. "Holy shit."

"I admit I looked," Cobb said sheepishly. "What does it mean?"

"It means that if we ever find Mark Torrey, he's going to have most of the city wanting a pound of flesh." But this was only half the story. Would these statements lead us to the money, and, ultimately, Mark Torrey, or was it just some sort of smoke screen? And what was on those tapes?

Having the checks proved only that Torrey had gotten the money, which was common knowledge anyway. Torrey could turn around and say he invested it, which is what he was supposed to do. Rummaging a little further, I saw what looked like investment statements. Were they for real? And what had Melissa Peabody found out? Did she know about Torrey and that's why she was found on the pavement? And what about Allison Sanders? What did she know that got her killed? All the other victims were rich and still alive. If their deaths were tied to this, Melissa and Allison had paid the highest price for Mark Torrey's greed.

I needed to get this envelope to a safer place. "If Vinny shows up, tell him I've got this," I told Cobb. "Thanks for holding on to it." I felt like I was praising a puppy for peeing outside instead of on the carpet.

I hoped Vinny was safe somewhere and hadn't suffered the same fate as Melissa and Allison.

I left before Cobb could argue with me. I stuffed the envelope into my bag so no one would see me leaving with anything, just in case the place was being watched. I didn't think I was being followed as I pulled into the bank parking lot. I'd rented a safe deposit box here for the past few years. When I slid the envelope into the box, I took a deep breath. The pieces were falling into place, but I'd lost a key player. Where the hell was Vinny?

Chapter 17

Dick Whitfield's butt was in my chair, he was talking into my phone. I cleared my throat loudly, and his eyes moved up to my face. It pleased me to see the fear run across them as he quickly said, "I'll call you back, okay?"

"Get out of my chair," I growled. "I'm sick and tired of finding you at my desk every time I come in." He jumped up like a damned kangaroo.

"You're never here," he tried feebly.

"Shut up. I'm not in the mood." I sat down and started leafing through my Rolodex.

"What're you working on?" he asked. He was like a fucking tree. His feet were planted firmly next to me and they hadn't moved.

"None of your business." I wasn't sure just what I was looking for among my phone numbers, I just wanted to look like I knew what I was doing so everyone would leave me alone.

"The cow doctor called."

"What?"

"I answered your phone and he said he could meet you later, about four at the cow hospital."

"Are you my secretary now?"

"Aren't you going to the press conference?"

It was the first I was hearing about a press conference, but I wasn't going to let him in on that. "Not sure."

But Dickie Boy was on to me. "Melissa Peabody's parents. They're holding a press conference at four."

Oh, Christ. It had to be that lawsuit. I got up, and lo and behold the tree sprouted legs. "Where are you going?" I asked.

He shrugged and stopped. I kept going, over to Marty's desk. He saw me coming and shook his head, a loud sigh emanating from his throat. "No. You can't go."

"You don't know what I'm going to ask about."

"The press conference. Dick's going. The cow doctor is priority one with you today."

"It's my beat. It has nothing to do with

Mark Torrey, it's her parents, for Christ's sake. Can't I do my job?"

"There's a fine line here, Annie. And I'm not going to cross it. You're taking a break from the cop beat. It's from upstairs."

"Oh, great. That way you're completely exonerated from any guilt you might feel about taking me off this story."

Marty smiled and took off his glasses. He twirled them in his left hand as he scratched his chin. "You know, you haven't taken a vacation in six months. Maybe it's time. Let things cool down for a week or so, then come back and we can start over. You won't lose your beat, I promise. But we need to give the illusion that you're repentant."

"For what?" I tried not to raise my voice, but two of the suburban editors looked up.

"For insubordination."

"Is that what he told you?"

"Annie, I know you. I'm sure it wasn't on purpose, but you have a tendency to say what you're thinking, and most people can't handle that. Especially the suits. You used to know that and stay out of their way."

"But he's dating my mother," I whispered so no one else would hear.

The corners of Marty's mouth twitched

and his eyebrows reached into his forehead. “Really?”

I scowled at him, and after a few seconds he realized I wasn’t going to get into it.

“Listen, Annie, take a vacation. A few days off. Do this story about the cow hospital and then take the rest of the week off. Go to Florida, go to Vegas and see your father. Get some sun and warm weather. When you come back, we’ll see.”

It didn’t sound like a request.

“I don’t want to go to Florida. It’s hurricane season.”

“Then you’ll feel right at home.” He went back to whatever it was he was doing and I stood there, mute, for a minute or two before returning to my desk.

“What’s going on?” Dick didn’t have the sense to keep his mouth closed when he should.

“Shut up,” I said, picking up my bag.

“I just don’t get it,” he started, and I walked around him toward the door. “What’s going on?” I heard again from behind me.

I turned my head but kept walking. “Shut up,” I repeated.

I found myself at Atticus with a cup of coffee and a scone. Usually I like to read something when I’m eating alone, but I didn't have anything and I didn't feel like browsing the shelves behind me. I sipped in silence, spread a little butter on the scone and waited for it to settle on my hips. I hadn't seen Tom too much lately, so no one would notice but me. I thought again about Vinny and wondered where he could've disappeared to. I should've been looking for him instead of sitting here doing nothing, but I couldn't move. I ate more of my scone.

I heard someone laughing, and I looked up to see Sarah across the room. She was holding a to-go cup with one hand, the other was touching the face of a guy with a mole on his chin. I sat up straight. It had to be the guy who left me the note, David Best's roommate, what the hell was his name? I scrambled in my bag for a few dollars, all the while watching them move out onto the sidewalk, taking a right down Chapel Street. I hurried out and spotted them crossing Chapel and walking up Temple. I jaywalked across Chapel and scurried toward them, but I'd lost sight of them, since they were now around the corner.

Just as I turned onto Temple, I saw them up ahead, getting into a white Toyota. It looked like the car I'd seen outside the Peabody when I was waiting for Hickey.

The sun reflected off the glass and I couldn't make out who was driving, but both Sarah and the mole guy got into the back. When the car sped past me, I noted two guys in the front, the mole guy's arm around Sarah. I wondered if this was a new romance, or something that had been going on for a while.

Thinking of romance made me think of Tom. I pulled my cell phone out of my bag and dialed the familiar number.

"Hi, stranger," I said when he answered.

"You shouldn't use this number." His voice was cold.

"I just saw David Best's roommate with Melissa Peabody's roommate. They're involved with each other."

"So?"

I bit my tongue to keep back a smart retort. All my relationships seemed to be deteriorating, and I was the last to know.

"Did you ever talk to him, David's roommate, I mean? About the note?"

"No."

He was not forthcoming with any more information, so I took the bull by the horns, or, more appropriately, the cow by the horns, since I was staring at a fiberglass cow covered in moss on the Green across from me.

"What's up? I mean, I haven't heard

from you, and don't say you've been too busy. You've never been that busy before."

He sighed. "I understand you're somehow involved with Vinny DeLucia's office break-in."

I started walking back toward Chapel, back to my car. "Somehow involved with his break-in? I was there, I discovered it; he's missing, do you know that?"

"I'm surprised you don't know where he is."

He was jealous. If I wasn't so pissed at him for his attitude, I might have found this enjoyable. "He's got a girlfriend," I blurted out. "They're getting married in May. But that's beside the point. He is missing, and I'm worried Mark Torrey might have gotten to him. He had something that incriminates Torrey."

"What?"

"That's not for me to say, but he was going to talk to me this morning about it, which is when I went to his office to talk to him and he wasn't there but the place was trashed." The stream-of-consciousness just moved out of my mouth like the runs.

"We're working on it," Tom said quietly, almost too quietly. The road noise was swallowing mostly everything he was saying.

"Listen, Tom." I felt I had to somehow

try to make things right. "I've got to go see this cow doctor at four, but why don't we have dinner tonight? I have to take the rest of the week off, maybe I could start my little vacation with a little R&R." I tried to make my voice light, but too many things were weighing on me and I wasn't sure it was coming out right.

"The cow doctor?" Of course he picked up on that one.

"Yeah. A feature thing. Anyway, what do you say?"

"I'll come by at seven, okay? We need to talk anyway."

As I ended the call and climbed into my car, the weighed-down feeling got worse. "Needing to talk" was a bad sign. Maybe the pressure of our relationship had finally gotten to him. Maybe he was really worried about what was going on with me and Vinny. But I wasn't sure what was going on with me and Vinny, especially now that I knew he was engaged. This was probably the worst day I'd ever had.

So I went for ice cream.

There is something soothing about a banana split: three scoops, chocolate, vanilla, strawberry, with hot fudge, caramel, and strawberry sauce, topped with a huge wad of whipped cream, walnuts, and a cherry. I can't eat a banana split anywhere but Friendly's. I know exactly how they make them since I spent three summers during college making them myself. The East Haven Friendly's was renovated in an attempt to compete against the Chili's that moved in across the way. I fear Chili's will force Friendly's out, so I try to get there as much as possible.

I was slurping some ice cream when I spotted him in a booth across from me. He smiled at me sheepishly, as if I'd caught him doing something other than having a cup of coffee by himself. I raised my eyebrows and swallowed.

He slid into my booth.

"Hey, Hickey," I said, scooping up some whipped cream. "What's up?"

His belly hit the table as he leaned in toward me. Instinctively, I sat back. He smelled pretty bad.

"I can't go home," he said in a hushed voice. "He's after me."

"Torrey?" I guessed.

He nodded. "The business is shut down, I can't get at my bank accounts. I tried to cover my ass but the feds managed to find them and freeze them. I've been living with friends, but friends aren't there when the finances run out."

Then they're not friends. I kept my mouth full so I couldn't say it. No use kicking him when he's down.

"Tell me how he did it," I urged once I got to the silver dish and there was nothing left. "Tell me why he killed her."

Hickey frowned.

"Come on," I prodded. "I know you know he did it. What did she have on him?"

He shook his head. "I don't know anything about that. I don't know if he killed her. She was asking a lot of questions, but she was a kid, she didn't really know anything."

It wasn't the answer I wanted.

"I was supposed to leave town this morning," Hickey said, inconsiderately concentrating on himself and ignoring my need to get the goods on Torrey. "But the guy who was helping me, well, he never showed. Maybe you could get him a message."

I don't like playing errand boy for anyone. That's Dick's job. But I shrugged, a little curious. "Where were you supposed to go?"

"He said he had a ticket to Vegas for me. I could disappear there, get a car, maybe go to L.A. He was going to let me know when I could come back."

"Who?"

"A private dick. Vinny DeLucia."

I sat up straight, my brain racing. "Vinny? He was going to help you?"

"I got him some information he needed, so he said he'd help me."

The envelope. It was falling into place. But I still didn't know where Vinny was, and obviously Hickey didn't have a clue either. "I know Vinny," I volunteered. "I've been looking for him myself, and I don't know where he is. Someone broke into his office and left it a mess."

The fear ran across Hickey's face, and I knew what he was thinking.

"I've got the stuff," I said quietly.

He stared at me.

"Vinny wanted me to have it. I'm working with him on this." So it was half a lie, at least it wasn't a whole one. "It's safe." I stared at him. "What do you know about it?"

Hickey shrugged.

"It's Torrey's accounts, isn't it?" His silence answered my question. "But you don't have any idea where Vinny might be?"

Hickey slumped back into the seat, visibly relieved. "Shit, no, but they'll be after me and I still have to find someplace to hide."

I couldn't have stopped it from coming out of my mouth, even if I'd known I was going to say it. "You could hide out at my place."

Hickey shook his head, and the relief spread through me. "No, Torrey knows about you. He's probably got someone watching you."

It made me catch my breath. Torrey had my home phone number, who knew what else he knew about me. I tried to push it out of my head. "A motel or something?"

Hickey shrugged.

I sighed. "You know, when Vinny comes back, he'll want to talk to you and you should be around here somewhere."

"Yeah, I guess I could shack up somewhere. Branford Motel's not a bad place."

I had my doubts about that but didn't voice them. "Do you have any money?"

He nodded. "I've got a little. Enough anyway for a room. I know the manager."

Figures.

I pulled out my wallet. "I'll get your coffee."

He grinned. "Hell, Annie, when this is all over I'd still like to hire you."

The old Hickey was back. I was becoming an old softie. I just hoped no one would find out, it would ruin the reputation I'd spent years honing.

Hickey was about to leave, but I put my hand on his arm and he sat back down. "Wait a minute. You said Vinny had a ticket to Vegas for you."

"Yeah, he was going to pick me up for a flight at ten but he never showed."

So maybe Vinny wasn't going anywhere himself; he was just taking Hickey to the airport. But that still didn't explain where he might be now.

I put some money on the table for the banana split and the coffee. "Do you need a ride to Branford?" Once I started, I couldn't stop. The niceness was oozing from me. Well, not really, but it was the closest I would ever get.

Hickey nodded. "Thanks. I'd appreciate that."

We didn't talk on the way, both of us lost in our own fears and thoughts. My brain wheels were spinning about Vinny and how he was helping Hickey and the evidence that sat in my safe deposit box. What the hell was I going to do with all that?

It was inching closer to the end of the day, I didn't have any answers and I still had to go talk to that stupid cow doctor. Moo.

Chapter 18

I pulled into the parking lot behind the building that housed the cow hospital. I knew it was the right place because there was a stupid cow in front dressed in scrubs. Well, it had scrubs painted on its body and a stethoscope around its neck. I stared at it for a few minutes from the car, not really afraid to get out, but the damned cows were just too spooky. Maybe I really did need to go on vacation.

I started a list in my head of places I wanted to go. Hawaii was first on the list, but I knew I could never afford it. Paris was second, London was third. Palm Springs was fourth, because I'd spent some time there a few years ago and had fallen in love with it. Disney World was fifth, I had to admit it. There was something about that damned Mouse.

I saw someone moving in the window. He probably saw me, too, and wondered why I was sitting in the car like a moron. I took a deep breath and got out, careful not to get too close to the Doctor Cow. You never know when you'll end up in the Twilight Zone and one of those things would come charging at you.

I was losing my mind.

I pushed the door open and then I really wasn't in Kansas anymore. Naked fiberglass cows, some standing, some lying down, surrounded me. I thought they'd all been painted, but these must be extras.

"Hello?" I shouted, my voice bouncing off the walls in the huge room.

"Up here."

I looked up to see the loft, but I couldn't see anyone. I found the stairs to my right and ascended them out of the cows and into darkness. A single lamp burned at the far end of the loft, and I approached it tentatively. Being jumped made me a little more wary than I would've been before.

"Hello?" I asked again, still not seeing anyone.

He stepped out of the shadows and into my light. "I was wondering when you'd show up."

Vinny had a five o'clock shadow that made him mildly attractive in that Don Johnson/*Miami Vice* sort of way. If I hadn't known about the fiancée, I might have taken advantage of the darkness since it had been a while since I'd had my eggs poached.

"What the hell are you doing here?" I demanded.

"Hiding out, what do you think?"

"Hiding from whom?"

He shook his head. "Are you dense or are you just baiting me?"

I shrugged. "Maybe a little of both. It's Torrey, isn't it? I saw Hickey this afternoon. I took him to the Branford Motel, and who knows if he's still there. We probably won't hear from him ever again."

"He'll probably stumble into some lucrative escort service business he just can't pass up," Vinny said, chuckling. "He really does need to lie low. Torrey's got people everywhere and he can't afford to have anyone around who can nail him."

"But the cops can't find him, so what's the problem?"

Vinny smiled condescendingly and it pissed me off but I kept my mouth shut. "They will, eventually. After I find him."

"But how can you find him when you're in hiding, too?"

He was quiet for a moment. "Touché."

"Why didn't you tell me you're getting

married?" It just came out in a rush, I couldn't stop it.

"Why, Annie, I didn't think you cared."

"Shut the fuck up. So tell me what's going on." I was embarrassed I let that out. I couldn't possibly really be interested in him. He was so annoying, lurking everywhere.

"Rosie and I have been together a long time. She gave me an ultimatum, and I took it."

"That's not what I wanted to talk about."

"I thought it was."

"Don't be an asshole."

"You see, I didn't know I'd meet anyone as colorful as you, so I gave her a ring." He was baiting me this time, and I didn't want to fall into his trap.

"Torrey. I've got the envelope."

"Good. Is it in a safe place?"

I nodded. "Yeah." My eyes had become accustomed to the dark now, and I could see jars of paint and newspaper on the floor in the back of the loft. "What did you do to the cow doctor? Do you have him in some sort of stable or something?"

"I made him an offer he couldn't refuse."

"Funny, funny, ha-ha."

"You think I'm kidding." He wasn't smiling. "You know, you're not the only one with connections."

This time I knew he didn't mean Tom. Vinny was from Wooster Street, so of course he knew about my father. His father probably had something on the side himself. I know, I know, you can't stereotype, but it just seemed that if someone from the neighborhood wasn't mobbed up, they knew someone who was or were related to someone who was. That was just the way it was.

"I glanced at the affidavits and saw the other stuff. What's on the tapes?"

Vinny smiled evasively. "Some pretty damning stuff."

"But he's gone. He could be gone forever."

"No one's that lucky. It'll catch up to him."

"Did he kill Melissa and Allison?"

Vinny moved toward a stool and sat down. "I'd offer you a seat, but there only seems to be one."

"I don't care. Did he kill them?"

"I'm still not sure. Maybe. Maybe not."

I started pacing. I do that when I'm trying to think. "You said he's got people checking things out for him. Can he trust them not to talk?"

"Of course not. That's how he's stupid. Can you stop pacing? It's making me nervous."

I stopped next to him, close enough to smell him. It wasn't unpleasant, I hate to admit it, rather a musky man-type smell that made me catch my breath.

"What's going on with us?" he asked quietly.

I shook my head to shake him out of my system and backed up. "Nothing. What the hell would be going on? You're getting married."

"But you didn't know that before." He paused. "How did you find out?"

"I was in your apartment. With your mother. We were looking for you. I saw a picture. She's pretty."

"She's a knockout. So you've seen my apartment."

"You could've told me you live so close."

"Did you snoop?"

"Your mother was there."

"So if she wasn't, you would've snooped."

"We were looking for you. And I'm a journalist. I'm paid to snoop."

"Fair enough. I would've snooped, too."

This was going nowhere. "You know, I have to go back with a cow doctor story."

"He can see you tomorrow morning at ten. Just tell your editor he couldn't make it."

"If you're not going to tell me any more, then I'd better go." I turned and started walking away, but I felt his hand on my arm and stopped.

"I need your help. It won't take long, but I can't do this alone. You're the only one I trust with this." His voice was soft.

I turned, his face close to mine. "Shouldn't you call the cops?"

"That's not my job."

"It's mine."

"Yeah, I know." He moved closer, and I tried to move back, but he slipped his arm around my waist and leaned in toward me. "But you'll help me, won't you? I mean, this means a good story, and the cops won't let you get it. I will."

I squirmed, and he tightened his hold on me. I could feel his leg pressed against mine and I lost it. I kissed him, hard, and he kissed me back like someone who wasn't about to get married to someone else in a few months. I don't know how long it lasted, but there was some groping and heavy breathing involved. I don't know which one of us pulled away, maybe we both did at the same time, but all of a sudden we were two separate people again.

"I shouldn't have done that," he said quietly.

"So you've got a conscience after all." I tried to keep my tone light, but it bothered me that he was playing me while he had a fiancée.

"Oh, Christ, Annie, we've both thought about it."

"Okay, so that wasn't my imagination?"

He sighed. "I love Rosie, but it's different now than it was. We've known each other a long time. I was happy the way things were, maybe, because, well, I didn't want to tie myself down to her forever." He arched his eyebrows at me. "Typical man, right?"

He was reading my mind again.

"She kept pushing me, and I finally said, okay, let's do it. But then I saw you again and I was attracted to you. It made me start questioning my real feelings for Rosie." He stopped and rubbed his forehead as if it was difficult to tell me this. This was a kinder, gentler Vinny DeLucia. And I was warming up to it. Not that I hadn't been in heat three minutes ago.

He smiled. "But I suppose you don't really want to hear all the sordid details of how I'm screwing up my personal life."

I shrugged. I did want to know, and he knew it.

We pondered what he'd said for a few seconds before he spoke again.

"Let's deal with Torrey first, and then see where we're at, okay? We both have a job to do and we can't be too distracted."

"This fiancée thing needs to be worked out," I started.

"Give me a break, Annie. Don't you think I know that? Now, do you want to help or not?"

I sighed, one of those long, deep sighs that I hoped would make him think I was being put out. "I've got some free time. I guess I could help. What's your plan?"

He cocked his head and smiled in a way that made me want to kiss him again. But I had to put that kiss out of my head. I tried to think of Tom, but he certainly wasn't thinking too much of me these days, so it wasn't hard to drift back to Vinny.

"I can't tell you now," he said.

"Fuck you." I turned and started back down the stairs.

"Wait."

I stopped and turned my head so I could see him from where I was. "Don't play these games, Vinny. If you want my help, I'll help. But you have to tell me what's going on. Those are the rules."

"Meet me at ten at my parents' restaurant. I'll be in front."

"It's so clandestine," I said sarcastically.

"Two girls have died, maybe because of Torrey. Can we afford to take any chances? He knew I had the tapes and probably knows you've gotten them. Like I said, he's got spies everywhere."

I remembered what Hickey said. "Yeah, yeah, yeah. I'll see you tonight." My voice was steady, but my knees were shaky as I went down the stairs and let myself out. My eyes squinted in the daylight that was quickly turning into dusk. I had no idea what I was getting myself into, I wasn't sure Vinny even had a plan. This could be something he was thinking up as he went along. Which wouldn't be too good for either of us.

Marty wasn't happy I didn't have a story.

"You're off as of tomorrow," he said when I explained the cow doctor could meet me in the morning.

"It won't take long," I promised, and it was a promise I knew I could keep. This story was a piece of cake, I could do it with my eyes closed.

"No. Bennett himself has said you're not to work the rest of the week."

"Do I need to get my résumé together?" I asked.

Marty shook his head. "No. This'll pass. But we have to humor him."

I hoped for my career's sake that Vinny found Torrey sooner rather than later. I wasn't sure how much of this I could take.

"We can send someone else tomorrow morning," Marty said.

I shrugged. It was no skin off my nose anyway. I didn't even want to do the story. I went to my desk and sat down, wondering where my official seat-warmer, Dick Whitfield, was. Oh, yeah, he had that press conference. Could he have finished the story already?

I strolled over to Marty's desk again. "Hey, what happened at the press conference?" His eyebrows shot up and I scowled. "I just want to know, okay?"

He hit a few keys on his computer and pulled up Dick's story. "I've been trying to figure it out. It's all over the place. But mainly it seems the Peabodys are pissed at the school and the city and intend to sue both."

Which confirmed what Melissa Peabody's uncle had told me at the memorial service. I wanted to point that out, but I held my tongue. I was in too much shit already. "My mother's firm is involved, isn't it?"

He peered at me over his glasses. "Did she tell you about that?"

"She said the family called them, but it was off the record."

Marty frowned but didn't say anything.

I went back to my desk, playing back my conversation with Vinny in my head.

My phone was winking at me, and I dialed my voice mail.

"Hi, Annie. It's Richard Wells."

A second after I wondered what the fuck he would want, he gave me the answer. "I was hoping maybe we could get together on this Mark Torrey story. I saw your piece and figured you know how to reach him. And maybe some time down the road I could help you out."

Christ, this guy wouldn't let up, would he? What did he think I was going to do? Hand over all my notes and bow down to him just because he worked for the goddamned *New York Times*? But this did tell me that he probably didn't have as much as I did. For a second, I was happy about that, until I remembered Bennett didn't want me writing about Torrey anymore. And it was only a matter of time before

Richard Wells found someone who would talk to him.

I didn't even wait for him to give me his number, I just hung up and quickly dialed another number. Paula answered on the first ring.

"You guys close to Torrey yet?" I didn't even say hello.

She didn't seem to mind. "We've got a good lead. What do you hear?"

"I've got something you might be interested in." Vinny would kill me, but this game was getting old. I just wanted it over, I wanted my life back. Rather, I wanted my job back. If the feds got their hands on Vinny's information, I could be exonerated and back on my beat. And maybe, just maybe, I could beat Richard Wells on this story.

"I'm listening."

"I can't tell you right now. I'm at work. How late can I call you? I've got a meeting at ten."

"Jesus, Annie, are you okay? Has Torrey been in touch with you again?"

"No. Really. But I got my hands on something you may need."

"You can call my cell phone anytime. Be careful, okay? There's a lot of money at stake and the guy is running scared. Never know what anyone like that will do. He's got connections everywhere."

The warning reverberated through the dial tone. I glanced at the clock and saw it was close to seven. Time for my dinner with Tom.

He'd left a message on my cell phone to meet him at a Thai place on State Street. Despite all the food I'd inhaled during the day, the menu looked appetizing. Tom, on the other hand, did not. In Vinny I liked the unshaven look, but on Tom it looked menacing, complementing his scowl.

I pushed the menu to the side. "Something tells me we might not be eating." Too bad.

"This isn't working anymore."

I bit my lip. "I know."

"I think we need to just call it quits. It's been fun while it lasted."

The waitress hovered. I ordered two beers. I wondered what Tom would drink.

"This case has been tearing us apart," Tom continued when she left, "and I guess we're just not strong enough to get through it."

"I don't know what to say." How original. I hate being dumped. It's why I don't like monogamous relationships. How had ours become that without us knowing it?

Tom kept going as if I hadn't said anything. "I've been figuring you'd be breaking up with me because of Vinny DeLucia anyway."

I took a deep breath before lashing out. "There's nothing going on with me and Vinny."

"Give me a break, Annie. You're spending all sorts of time with him, he's in your apartment, he's saving your life. Christ, the guy is hooked on you, can't you see it?"

For a moment I forgot what was going on and wondered if I really was getting under Vinny's skin. But Tom's face brought me back. "No, Tom. I can't. He's getting married in the spring. He's working on the Torrey thing and he thinks I can help. God knows why."

Tom stood up. "Shit, Annie. Stop lying to yourself. I'm sorry about dinner, but I've lost my appetite." He took a couple of bucks out of his wallet, I guess for the beers. "Just be careful, okay? Torrey's unstable. He's backed up against the wall, and we don't know what that'll do to him." He handed me the money and walked away.

As I watched him leave, the beers came. The waitress was going to take one away, but I told her to leave it. As I sipped, I realized that was the second warning in less than an hour about the same thing.

Tom and Paula should both know I never listen.

Chapter 19

Since I didn't have dinner, I stopped and picked up a powdered doughnut and a cup of coffee on the way to see Vinny. The doughnut was stale and the coffee was lukewarm and I spilled some on my crotch in the car so it looked like I'd pissed on myself.

I drove down Wooster Street, noting the activity at Sally's and Pepe's and at Libby's. I had an immediate craving for a cannoli, but it probably wouldn't sit well on top of the doughnut. If I was lucky, Vinny could get me a slice of pepperoni pizza. My pants waist was a little tight anyway so it wouldn't matter. With Tom breaking up with me, getting beat up, being way too confused about Vinny, and my job on the line, putting on a few pounds was the least of my worries.

I eased into a parking spot in front of Vinny's parents' place, but before I was even out of the car, Vinny's hand was under my elbow, helping me out.

"Anyone follow you?"

"Give me a break." He led me around the back of the building, opening a back door. I stepped into the darkness and squinted, hoping my eyes would adjust quickly so I wouldn't trip on anything.

"I'm not kidding." His voice was serious.

"No, at least I don't think I was followed."

I tried to shake off his hand, but it got tighter.

"There're stairs here."

No shit. I managed to keep myself upright while stumbling down three of them. I felt a strong arm around my waist and I regretted the doughnut.

We went through another door and a light turned on, blinding me. "What the fuck . . ."

I blinked a couple of times and when I focused, I saw the room was full of boxes, canned tomatoes, olives, all the wonderful stuff that makes pizza. My mouth started to water.

"There's no time to eat. Didn't you get supper?" I hated it when Vinny read my mind. Or maybe he saw the saliva dripping out of the corner of my mouth.

I shrugged. I wasn't going to admit to my unhealthy meal. "What are we doing?"

"I've got a meeting set up."

"Torrey?"

"No." Vinny stopped riffling through some papers on one of the boxes and stared at me. "Are you on drugs or something tonight?"

"Tom just broke up with me."

His face changed for just a second before the grin was back. "His loss."

I sighed.

"Hey, I'm sorry."

"Yeah, right."

"Believe it or not," Vinny said simply. "Let's get to work. I need to find Torrey and fast."

"You mean you won't get paid if you can't get Torrey."

Vinny smiled that long, sexy smile that made my knees weak. "That's what I like about you, Annie. You've got my number."

"And your fiancée doesn't?"

"I don't want to talk about her. We don't have time to get into it now."

"You screwed up my cow story."

"Stop changing the subject."

"I don't know why I'm here. Why don't you just let the feds find Torrey?"

"Hickey's waiting for us. We can't be late."

"Hickey?"

Vinny nodded. "Okay, quickly, this is what's up. Hickey and Torrey go way back; they went to high school together." He winked. "Kind of like you and me."

I didn't want to think about it. "Okay," I prompted.

"After they both got out of college, different colleges, Hickey managed to start up a lucrative business for himself, and Torrey went off to law school. They hooked up again a few years ago at a school reunion. Hickey had one of his girls with him." He paused. "Torrey went home with her."

"Torrey told me he never paid for the girls," I said. "He's kind of good-looking, if you like that type, he's rich, he's got a job." I remembered how he'd sucked me in for that split second; I still couldn't explain it.

"He's a control freak," Vinny said. "He likes the young girls because he can control them." He paused, and I wondered if there was something else to it. Something uglier. But Vinny just shrugged. "Anyway, you're right, Torrey's never paid for it, at least not in the way we'd normally think.

He offered Hickey a business proposition in return for the girls, and, being Hickey and greedy, he went along with it. Hickey's been laundering money through his business for Torrey, along with some of Torrey's other buddies. The feds got one of them this afternoon, but they still don't know where Torrey is."

"And you do? Come on, Vinny, he's probably in South America by now."

"Actually, he's in Italy."

I was impressed. It seemed like he really knew this for a fact. "Are we going to Italy? I've always wanted to go there."

"Not yet, maybe one of these days, but I've got a meeting set up with someone who can lead us to him." Vinny picked up a set of keys. "Come on, we're taking my dad's car."

We went back up the stairs, the smell of pepperoni invading my nostrils. My stomach grumbled loudly.

"Oh, Christ, you should've eaten before you came." Vinny left me alone in the hall, disappearing toward a distant light. I stayed put. I didn't want to run into his mother again. I had the distinct impression she didn't like me too much. She was probably best friends with Rosie.

Vinny's silhouette filled the doorway and

he opened the door. I followed him, not seeing the pizza box until he put it on top of an old Buick. I pulled the top open and felt hot steam hit my face.

I grabbed a piece before he took the box and put it in the car. The tomato sauce moved down my throat and I groaned. I couldn't help it. It just came out.

"I didn't realize a pizza could give you an orgasm." He started the car.

I couldn't think of anything smart to say back, and anyway, my mouth was full of pizza. I didn't see where we were going until I swallowed the last bite.

"This isn't the best neighborhood," I thought out loud, moving my hand to lick the last of the sauce off.

That's when Vinny took my wrist and guided my fingers into his mouth.

"Pretty good sauce," he said when he was done. I gripped the armrest and tried to keep myself from lunging at him. Men think about baseball, but the only thing that came to mind was Dick Whitfield sitting at my desk, using my phone and my pens. It had the same effect.

"We're here," Vinny said casually.

I peered out into the darkness at a row of storefronts. "Here?" Grand Avenue is not known for its hospitality at night.

I saw a shadow move and instinctively pulled back.

"It's Hickey." Vinny was out of the car.

I opened the door and stepped carefully onto the sidewalk. As a cop reporter, I spend a lot of time in dicey neighborhoods, but I'm always cautious. Hickey's protruding stomach made me a little more relaxed.

"You didn't say she was coming along." I noticed he didn't seem too upset about it.

"Might help."

"Might not."

They were worse than a Laurel and Hardy routine.

"I am here," I said. "You don't have to talk about me like I'm not. And can someone please tell me what the game plan is?"

Vinny and Hickey were walking, shall we say, briskly up the sidewalk. I was glad I was wearing my flat shoes. Pumps would've killed me. I wanted to whine a little more about how they were keeping me in the dark, but I was still a little hungry and very tired. I wished all this detective stuff could wait until morning.

They turned into an alley, and I had no choice but to follow them. We went through a door and up some stairs. Hickey turned on a small light on a desk. There were five phones, notebooks full of pen marks scattered about.

"Welcome to Come Together," Hickey said proudly.

"Nice digs," I said, sitting down. We should've brought the rest of the pizza up.

"We're not staying long," Vinny warned.

Hickey picked up a phone, dialed and hung up. "She's got a pager," he told me.

"Who?"

Vinny shook his head. "For a smart person, you're really being stupid."

"Can't you give me a little clue about what the fuck we're doing here?"

"I love it when she talks dirty," Vinny told Hickey, who made an obscene gesture just as the phone rang.

"Twenty minutes. Twin Pines Diner." That was the place I met Hickey for the first time. What was it he'd said? Something about meeting all his girls there. I wasn't sure I was going to like this.

Hickey turned off the light, throwing us back into darkness.

"Couldn't someone have brought along a flashlight?" I asked.

They acted again as if I wasn't there. If I was only good for a joke, they shouldn't have brought me along.

We got back to Vinny's car, and he turned to Hickey. "Your car's close by?"

Hickey nodded. "You follow me." He moved down the sidewalk to his car.

I slid into the front seat of Vinny's car, and Vinny started the engine. We watched Hickey pull out into the street.

"Okay, here's the story," Vinny started as the car lurched forward, throwing me nearly into his lap. "Sorry," he said.

I took a deep breath, but didn't say anything.

"One of Hickey's girls is with Torrey. She called her sister and told her where they are, said she needs some money, wants to get out of there before the feds come in after Torrey. I guess she's gotten cold feet about the whole thing. She told her sister to call Hickey, she trusts him, and he'll know what to do."

"Why doesn't the sister just send them some money?"

"She doesn't have any. Apparently she's just a kid in high school."

I thought for a second. "Why didn't Torrey's girlfriend call Hickey herself? Are you sure it's on the up-and-up?"

"Hickey says he hasn't heard from her since the night you met Torrey on Orange Street. I did some checking and she flew under her own name to Rome that night on an Alitalia flight. When she called her sister, she said she didn't want to risk Torrey finding out that she wants out. She must know Torrey's guys have been watching Hickey."

"But Hickey told me that he can't get at his money."

Vinny chuckled. "He tried that with me, too. But there seems to be another bank account, one the feds didn't find."

I shook my head. "Jesus, I can't keep this straight." I paused, then asked, "So where do you and I come in?"

"We're Hickey's beards."

"We're what?"

"He set this up to meet the sister, but we're going to make it look like he's meeting us. Torrey's guys already know that we've been in contact with Hickey, so it won't look out of the ordinary if we meet him. Then, while we're in there with him, this girl can slip him the information and no one will be the wiser."

I shook my head. "I'm still a little confused how you and Hickey managed to hook up on this. And why you're helping him."

"I talked to him after Melissa died, and he was scared. He's pretty sure Torrey killed her, and he made the stupid mistake of telling Torrey he'd been taping their conversations and threatened to take the tapes to the cops." Vinny paused. "So when I showed up, he offered to help me get Torrey, and in return, I'd do what I could to help get him off as easy as possible."

"Jesus," I whispered.

"He gave me the tapes, but I started noticing that I was being followed. That's why I wanted to meet you at my office that day and give the tapes to you."

"Don't do me any favors. I got a threatening note, was almost abducted, and I didn't even have the tapes then."

Vinny scratched his head. "I don't understand that, either. Torrey must have thought I'd told you all this before." He reached over and touched my cheek. "I'm sorry."

"These tapes had better be worth all this." I was trying not to notice that his fingers had sent electric shocks through my body.

"He's got Torrey on everything. I'm surprised Torrey didn't figure out what Hickey was doing, but he probably thought he was stupid and wouldn't risk his own business."

"So why did he?"
"Why did he what?"
"Why did Hickey risk his business to make the tapes?"
"Why do you think?"
Okay, I wasn't too fast on the uptake. "To save his own ass." I paused a minute. "But didn't you say they were friends?"
Vinny chuckled. "As only criminals can be. Hickey isn't stupid, and he knew Torrey well enough to know he's a slick son of a bitch and would sell him up the river without even thinking twice if the shit hit the fan. Hickey wanted to get him first."
"So what are you getting out of this to-night?"
"Torrey's location."
"And I'm here, why?"
Vinny's eyes glanced from the road to me, and I could feel his stare. He smiled. "I like your company."
"Give me a break."
He laughed, then grew quiet. "I wanted to keep an eye on you. Torrey's getting antsy, he trashed my office, he did try to abduct you, who knows what he'll try next. If you're with me, then at least I feel like I can protect you."
"But I was alone after I left you at the

cow hospital until I met you at your parents' place," I said.

Vinny smiled. "Only some of the time."

Shit. He was following me again. I think he was trying to make me feel better, but it didn't work.

"Why didn't you tell Hickey I was coming along?"

Vinny shrugged. "Don't worry about him. He's cool about it."

I wasn't sure *I* was "cool" about it, but my curiosity was getting the better of me. And the thought that I could maybe salvage my dying career with an exclusive story out of all this. I'd never done anything like this before. Some reporters lived at homeless shelters for a week to write stories about their experiences; some hung out with drug addicts to get inside their world. I started out as a town reporter, covering planning and zoning commissions, before moving into the city to cover the court beat, which is pretty cut-and-dried. I made the change to cop beat about four years ago, but I was always an observer, not a participant in any illicit incidents. The butterflies in my stomach seemed to have a double meaning: I was scared, but excited at the same time.

We pulled into the diner's parking lot behind Hickey. The lights in the lot were out, bathing us in darkness. There was only one other car, on the other side of a Dumpster in the back. We got out of the car, and I glanced at Route 1, which was about a hundred feet away. A couple of cars whizzed past, but it certainly wasn't rush hour. They probably didn't even see us tucked back here near the trees.

Hickey was a few steps ahead of us.

"Annie." Vinny turned to me, but before he could say anything else, something whizzed past my ear, and Vinny pushed me to the ground. He reached behind him, and I saw a flash of silver in his hand.

"What the fuck?" I managed to say just before I heard a popping sound nearby.

"Christ, someone's shooting at us," Hickey muttered, the panic rising in his voice. He was on the ground, too.

"Where the hell is the shooter?" I heard myself shout.

More pops. They were coming from the back of the parking lot, near the Dumpster.

Vinny's gun exploded near my ear. "Stay down," he said harshly. I wasn't about to get up.

Suddenly it was quiet. Vinny grabbed my arm. "Get back to the car. Now!" he shouted, and I pulled myself up. I don't remember getting into the car, but I was sandwiched in the back on the floor between the front seat and Hickey's stomach as he lay on the seat facing me. In seconds we were moving, Hickey's flesh pillowlike against my back, Vinny's neck tense as the car careened out onto Route 1.

"So I guess Torrey wants us dead," I said sarcastically once my voice came back. I climbed over the seat into the front. "They were waiting for us in the dark. It was a fucking setup."

Hickey drew in a breath. "She didn't know you were coming. She thought it was only me and Vinny. So we're the dead ones."

Vinny's mouth was set in a hard line. "No one's going to die." He turned to me. "Are you all right?"

I nodded. I didn't even have time to think about what was happening, which is probably why I didn't wet my pants.

"Hickey, you okay?" Vinny asked. The car was pulling onto Interstate 95 over the Quinnipiac River bridge (how had we gotten this far so fast?) and we pulled off at Hamilton Street.

"Yeah," Hickey said quietly. "Sorry."

"It's not your fault," Vinny said. "Obviously, she had us both going."

We watched the buildings move along beside us until Vinny turned onto Chapel Street, up toward Wooster Square. He pulled up in front of my building and all the doors opened at the same time. I waved them back. "Come on, guys, I think I can make it up to my apartment okay on my own." I sounded brave, but I was thinking about the ambush and hoped they would insist on coming with me.

I tried to act pissed off as they walked me up to the door. I saw Amber's curtain move and Walter's light flicker.

I unlocked the door and the three of us rushed up the stairs, not caring if we made noise. I turned the key in my door and opened it. The light switch was just over to the right, and I flipped it.

It was worse than Vinny's office had been. The couch cushions were ripped, their insides strewn about the room. My books were in a heap on the floor, I could see bindings were broken. A favorite glass vase from my grandmother was in pieces next to my rocking chair, which seemed to be the only piece of furniture untouched. I felt a sob rise in my throat, and I forced it to change into "What the fuck?"

"Oh, shit, Annie, I'm sorry," Vinny said quietly.

Hickey just stared at the mess, his eyes wide and sympathetic. I was glad they'd insisted on coming up with me. I couldn't have taken this alone.

"I'll kill him," I blurted.

"You have to stand in line," Hickey said. "Cops?" he asked Vinny.

Vinny shook his head.

I picked up the phone, but Vinny took it out of my hand. "Torrey's just trying to scare you."

"And he just tried to kill me. Next time he might actually do it." I tried to stay calm, but my voice was rising. I didn't like being shot at and I didn't like it that someone was in my apartment, tossing my things around, looking through my belongings. I remembered my nosy neighbors. "Do you think Walter and Amber saw whoever did this?" As I asked, I knew they probably did. They didn't miss the guy with the mole, and this guy probably made some noise.

"Stay here, okay? Don't touch anything." Vinny disappeared out my door, leaving me with a wide-eyed Hickey.

"Does Vinny really think I'll help him now?" I demanded. "What's really going on?"

Hickey shrugged. "He seems to know what he's doing."

"Doesn't seem that way to me. This is entirely fucked up." I moved into my bedroom to encounter even more pandemonium than in the living room.

Every drawer was open, and my heart moved up into my throat as I looked in the one next to my bed. My gun was gone.

Absently, I started picking up strewn underwear, ignoring Vinny's order.

"You could make a lot of money with that." Hickey's voice made me jump, and I turned, clutching a red silk teddy.

"This is none of your business."

"It most certainly is." His grin was a little too wide. His attempt at levity was ill-timed.

I shoved the teddy into my drawer just as Vinny came in. I saw his eyes taking in the bed and the underwear I hadn't had time to put away.

"They said they didn't see anyone. I guess we should call the cops. Your boyfriend's probably going to find out anyway and be pissed you didn't call."

"He's not my boyfriend anymore, remember?" I said curtly. "By the way, they got my gun," I added as I picked up the phone and dialed my ex-boyfriend's number.

"Tom Behr."

"How professional."

"It's late and I'm busy." How soon we forget. He used to like it when I called him late.

"My apartment is a mess. Someone broke in. I'm officially reporting it."

"You always have a crisis." It sounded like he wasn't going to do anything about this.

"Fine. Forget about it. I'm taking back my report." I slammed the phone down and turned to see Vinny and Hickey wide-eyed behind me.

"What'd you do that for?" Hickey asked.

"I can't deal with this anymore." I picked up my purse.

Vinny shook his head. "You've got to report the missing gun."

I nodded. "I know. I just can't think about it right now. I have to get out of here."

"Where are you going?" Vinny and Hickey followed me back into the living room.

"I'm going to stay in a hotel."

"You don't have to do that," Vinny said. "I live just across the park. You can stay at my place."

"Yeah, and what would your fiancée think about that?"

Vinny scratched his chin. "I could stay at her place."

It wasn't exactly the answer I wanted, but being cheap, at least I wouldn't have to spring for a hotel room. "Okay, sounds good."

He looked surprised for a split second, as if he didn't expect me to accept so easily, but then a smile appeared. "Good." He turned to Hickey. "I'll take you back to your car. Let's all meet at my place in the morning, about nine, okay? On to Plan B."

His voice was light, but his eyes were darting around my apartment, taking everything in. "We can get this place cleaned up, too."

I thought I saw the blue flashing lights of a police car pull up in front of my building as we went into Vinny's. Screw Tom. He'd just have to break the door down.

Chapter 20

Vinny's bed was the most comfortable I'd ever slept in. He'd set the alarm for me, but when it went off, I hit the snooze button and rolled back over. His sheets smelled like fabric softener, just like my grandmother's used to. For a single guy, he was very tidy. Even when my apartment wasn't broken into, there were always dirty clothes piled somewhere, an empty glass here, a plate with half a muffin over there, newspapers strewn about, usually near where I'd been sitting last. I didn't know what it would be like to live with Felix Ungar. I'd probably go crazy, and I would have to sabotage the relationship somehow.

Rosie's face smiled at me from the bedside table when I opened my eyes for the second time. I squinted at her, noticing now that she was about as thin as I was, on one of my good days anyway, and she had a crease in her forehead. But her breasts were definitely bigger, her legs longer. She looked like the kind of woman who could wear a paper bag and look fashionable. I ran my hand through my mass of snarls. Maybe I'd try to comb it today.

Or maybe not.

I wanted coffee, but I didn't want to get up to make it. I wanted someone to deliver it to me, along with a three-egg Western omelet and some home fries.

"Are you going to stay in bed all day?" Vinny's face appeared in the doorway, startling me. "Breakfast's getting cold."

Breakfast? Really? I swung my legs over the side of the bed, suddenly aware of my attire. Vinny had given me a T-shirt and sweatpants to wear to bed. They made me look like a cow.

Hickey was downing a cup of coffee when I emerged from the bathroom, not much neater than I'd been five minutes earlier.

"Hey," I muttered as Vinny put a cup in front of me. I took a long drink, ignoring how hot it was, craving the caffeine.

"Bagel?" Vinny offered. Poppy seed, with raspberry jam. If it wasn't for that kiss yesterday, I'd think he was gay. No straight guy was this neat and organized. The few times I'd stayed at Tom's, the only things in the refrigerator were a six-pack and a stick of butter.

I chewed slowly. Hickey still hadn't said a word.

"So how are we going to catch the elusive Mr. Torrey?" I asked after practically licking my plate. I nodded when Vinny offered more coffee.

"He doesn't know."

"He speaks," I said, raising my cup to Hickey, then turning to Vinny. "You don't know, do you? He's right. You're making this up as you go along."

"We're not going to find him because he doesn't want to be found," Hickey said. "We may have the evidence that proves he's been scamming everyone, but unless we find him, there's nothing we can do about it."

It was a fairly pessimistic view, but the truth.

"I'm still curious about Melissa Peabody," I said. Vinny continued to munch on his bagel, listening to us. "Did he or didn't he? Maybe it really was David Best. Maybe it was his roommate, the guy with the mole. He's pretty fucked up. He could probably kill someone." I drained my cup again. "Oh, Christ, we're right back where we started."

Vinny chuckled, and Hickey and I stared at him.

"What's so funny?" I demanded.

"Both of you. You have no faith, do you?"

"Frankly, no." I just wanted everything to go back to normal: my job, my apartment, my antisocial life. Maybe even Tom, even though he was being an asshole. Mark Torrey had fucked up my life. I wanted more than anything to get even, but Hickey was right. Torrey was still in Italy, and we were getting nowhere.

"How do you think we can entice Mr. Torrey back to New Haven?" Vinny asked.

I felt like I was back in school, and it wasn't a good feeling. I didn't like this game, but if I played along maybe it would be over soon.

I shrugged. "Beats me."

"Oh, come on, Annie, think. He's a smart guy, he's feeling cocky. He has a lot of cash stashed somewhere. I've traced some through four banks and three dummy companies, including McGee, and still don't know where it ended up. Don't you think he wants to play the cat-and-mouse game? He met with you, didn't he, before he left, knowing you'd put something in the paper. I still think he wants the notoriety, he wants to know that everyone's talking about him." Vinny paused. "There's been nothing in the paper recently about him. It's probably pissing him off."

"Okay, so you took Psych 101 in college. But he wouldn't risk coming back just to get his name in the paper again."

"But he might risk it if he thinks we have even more than the tapes."

He was talking in riddles again, and Hickey frowned. "What more would we have?"

Vinny shrugged. "Maybe I sent him some e-mail. Maybe I told him we've got proof that he killed Melissa."

"Like what kind of proof?"

"Shit, I don't know. That's all I said. He'll contact us, because if he didn't kill her then he won't want to go down for murder, and if he did kill her, well . . ." His voice trailed off and we pondered what Mark Torrey might do if truly backed up against a wall. I didn't want to think about it.

"You've got his e-mail address?" I asked.

Vinny laughed. "Annie, you can find out anyone's e-mail address, phone number, address, just by doing a simple search on the Internet."

"I know that." I pushed back my chair

and got up to pace. "He's got his lackeys working here, you know that. He won't come back. He'll just get his guys to finish the job they started last night. Maybe we can leave it up to the feds and move on with our lives."

"You seem to forget that I was hired to find him."

"But I wasn't." I went back into the bedroom and found my clothes folded neatly on a chair, not in the heap I'd left them in the night before.

"You can't give up now," Vinny pleaded quietly. He moved in behind me, softly, quietly, and I could hear him breathing.

I took a deep breath. "My job is on the line here, Vinny. Bennett thinks I'll write something and he'll get fired for raping our pension. He has to keep me from doing that, but he can't fire me outright because he knows then I'll blab to every other news organization in the area and he'll really get caught. If I quit, he can say it's just sour grapes."

"He could say that even if you're fired."

"Yeah, well, I guess so. I'm not thinking straight. I just want my life back." I willed myself to turn around and keep myself in check. He was very close, and I could smell him, it was a faint but musky odor, and it drove me crazy. I glanced at the picture of Rosie to keep me strong.

I pulled back. "Why haven't you gone to Italy to find him?" It was the first time this dawned on me, that my mother would gladly pay out of her own pocket to get Torrey any way she could.

Vinny sighed. "He's moving around a lot. Your mother wants me to stay here to try to draw him back. If he's in Europe, it might be pretty hard to get him extradited quickly."

"What's my role in all this?"

"I may have said in the e-mail that you want an interview before going to the feds, but it has to be face-to-face."

I scowled at him. "Thanks a lot."

Vinny's face changed, becoming softer. "I'm sorry about what happened."

"The shooting or the break-in?"

"All of it. Tom, too." His hand touched my cheek, and he moved closer. I didn't stop him.

We didn't even come up for air when we heard the doorbell, but Hickey's voice in the doorway was urgent.

"She says she's your fiancée."

Vinny pulled back with a deer-in-the-headlights look about him. His mouth was bruised, and mine felt like sandpaper. It was not unpleasant. "Oh, shit," he said quietly.

I let him walk out into the living room alone. I held back for a couple of minutes before venturing out. She was drop-dead gorgeous. She'd lost weight since the photograph was taken, had long strands of dark hair, and legs going on and on. Oh, Christ, something else to obsess about. I hoped my nipples had calmed down so she wouldn't suspect anything, but then again, why would I threaten her?

She held her hand out, the manicured French tips dainty against my chewed ones. "Vinny says you're working on this latest case with him. I don't know why he continues in this silly business. He could do a lot better."

I wanted to say, he's right here, in this room, and he likes his job. So she was a bitch. In a different way than me, in a possibly worse way than me. It made me smile.

"So lovely to meet you." I picked up my jacket and bag and turned to Vinny. Hickey was still hovering, but he didn't need any explanations. "I'll be seeing you."

Vinny walked me to the door and out into the hallway, where she couldn't see us. I felt him press something into my hand

and I looked down to see a small gun, a .22, like the one that was stolen from my apartment.

I frowned. "What's this?" I asked, trying to give it back.

"You've got to take it," Vinny said firmly. "You need some sort of protection."

"I've got my pepper spray."

"Not enough." I could see how concerned he was about me, and I nodded, slipping the gun into my bag.

"Okay," I said softly.

"Noon, okay? At your apartment?"

I certainly didn't have any plans for the day. "She won't mind?" I jerked my head in the direction of his apartment.

I could see genuine angst cross Vinny's face. He lowered his voice. "I've got some stuff I need to work out, but it doesn't mean I'm not thinking about you." His lips brushed mine, and an electric current ran through my body. Okay, so maybe I wasn't as torn up over my breakup with Tom as I thought.

"I'll see you at noon," I said. As I went down the steps, I realized he hadn't asked where I was going, and I wasn't sure myself.

I let myself into my apartment, bracing

myself for the mess. Yup, it was still there. Time for some down-and-dirty cleaning up. I went into the bedroom and found a pair of gym shorts and a T-shirt, put them on and pulled out the vacuum.

It had been a long time since I'd cleaned, an embarrassingly long time. Which reminded me again of my laundry and lack of clean clothes. I dropped what I was doing and put the dirty clothes in my laundry bag and hauled it down the stairs and threw it in my car. I had no excuse now.

The phone was ringing when I let myself back in.

"Hello?" My eyes were scanning the room, figuring out what to tackle next.

"I understand you have some things I want."

I flopped down on my rocking chair, wondering again how Mark Torrey had gotten my phone number. "There are a lot of people looking for you."

"I know. I'd like to meet with you again and get this whole mess straightened out. I want to clear my name, because I did not kill Melissa. But perhaps after you get your apartment cleaned up. And maybe after you get that laundry to the Laundromat. I hope you won't leave it in the car too long."

I sat up straight, the hairs on my neck standing at attention. "Where are you?" I finally sputtered.

He chuckled. "Don't worry about that, Miss Seymour. How about tonight?"

"What about tonight?"

"A meeting, Miss Seymour."

"I thought you were in Italy."

"Edgerton Park. The Whitney entrance. Nine o'clock. And don't bring any company. I'd like to see just you. And, of course, the tapes."

"Why would I do that? Do you think I'm stupid?" My bravado surprised me, but it's easy to be brave on the phone.

"We've got your friend, the private dick. If you want to see him again, you should do what I ask."

He hung up. I held the phone for a few minutes, his words sinking in, and then a panic swelled in my chest. Edgerton Park. That was where Vinny's meeting was supposed to be the other day. I ignored my shaking hand as I fumbled in my bag for the card with Vinny's phone numbers on it.

I left messages at both his apartment and his office. I wanted to call his parents' place again, to see if he was there, but didn't want to scare his mother again. She didn't think too much of me anyway.

I dialed another number, though, and when Paula answered, I sighed with relief. "Paula, Torrey contacted me. He says he's got Vinny. He wants to meet tonight." I told her every word. I'd committed it to memory without even realizing it.

"You can't go," she said when I finished.

"I have to go."

"We'll go."

"He said me. Only me." I did want company, but they could just stay hidden until Torrey showed up, then they could take him away and lock him up. I didn't want this screwed up, I wanted to get this guy. I wanted to see Vinny. Make sure he was okay.

"You are not to go. Do you hear me? Leave it up to us. Jesus, don't fuck this up." I'd never heard Paula this angry.

"Okay. Okay, but won't he get suspicious if I'm not there?"

I heard her sigh; it was not unlike something my mother would do, but I didn't say anything, that would piss her off even more. "We'll come to your apartment and wire you."

"You can't do that. He's watching me. I don't know how, but he knows every move I make."

"Shit." My thoughts exactly. "Okay, how about this? We can meet you at the paper. He wouldn't think anything funny if you went there."

Marty and Bill Bennett would, but I'd just have to deal with that later. "If you go in the main entrance, I'll wait there, near the security guard. You should come alone or with just one other agent, so no one will get suspicious." I could see it now: A crew of FBI agents with all their gadgets showing up at the newspaper would definitely set off the red lights.

"Four o'clock."

"Sure."

I heard the dial tone and I hung up.

He was right. Vinny. About Torrey being dangerous. About him contacting me again. How did he know Torrey would be that predictable?

I thought a little more about Vinny. He wouldn't have let his guard down, would he? Enough to let them get him? I thought about his kiss this morning, and I didn't think I'd ever wanted to see anyone again this much. No, he had to be all right. Torrey had to be lying. It had to be a trap and I was happy I'd called Paula so she could sic the feds on Torrey's lackeys. Torrey couldn't possibly be in town. Could he?

Chapter 21

I was in the middle of plucking my eyebrows, trying to keep my mind off Vinny, when I heard the doorbell. Thank God. He was here. He was okay.

I buzzed him up, opened my door. But when I saw who it was, I wanted to cry.

Dick Whitfield knew where I lived and that was a bad thing.

"You have to tell me what's going on," he insisted, pushing his way into my living room. "Why are you on vacation? What's going on with Mark Torrey?"

I still held the tweezers and wondered how much of a weapon they would make. Seriously, Officer, I didn't think I really could take his eye out with that pointy end . . . I shook myself back to reality. "I can't tell you. Now, I'm terribly busy and you have to leave." I didn't like it that he was in my space, looking at my things. This apartment had gotten way too much bad karma recently. Maybe it really was time to think about buying a condo somewhere.

A thought dawned on me. "Do you know the Laundromat on Grand Avenue?"

He frowned but nodded.

"I really need a favor. I've got a huge laundry bag in my car, and I just can't get over there now. Could you drop it off for me on your way back to the paper?"

He stood up and for a moment I thought he was going to do it. But just for a moment.

"Listen, Annie, I've taken just about as much abuse from you as I can."

Oh, Christ, he was going to tell me I'd hurt his feelings. No shit.

"I've been doing your errands now for a while, and you don't seem to take me seriously."

Okay, and the problem is what?

"I'm a serious journalist, and I take my job seriously."

He was repeating himself and seemed unaware I hadn't responded.

"Could you just give me a little respect, the respect I deserve as your colleague?"

He had to be kidding. Maybe he could expect that from Marty, Renee, some of the other people at the paper who weren't as disagreeable as I was. Maybe he could stop trying to step on my toes and I'd think about it. Maybe he could leave me alone now, right before I was going to have to deal with Mark Torrey and the FBI. If he thought I was really going to tell him anything of any substance, he was as stupid as I thought.

He'd stopped talking and I was lost in my own world, which just emphasized his point. Like I cared.

"All right, so you don't want to deliver my laundry. Fine. It's okay with me."

He sighed and ran his hand through his hair. "I really try to like you, Annie. I really think you do good work."

He wanted me to give him a compliment back. But I couldn't, even if I pretended I wanted to. It was just too much.

"Listen, Dick. This has been a very bad day, a very bad week, in fact. Someone broke into my apartment last night and I just got it cleaned up. I've been almost abducted, had hate mail pushed under my door, been chased after by an escort service operator, seen two dead girls, and been told by the publisher I have to take a vacation. And that doesn't even match having to cover the stupid cows. So I would appreciate it if you would just accept me for the way I am, like everyone else, and leave me alone at the moment."

It was the most I'd ever said to him at one sitting and it surprised him into walking to the door. "I didn't realize it was so bad." Oh, God, now he was trying to offer some sort of weird sympathy.

I lowered my voice conspiratorially. "And my mother's dating Bill Bennett." I paused dramatically. "But you can't tell anyone that. It's terribly embarrassing." I knew it would be all over the newsroom within the hour, but throwing him a bone didn't seem like a bad way to get him to leave.

His eyes grew wide. "Really?"

I nodded, pushing him into the hall. "I'll see you in a week."

I closed the door and heard him go down the stairs. I watched from the window as he walked down the sidewalk and disappeared around the block. I went back to the bathroom to finish my grooming.

Noon came quickly, but Vinny didn't. I started having second thoughts about whether Mark Torrey was just trying to trap me into going to the park. I tried not to think about it. I made myself a sandwich and sat down with a pad and a pen. I started charting out the events of the past days, starting with Melissa Peabody. It was sort of my version of diagraming a sentence, with a lot of arrows and initials and stuff. It got pretty crowded. And just as it started to make sense, just as I was figuring it out, the doorbell rang again.

Tom looked around when I let him in, his eyes taking in how neat everything was. How out of the ordinary that was. "You really did have a break-in, didn't you? Why didn't you stick around last night?"

We had never given each other keys to our apartments. We figured we would keep the relationship light that way. I couldn't let myself into his world, he couldn't come into mine uninvited.

I shrugged and closed the door behind him. "You were a real shit."

"Yeah. I know. And Paula called me."

"So she sent you over here to baby-sit me, to make sure Mark Torrey doesn't do anything awful, or is it to keep me from disappearing before our allotted meeting time?"

Tom's eyes were dark, and he caught mine. "You don't have to be so hostile. I'm not the enemy."

I sighed. "Yeah, you're right. Sorry about last night. But I just couldn't deal."

"Where'd you go?"

I shrugged, remembering something. "My gun got stolen in the break-in."

Tom's eyebrows rose. "Your gun?"

"My dad got it for me, made me go to the firing range to learn how to use it. It was in the drawer next to the bed. I think it's the only thing that's missing."

Tom was shaking his head. "Jesus, Annie." He pulled a pad out of his pocket. "I need to see your permit."

I went into the bedroom and rummaged around in the file cabinet in the corner, finally finding the permit. Tom was sitting in my rocking chair, incredulity on his face. "Why the hell didn't you ever tell me you had a gun?"

I thought briefly about the gun Vinny had given me that was in my purse, but opted not to tell him I had a replacement. Especially since I didn't have a permit for that one; who the hell knew where Vinny had gotten it. I handed him my permit.

Tom wrote down all the information he needed and gave it back to me. "If you're lucky, no one will use it while committing a crime."

The way he was looking at me, I was sure he wouldn't mind if someone used it on me.

"So you're really going to do this? Meet Torrey?"

I nodded.

"You have to be a hero?"

"He says he's got Vinny," I said softly.

Tom turned away, but not quickly enough so I didn't see the sadness in his face. I'd spent a year with Tom, more time than that fantasizing about him, and I was hurting him. And it hurt like hell. But I couldn't dismiss how I felt about Vinny; if Torrey did have him, I had to help.

Tom's beeper went off, and he picked up the phone, spoke softly a few minutes, and then said, "I have to go."

"What?"

"I'll be back." He opened the door and disappeared down the stairwell.

I needed to stay busy until four o'clock, and I wasn't in the mood to watch *General Hospital.* I thought about my laundry in the car. The Laundromat was just around the corner. Doing my laundry couldn't be a threat to Mark Torrey, and if his lackeys wanted to watch my clothes go around in the dryer, well, that was their problem. But I wasn't going to let myself be a sitting duck. I opened my bag, to make sure the gun was still there. There it lay, gleaming silver next to my wallet and tampon container. I closed the bag, picked up my keys, and let myself out.

I waved off the woman behind the counter, anxious to lose myself in actually doing my laundry. I almost fell asleep listening to the gentle whishing of the washing machines and the loud whirring of the dryers. The noises soothed me, the normalcy of doing laundry lulling me into a major daydream about how Vinny's fiancée meets some guy on a business trip and tells Vinny she's found the real true love of her life and she'll have to break up with him. Vinny comes to my door, disheveled, unshaven with that sexy Don Johnson thing happening, and takes me to bed for three days.

I can't say any more because it was definitely X-rated and definitely more interesting than doing laundry.

The hand on my shoulder made my heart stop for a second.

"Come with me." The voice was rough. I was at a distinct disadvantage, especially since my gun was in my bag on the floor and I couldn't reach it. I tried to lean over, but the hand on my shoulder nearly pulled my arm out of its socket.

"Let's get going."

I stood up as quickly as allowed. I looked

around the Laundromat: an exhausted mother with twins, no, she wouldn't notice this; an old man with his back to me, folding laundry, I could see the hearing aid sitting on the chair next to him. The woman behind the counter looked like she was sleeping. This truly sucked.

I was shoved into the back seat of a car. A white Toyota. With a dent in the passenger side, like the one I'd seen at the Peabody Museum. The guy at the wheel started the engine and we began to move. I turned to get a good look at who was abducting me.

It was that lawyer, the one at my mother's dinner party, the one who hooked me up with Torrey. What the hell was his name?

"You called the cops." He said it simply.

"I'm sorry, but I can't remember your name. My mother's dinner guests all start to look alike after a while."

He made a rude snorting noise and I noticed the gun in his hand.

"Where are you taking me?"

"Mark said you shouldn't call the cops." Christ, he was a broken record. Maybe he was stupid. I could deal with stupid. Certainly Mark Torrey was the brains behind the operation. He picked morons to do his dirty work. He's in Europe, this guy's here, watching me. Yeah, he was stupid.

Letting my brain do all this conjecturing allowed me to ignore, for the moment, how deep the shit was that I was in. No one had a clue I went out to do my laundry, so they wouldn't have a clue where to look first. Much less find me.

Albert Webber. That was his name. I glanced at the guy at the wheel. I recognized him. He'd also been at my mother's party. Christ, if she only knew. It must be Nicholas Curtin, the other guy Hickey had told me about.

"Listen, Al, I'm sure whatever this is about we can clear it up. I didn't call the cops, like you think. Since you've been privy to things in my life, you must know I've been dating a cop for a year. He came over this afternoon to see how I was doing, since he knew my apartment was trashed last night."

He seemed a little startled at my speech, but recovered quickly. "You're going to get those tapes. Where are they?"

Seemed like as good a time as any to go to the bank. I told him where we needed to go, and the car maneuvered its way around the city streets. I eyed the back of Nick Curtin's head as we pulled into the parking lot.

"They might not like you having a gun

on me in there," I said matter-of-factly, surprised that I wasn't peeing in my pants. I recognized the gun, too. It was mine. It had a little piece of pink ribbon tied around it; my dad had thought it would be funny to wrap it, but the knot was so tight I couldn't get the damned ribbon off.

He looked down at his hand, this time seeming startled that a gun was there.

"You don't really like this much, do you?" I asked.

His grip tightened on the gun. I could see the veins rise in his hand. "Shut up. I'm going in with you."

He shoved the gun under his jacket and grabbed me by the arm, pulling me out of the car. It hurt, but after all the other physical abuse I'd taken lately it wasn't too bad.

"If you try anything, I'll start shooting. I don't care who I hit, and I hope I hit you."

I wasn't sure I believed him, and he sensed that.

"We've got the private dick. If I don't come out of there with you and the tapes, he's not going to make it, either."

Nick Curtin turned his head a little, and I could see his eyes were dark. While Webber seemed a little nervous, Nick looked much more likely to actually harm me. Anyway, I didn't have any reason not to believe they'd carry out their threat. Two girls were already dead. Two girls they both knew intimately. Why would they hesitate about killing me or Vinny or both of us?

I had to go through all the rigmarole to get to my safe deposit box. I vaguely referred to Albert as a "friend" when the bank clerk frowned at him. "He has to stay out here," she said firmly.

I shrugged and glanced at Albert, who patted his jacket to remind me to behave.

I went into the vault and opened my box. There it was, the envelope that Albert wanted. And underneath it was the envelope that held my will, the one my mother insisted on drawing up for me after she became a lawyer. It basically said I left all my worldly belongings, aka my travel mug collection and some jewelry given to me in a long-ago ruined relationship, to my mother. She had a copy of it in her safe, just in case I lost this one, which wasn't out of the realm of possibility, since I would be giving it to Albert.

I also had some cassette tapes in the box. They were recordings of interviews I'd done with an accused murderer a few years ago. The thing was, he'd turned out to be innocent. I harbored thoughts of writing a book about it, which is why I'd kept the tapes. But since it seemed like they'd do more for my future right now than a book would, I scooped them up without feeling nostalgic and put them in the envelope with my will and sealed it. I convinced myself it was the right thing to do; at the very least it could buy me and Vinny some more time. I grabbed it and went back out into the bank lobby.

Albert smiled. Actually smiled. "Now that wasn't so bad, was it?" he whispered as he held my arm back to the car.

I stopped at the door, his grip firmer. "Listen, you've got it now, can I go? I don't know where you're going, I don't know where Torrey is. I'm in the dark. This is all I know, and if you're never caught, it doesn't matter anyway, does it? Can I go back and put my laundry in the dryer?"

For a minute I thought I was going to get away with it. His eyes wavered, his mouth moved in a chewing motion. Then he shoved me back into the car.

This wasn't good.

"So are you going to get rid of me like you got rid of Melissa and Allison?" I didn't want to say it out loud, but I had nothing to lose.

He shook his head. "I don't know anything about that."

"Oh, come on. You're obviously the muscle behind the brain." I was thinking "musclehead." "Torrey must have told you how to handle those girls."

He'd get double vision if he kept shaking his head like that. "They were nice girls. I'd like to get my hands on whoever killed them."

He seemed sincere, so sincere that I believed him. I wasn't sure why, it was my reporter's instinct. I could smell a rat a mile away, but on the flip side, I could also tell when someone was telling the truth. These were skills Dick Whitfield often got confused.

"So you don't have much experience with killing people, then," I said flatly, a bubble of hope rising.

He jabbed me with the gun. "Don't think I can't." But he didn't look me in the eye. I held on to that.

"You know that if you turn yourself in and testify against Torrey, you'd probably get some sort of good deal." God, I sounded like my mother.

It didn't sway him, the lawyer talk. "I wish you'd shut up," he said. "I thought reporters were supposed to be seen and not heard."

"That's children." Although reporters

were not unlike children in many ways.

He shrugged. "Whatever."

We were on State Street, near the Mexican place where I'd met Allison. It seemed like a million years ago. A cow stood in the small patch of grass in the intersection. It was painted like a car, spokes on its legs, a steering wheel glued to its horns, a huge rearview mirror facing the street. I saw the reflection of the car in it as we moved past. We got onto the highway going north.

"Where are you taking me?"

I didn't think Albert could sit still and stay mute so long.

We got off the highway at Exit 10, Route 40, and sped down to Whitney Avenue in Hamden. We turned right, going past the funeral home, the cemetery. I finally figured it out. They were taking me to Sleeping Giant State Park. Not being a hiker, or even remotely interested in spending an afternoon in the woods with the deer ticks and snakes enjoying nature, I'd never been there. Accidents happened all the time, hikers fell off rocks, kids got lost for hours at a time. I didn't want to be a statistic.

"Do you know your way around here?" I asked when we pulled into a small dirt drive about half a mile from the main entrance to the park.

Albert gave the gun to Curtin and began putting on hiking boots. So he knew his way around.

"You could still cut a deal," I cautioned him. "But once I'm dead, I bet all bets are off."

"By the time they find you, I'll be long gone," he muttered, pushing me out of the car, my gun stuck in his waistband. He probably saw that in some movie or on TV.

Sneakers are completely useless in the woods. I kept slipping on the underbrush. My thoughts were ironically on how to maneuver, rather than on the gun. I still wasn't 100 percent convinced that Albert could kill me, and I hung on to that when he forced me off the trail and into the forest.

Even if he couldn't kill me, I'd never find my way out of this place and I'd probably die here anyway. A mountain lion or a snake would take me out. It was like that *Survivor* show on TV but without the cameras and the million-dollar pot at the end.

"Where is Mark Torrey?" I asked Albert as I stepped over a fallen tree trunk.

He shook his head.

"Oh, come on, Albert. Give me a break. Who am I going to tell?"

"He's in Europe."

"Can you narrow it down some?"

"Why do you want to know?"

"Because he's got my life in your hands from way far away. Do you always follow his orders? How did you get to this point, holding a gun on someone? I thought you were a lawyer, a do-gooder, didn't you want to get into my mother's firm?" I couldn't stop once I started.

"I should kill you here," he said, but kept moving. I could hear the traffic then, and I saw some hikers in the distance. I supposed if we could see them, they could hear the gun.

"No, really, Albert. What's motivating you? You must be getting some huge stash of cash out of this. Do you really think Torrey will let you have it? Do you really think Torrey won't sell you down the river if he gets caught?"

He stopped, the gun suspended in the air between us, his finger stretching toward the trigger. I took a deep breath. This was every public official's dream: Kill the reporter before she writes again.

Chapter 22

But I wasn't about to get shot. So in a moment of pure adrenaline, I lunged toward him, pushing his arm with the gun perpendicular to my person. The gun went off as we fell, and I rolled slightly, slamming my head against a rock.

"Hey, what's going on over there?" The shout came from somewhere to my left, and I heard Albert scramble up. I opened my eyes to see him looking around on the ground, but a rustle of leaves caused him to glance up and take off back in the direction from where we'd come.

I turned toward the sound of footsteps, glad that someone had shown up to thwart any further attempt on my life.

Actually, it was more than one person. It was a whole fucking pack of Cub Scouts. Albert would have a hard time explaining how a bunch of little midgets in blue uniforms and yellow neckties kept him from doing me in.

"Are you all right?" The Cub Scout leader was leaning over me, and I could smell onions on his breath. The pack was laying back, obviously not Boy Scout caliber just yet. "We heard a shot. No one's supposed to hunt here."

I couldn't explain that I was the intended target, not some poor unfortunate deer.

I sat up, dazed, wet drops on my face. I wiped them off with my sleeve and saw that I was bleeding. No wonder those kids were uncertain about me. I must have looked like hell.

It was good to know that I wasn't mortally wounded, and that my abductor was gone. But it wasn't that good. I was still out here, in the woods, with these little people and a guy who needed to brush his teeth. Albert would probably be waiting for me back at my apartment, or, worse, Curtin would be there. I hadn't liked the look in his eyes.

"I'm okay," I managed to sputter.

"You're bleeding." He turned to one of the kids. "First-aid kit."

I didn't want one of these little Cub Scouts touching me, much less applying bandages and shit that he'd get some sort of badge for.

"I'm okay, really," I insisted. "I just need to get back." Back where, I wasn't sure, but I wanted out of the forest and fast. The Cub Scouts would be useful in that, at least, since unless there was pavement and a street sign, I had no sense of direction.

I got to my feet slowly, my head feeling like a train was rumbling through it.

"Where's your pack?" the Cub Scout leader asked.

I shook my head. "Never take one along."

"You really should bring one, at least bring some water." I could see all the little Scouts nodding in agreement. This is why I dropped out of Girl Scouts. I didn't have the pack mentality.

"Is your car in the lot?"

I nodded. They didn't need to know what my real story was. It was way too complicated even for me.

Albert was probably discovering at this very moment that he had my personal items, not the tapes he was looking for. Mark Torrey would be pretty pissed off at him for botching the job so completely, so maybe he'd plan his own escape. Maybe.

My brain was working in overdrive and it was tiring me out.

I concentrated on the trees as we hiked

down. They all looked alike to me, big branches, some leaves. What was the appeal of "getting back to nature"? I just hoped I didn't see any large insects or wild animals.

If Albert didn't kill Melissa and Allison and Mark Torrey didn't kill them, then who did? Was it really David Best? Was it his roommate, the guy with the mole? He had a history, at least with me. And he didn't even know me. What was his relationship with Sarah? She told me outright she hated Melissa, but I didn't really believe her. She'd said it to see my reaction, and she probably did hate her on one level. But on another level, it was just typical girl jealousy. She wanted to be the pretty one, not just the smart one.

Stream-of-consciousness can be a dangerous thing.

The Cub Scout leader was talking to me. "Didn't you hear the shot?"

I nodded.

"So you were here hiking alone?" He didn't believe me, and I guess I wouldn't, either. I must have looked pretty dreadful, judging from the looks on those Scouts' faces. Since I didn't have a mirror, I could only suppose my hair was even worse than usual, I had blood on me, who knows just how much, and I was still healing from my first attempted abduction. Christ, what was it Vinny found attractive?

"I got lost," I tried. "I came up here with, well, someone else, who left me here. Must be playing some sort of trick on me." I tried to keep my voice light, even laughed a little, a high-pitched twitter that didn't sound altogether human.

It worried them. I think they thought I was some sort of escapee, not necessarily a criminal, but a crazy person loose in the woods.

"Do you need a doctor?"

"Probably." Why lie?

"Are you still bleeding?" He came over to me, his eyes studying the side of my head. "Pretty nasty, but I think it's okay."

Thank you, Marcus Welby, MD. Of course I'm dating myself. Anyone in her right mind would want George Clooney instead.

He stopped asking questions, and we hiked in silence, and somewhere along the line I noticed we were on a trail. I wished they would've given up one of those walking sticks. When I saw the parking lot, my first reaction was to sigh with relief. My second reaction was that I had no car here. I wasn't quite sure how to explain that to the Scouts. But Quinnipiac University was right across the street, and I could find a phone there.

"Oh, my car's over there."

"Are you a professor?"

Too old to be mistaken for a student. Shit. I nodded.

I could see he didn't believe me, but he didn't press me for any more information. I thanked my little saviors and, after checking the parking lot and road for the white Toyota, ran across the street to the campus. I had no clue where I was going. I turned a few heads until some real professor stopped and asked me what the hell I was doing there. In those words.

"I need to find a phone. Someone played a prank on me and left me in the park, wounded."

"You should call the police."

If I had a phone . . . well, it wouldn't do me any good to piss off anyone else today, so I kept my mouth shut and followed him to a pay phone.

No quarters. There was a stack of them in my bag at the Laundromat. But my phone card pin number was committed to memory. I dialed the only number I knew I could.

"Can I speak to my mother?" I asked her secretary.

"She's busy, Anne."

"It's an emergency. Please."

Her hesitation proved my voice matched the situation. "Okay."

I waited, but not as long as I thought I'd have to.

"What's wrong, Annie?"

I burst into tears. How pathetic. But it was probably the worst day I'd ever had, outside of my wedding day eons ago, and I was way overstressed.

"Please calm down and tell me what's wrong." She was getting even more worried.

Finally I composed myself. "I need someone to come pick me up. I don't want to tell you on the phone."

"Where are you?"

"Quinnipiac University."

"Why?"

"It's a very long story. Drive into the entrance on Mount Carmel Avenue and I'll come out to meet you." I didn't want to chance it that Albert and Nicholas were lurking.

I hung up the phone and ducked into a building and found a restroom. It was even more horrifying than I'd imagined. My hair hung in knots; leaves and tree branches stuck out among the splotches of blood, which covered one shoulder and the front of my sweatshirt, not to mention the sleeve I'd wiped my cheek with. I turned the water on and let it steam before plunging my hands in. I scrubbed my face and hair after getting the leaves out. A huge welt covered in blood was beneath my hair just over my ear, obviously where I'd come in contact with the rock.

When I was as clean as I could be considering the venue, I straightened myself up and walked out as if I always looked like shit.

The car pulled up about ten minutes later, and I stumbled toward it. My mother rushed out and took me into her arms. Sure, she's a royal pain in the ass most of the time, but she's still my mom and I know when I need her I can count on her to be there. I was settled into the front seat next to her before she asked me what happened.

In a rush, it all came out, the cows, Vinny, Tom, Dick Whitfield, being forced to take a vacation, my will, the tapes, my abduction and survival. I didn't tell her about kissing Vinny, some things have to stay private, but telling her Tom broke up with me would elicit more sympathy, so I kept that in.

"I told you to be careful if you were going to pursue going after Mark Torrey," was all she said at the end. It was pretty fucking anticlimactic, if you ask me.

"He's going to kill me," I said matter-of-factly. "And we really need to find Vinny."

"They lied to you about Vinny."

"What?"

"Mark Torrey does not have Vinny locked up somewhere. I just saw him not half an hour ago, he was in my office. He was looking for you."

I felt like an idiot. "I can't believe I bought Torrey's story, but when Vinny didn't show up when he said he would, I didn't know what to think."

"You had no idea Torrey was lying."

"But then where the hell was Vinny all day?"

My mother sighed. "I'm sorry, dear, but that's my fault. I asked him to check some city records online for me, about Lundgren's redevelopment project. There might be a tie-in to the investment scam. I offered him the use of the firm's computer system, so he didn't have to go back to his office. Well, it took longer than he expected. He said he tried to call you, but your line was busy."

Probably because I was talking to Mark Torrey about my laundry.

"You have to call Paula, you know," she said. "She's been looking for you, too."

"Do you have your cell phone?"

She handed it to me and I dialed Paula's number. Voice mail. I opted not to leave a message. "Maybe it would be a good idea if I stay missing for a while."

"But she should know you're all right, and obviously Mark Torrey isn't showing up at your rendezvous."

It sounded so clandestine. A rendezvous. Kind of like a ménage à trois. All those French words made life sound like one big orgasm.

"Why don't I go to your house and clean up first? I can call her and Vinny from there," I said.

"You might need a doctor."

I shook my head. "I'm fine. Really." I didn't feel much worse than I had the last couple of days.

She was looking at me with that I'm-your-mother-and-I-know-best look, but I stared her down.

"You need some clothes." My mother's eyes took in my bedraggled figure.

I thought a minute. "We can stop at the

Gap, you can run in, grab a pair of jeans and a sweatshirt. You can drop me at your house."

I waited while she shopped for me. The last time my mother bought my clothes was when I was twelve.

I didn't even look in the bag until I got into her house. She pecked me on the cheek and made me promise to call Paula. "If you don't, I will," she warned.

I shed my clothes, turned the hot water on in the shower, and stepped in, basking in the steam. I was beet red when I got out, but I felt human again. I opened the Gap bag and stared.

I'd told her a pair of jeans and a sweatshirt.

I stared at the gray wool slacks and pink sweater twin set like they were aliens. On the back of the sales slip she wrote, "You'll look better in this." I doubted it.

I pulled them on, having no choice since she and I were so different in size and I couldn't take something from her closet. The slacks actually hung nicely, the sweater was soft. But when I stared in the mirror, my hair, bruised face, and sneakers made the whole thing look like the sham it was. I looked like a bag lady who'd just ripped off the local thrift shop.

I dialed Paula's number again.

"Where the hell have you been?" she demanded after I said hello.

"It's a long story. Did you go to the park anyway, and was Torrey there?"

"We did go to the park, but he wasn't there. Where are you?"

"At my mother's." I quickly told her what had happened at Sleeping Giant.

"So they're still out there somewhere?"

"Yeah, I guess so."

"Stay there," she said firmly. "I'll get someone to go with me out to Wooster Square, to your apartment to see if they're there looking for you. A white Toyota?"

"With a dent in the passenger side."

After we hung up, I tried Vinny again and left another message.

I found my mother's brandy and poured a glass. Just as I took a sip, I saw the keys. The keys to the Mercedes. An idea began to take shape. Hell, I couldn't just sit here and do nothing. I'd go crazy. Albert wouldn't think to notice the preppy brigade driving a Mercedes. I downed the brandy and ignored the fact that I didn't have my driver's license on me. I was going to meet the fucking FBI.

Chapter 23

As I stopped at the light at Chapel Street, ready to cross over to my building, movement to my right caught my eye. A couple seemed to be in the middle of a knock-down, drag-out fight on the corner of Olive and Wooster. It was a long light so I watched for a while, not expecting to see the skinny woman throw a punch and make contact with the guy's face. I sat up a little straighter, wishing I had my cell phone to call 911, when he grabbed her wrist and held it tight. Her long hair was over her face, but when she turned, the street light caught her and I gasped.

It was Sarah Lewis.

Granted, I wasn't surprised she was here, in my neighborhood, rather than over at the ivy-covered buildings at Yale, because this *was* where everyone came for pizza and Italian ice. But I was surprised that she was in a fistfight with some guy.

And when he turned into the light, I saw it wasn't just some guy. It was the mole guy, Matt Minneo, David Best's roommate, the guy who left me that threatening note.

The light changed and the car behind me honked because I hadn't moved. I inched slowly across the intersection; let the guy behind me think I was some old person who couldn't see. As soon as I got past the corner, I slid into an illegal parking spot in front of a fire hydrant, threw the door open, and moved down the sidewalk, making sure the building on the corner was blocking me from their view.

Not that they'd notice anyway.

He was yelling, she was yelling, I couldn't make out what they were saying. I moved a little closer.

"Don't do it," he was pleading with her, and while I thought it meant he didn't want her to hit him again, she didn't look like she would. Her arms hung limply at her sides, her hair had fallen back across her face, her head hung low.

She answered him so softly that I had no chance in hell of hearing what it was he didn't want her to do. He responded with something else, and all I could make out were the words "blow over." But they were moving closer to my corner, so I closed my eyes, thinking that if I concentrated only with my ears I could hear better.

"It's just a matter of time."

Hell, it worked. Go figure. But in that second that Sarah's words resonated in my head, a memory slammed into them, pushing them aside.

It was the voice. The voice of the woman who'd tried to abduct me.

My eyes flew open as I watched them walk along the sidewalk, coming toward me. I inched back a little, uncertain what to do about this. I didn't have Vinny's gun, I didn't have my pepper spray; they were still in my bag at the Laundromat, if no one had stolen it yet. How could I confront them, it was two against one, and they'd already almost succeeded in taking me out.

Matt was rubbing his face where Sarah had hit him. My thoughts twisted around a little, wondering why he was still trying to talk to her, when she'd so obviously abused him. What a wuss.

They were just at the corner, and I scooted backward, behind the steps of the brownstone a few feet away. But instead of turning, they stopped. They were so close now I could almost hear them breathing. I held my own breath as I eavesdropped.

"Thanks for everything," Sarah said, starting to cross the street. Matt stood where he was as she approached a white Toyota. It looked a lot like the one I'd been in just a couple of hours ago, but it was facing the wrong way and I couldn't see if it had a dent in the side. As I stared at it, a question began to form. What the hell connection would there be between Sarah Lewis and Nicholas Curtin and Albert Webber? And if this was the same car, where were Nicholas and Albert?

As I was pondering that, Sarah paused a second and leaned down toward the driver's side window, straightened up and turned around again, looking up and down the street, like she'd lost something.

"What time's your flight?" Matt called across the street.

She didn't answer him, just opened the door and climbed in, giving Matt a little wave of her hand, sort of like the Queen Mother.

"Jesus, Sarah, don't go." But his words were lost as she started the engine and took off.

Matt turned back in the direction of Wooster Street. I pulled up from my crouch behind the stairs, uncertain whether to follow him or follow her.

But as I emerged from my hiding spot, someone else made my decision for me.

"You're not getting away this time," the rough voice whispered in my ear as he held my arms behind me and pushed me out onto the sidewalk. I felt something prick me just under my chin, and I tensed. He had a goddamned knife.

I managed to catch his profile and recognized Nicholas Curtin. He must have been waiting here for me to come home. And here I was, offering myself to him on a silver platter. Shit.

"So Albert fucked up and you have to take over?" I asked loudly, with much more bravado than I felt. I'd seen this guy's eyes in the car, and I knew he was capable of much more than Albert.

He stopped, and I almost fell over, but then felt myself being shoved into a car. But this one I knew. It was my mother's Mercedes.

"We're not taking your car?" I asked as he pushed me across the seat, over the stick shift, and into the driver's side.

The door slammed, and the knife gleamed in his hand. "You didn't even see me while you watched them, did you? Some reporter you are."

Jesus. He had a point. But it was no use

crying over spilled milk now, I was seriously screwed and I had no clue how to get myself out of this. I glanced around the square and didn't see anyone waiting to rescue me. Paula had told me to stay put, so no one knew I was driving my mother's car, no one knew I'd decided to come home. They'd find me in a ditch somewhere, stabbed like Allison, and Dick Whitfield would get my job.

"Start the car," he ordered. I could feel the knife under my right ear.

I started the car, I'd left the key in it, and eased away from the curb.

I had to do something. I couldn't just be a sitting duck and make this easy for him. Anger surged through me.

Taking my chances, I leaned quickly to my left, away from the knife, slammed my foot onto the accelerator, twisted the steering wheel, and as the car lurched forward, the force of the movement pushed us both back into our seats. The knife skittered somewhere and I heard Nicholas Curtin yell, "You fucking bitch!"

I didn't take my foot off the accelerator, instead gave it even more gas.

I heard the scraping of metal against sculpture as we skidded past the statue of Christopher Columbus and into the park, slamming headfirst into the Mooster Street cow. The airbags exploded and sucker-punched me, pushing me back into the seat, my face raw where the bag met my left eye and cheek.

I sat, stunned, for what seemed an eternity but was only a second or two, before the door swung open and a glaring light blinded me.

"Are you okay in there?" I heard a voice through the bullhorn. "This is the FBI."

So they were there. Someone punctured my airbag and I fell to the ground before being lifted back up. I saw Nicholas Curtin being pulled out of his side of the car. The spotlight made Nicholas's face look like a comic book character, his eyes wide, his mouth open. In seconds, three FBI agents had dragged him off somewhere.

"You okay?" Paula's voice was heaven-sent.

I bit back tears of relief. "Yeah, yeah, I'm okay." I felt my face.

"You've got a serious burn on your cheek," Paula said softly. "But at least that's all."

I blinked at her. "How the hell did you get here? Didn't you see him grab me?"

Paula shook her head. "We were on the opposite side of the park, figuring out our strategy. I happened to glance across the park and saw him push you into the car. I wish it hadn't gotten that far, I'm sorry."

I was sorry, too, but was just happy that they were there after all. "So you didn't see Albert Webber?"

Paula shook her head. "Did you?"

"Only Curtin. But it's funny, Sarah Lewis, you know, Melissa Peabody's roommate, well, she was driving a white Toyota. Like the one I was in with Webber and Curtin."

"Could it have been the same car?"

I shrugged. "Beats me. The other car had a dent in the passenger side, but I couldn't see if this one did."

I was brushing dirt off the dreadful slacks and then realized what I was doing and stopped. "Sarah was with that guy who left me the note. They were on the sidewalk. I think they were the ones who attacked me that night."

"How do you know?"

"I recognized their voices."

"Are you sure? Why would they attack you?"

"Beats me." I thought about my conversations with Sarah: First she'd been so reluctant to talk to me; then that day on the street she was actually eager to tell me how

Melissa wanted out of the escort service. I'd seen her in a white Toyota before, too, and now she was driving it. But damn, I still couldn't connect the dots.

"There's got to be something there," I said after I filled Paula in.

Paula took my arm. "Come on. Why don't you let us figure it out? We need to concentrate on what happened at Sleeping Giant today, and what happened right now."

Another thought dawned on me. "How the hell am I going to explain to my mother that I crashed her car into a cow?"

We stared at it. Pieces of cow sat on top of the hood of the Mercedes, which, while it did not suffer much front end damage because of its sturdy German craftmanship, was scratched all to hell. The head of the cow stared up at us from the ground, its pathetic pizzas invisible in the shadows.

"You killed it," Paula said softly, and I snickered a little, even though it wasn't really funny.

Paula had a couple of FBI agents check out my apartment before she took me up there. My laundry bag and purse were on the sofa. I rummaged through the purse, found the gun and my pepper spray. The money I had in my wallet was still there.

"How did these get here?"

Paula shook her head. "No idea."

But as she was answering, I saw the note on the kitchen table.

Your mother called me. I brought your things back for you but am checking on some stuff so I can't stick around. I'll see you later. Vinny.

"He's got a crush on you," Paula teased.

"He's got a fiancée." But I couldn't keep my face from growing hot, and Paula saw me blush.

"Your mother told me about him."

Jesus, she might as well put up a fucking billboard on the Q bridge. "He's engaged," I repeated. "End of story."

The red eye on my answering machine was blinking, and I hit it to keep this conversation from going any further.

"Sorry to have to break our date, Ms. Seymour, but I'm indisposed." Mark Torrey's voice echoed in my small apartment, and my fists clenched. "You shouldn't have tricked Albert with those tapes, and I'm disappointed, of course, with the turn of events with Nicholas. But you can't win them all, can you?"

Chapter 24

"Are you okay?" Paula was asking.

I turned to her and finally allowed myself to breathe. "How the hell does he know? This all just happened. How does he know? Where the fuck is he?"

Paula went to my cupboard and found the brandy, poured me half a glass, thought better of it, and filled the glass even more. She handed it to me, and I took a deep swallow.

She hadn't said a word, and her eyebrows were furrowed together the way they get when she's deep in thought. Finally she asked, "Besides Melissa's roommate and her boyfriend and Nicholas, did you see anyone else out there tonight? Besides us, I mean."

"No." I drank a little more of the brandy and felt a warm rush through my body. I wanted to get drunk and go to sleep for three days.

But it didn't seem like Paula thought that was a good idea because she kept talking. "Tell me again what happened when you saw Melissa's roommate."

I took a deep breath and related everything I'd seen and heard.

Paula shook her head. "I don't think it sounds like anything except a lovers' quarrel."

"But what if it was those two who mugged me that night?"

"Are you sure, absolutely sure that it was?"

I closed my eyes and thought about it, but now that I couldn't hear their voices, I just wasn't as sure. Maybe I wanted it to be them, maybe my ears had been playing tricks on me. I shook my head slowly. "I don't know."

"Listen, I need to get back to the office. It's going to be a long night with Nicholas Curtin. I hope he'll be able to point us in Torrey's direction." She glanced at my answering machine. "I need to take that tape. We might be able to find something on it that could help us."

I nodded and watched her pull the tape out. "If you get another call, call me on my cell." She patted the phone where it sat clipped to her belt. "Anytime," she added as she opened the door. "Oh, by the way," she said, pausing, "I'll be here at eight-thirty to take you to the bank to get Hickey's tapes."

I glanced at the clock. Nine p.m. How had it gotten so late? I nodded. "Sure, okay."

"I'll have a cop downstairs all night," she added, like it was an afterthought but I knew better. "Just in case."

Because Albert was still out there and I could still be in danger. She didn't have to spell it out for me. But thinking about the cop, I wondered where Tom was.

And thinking about Tom made me realize I didn't want to be alone. After Paula left, I locked the deadbolt and put the chain on the door, turning off the bright overhead light and keeping on the smaller lamp on the end table. I was almost done with the brandy and was about to get a refill when the buzzer made me jump about fifteen feet.

I glanced out the window and saw a familiar figure on the stoop. I pushed the button to let him in and was just unlocking the door when he got to the landing.

"Jesus, you look like hell," Vinny said when he walked in.

"Nice to see you, too," I growled. "If you

don't have anything nice to say, you don't get to stay." Despite my tone, he must have seen how relieved I was to see him.

Vinny put his fingers under my chin and lifted my face toward him. "You okay?" he asked softly.

I didn't want to do it, but the tears spilled down my cheeks before I could stop them, and he pulled me to him, his arms around me. I felt his lips on my hair, and I lifted my face to kiss him. To hell with Rosie.

We stood like that for what seemed like forever but was probably only about five minutes. I struggled to stop the tears and finally stepped back, keeping him at arm's length. "No," I said, "I'm fine now, I really am." But I wasn't completely sure about that.

"What happened out there?"

"Nicholas Curtin ambushed me while I was watching Sarah and David Best's roommate have a fight. He had a knife, I crashed my mom's car into the cow. End of story." The waterworks were going to start again if I wasn't careful. I took another drink of brandy, hoping the booze would keep me in line.

"Sarah?"

"Melissa Peabody's roommate, Sarah Lewis."

"She was here?"

I shrugged, not sure where he was going with this. "She was near Wooster Street. They were fighting." I paused. "You know, I think they were the two who mugged me that night."

Vinny was nodding. "They might have been."

I had started heading for the kitchen for another refill, but I stopped and stared at him. "Really?"

"Yeah." Vinny ran a hand through his hair, and the shadows under his eyes told me he was tired. "I spent all day on the computer. Following Mark Torrey's money. At least as far as I could get," he added.

I waited, uncertain where this was leading.

"What exactly were they fighting about?" he asked.

I struggled to remember. It wasn't that long ago, but so much had happened to me today that everything was starting to get mixed up. The brandy probably wasn't helping. "I don't know, really. But it sounded like she was going somewhere, he said something about what time was her flight."

Vinny's eyes grew wide. "A flight? You're sure?"

"Yeah. What about it?"

He started for the door. "I have to go."

This was unacceptable. I had been abducted twice in one day. I wasn't about to be abandoned, too. "Where are you going?"

"You'll be okay," he said absently as he opened the door.

I put my arm across the doorway. "If you're leaving, then I'm coming with you."

A smile slid across his face, and his eyes twinkled. "Come on, Annie. You must feel like crap."

"Because I look like crap?" I was aware that my voice was getting louder. Pretty soon those neighbors of mine would complain about the noise. But I didn't give a shit. I wasn't going to stay there all by myself, even if there was a cop downstairs. Vinny, for some odd reason, made me feel safe. I didn't want to lose that feeling right now.

"You can't come with me," he said, but I could see he was wavering.

"There's something about Sarah, isn't there, that you know," I said. "Tell me what's going on."

Vinny pulled my arm away from the open doorway and gently shut the door, obviously aware that my voice was carrying. "I found a bank account with her name on it," he said. "There are a lot of bank accounts, Torrey has been shifting the money from one to another until it's out of sight. Torrey had accounts in Melissa Peabody's name, too, and Allison Sanders's, Albert Webber's, Nicholas Curtin's, and a couple of others."

"No shit?"

Vinny nodded. "No shit."

"So the money he bilked from my mother is gone?"

"Hopefully we can still find it," he said, but I could see he wasn't that optimistic.

Something was nagging at me. "But what about Lundgren? He was really pissed when I asked him about that and put it in the story. And my mother said something about how Lundgren might be connected."

"From what I've been able to piece together from the tapes that Hickey made, Torrey embezzled from Lundgren, and they found out about it after he started working for the city. But instead of turning him in, they bribed him by helping him set up McGee with the idea that some of McGee's money would find its way into their pockets. Lundgren knew what Torrey was capable of and that he'd go the distance. His contacts at City Hall got him in good with the high rollers in the city. He's a smooth guy, he's a lawyer, and everyone trusted him, especially after the first year when all the investors made money. Then he started skimming, like he was supposed to."

"But he didn't give Lundgren what they wanted, did he?"

Vinny smiled. "Give the girl a gold star."

"So everyone's been looking for this guy." I paused. It was almost too much to take in at once. "He used Sarah's name on an account, too?" I struggled to remember if Sarah had told me she'd had contact with Torrey, but all I came up with was that she'd talked on the phone to him a couple of times. Maybe it was more than that, though, and suddenly her blush slammed into my brain, the blush she'd had when she was talking about him. Dammit, that was it. Did Mark Torrey fuck every Yalie this month? "Do you think she knows?"

Vinny's smile turned into a grin. "I think she's going to meet him. I think she knows where he is."

I wanted to go with him. Call me crazy, but I wanted to confront her, see if she really was the one who'd mugged me, find out why. And if she did know where Torrey was, well, I wanted to find him, too.

"You have to let me come along," I said firmly.

"I don't think so," Vinny said, his hand on the doorknob again.

"Yes, you do. Because I know where her dorm room is, and you don't." I wasn't exactly sure that he didn't know, he might have been to her room after Melissa's body was found, but figured I'd throw that out there and see where it landed.

And to my surprise, he paused. "Okay," he said. "Okay, you can come."

I grabbed my bag off the floor and was out the door before he could change his mind. But I hadn't remembered about the cop downstairs, who scowled at us when we came down. "Where are you going?" he demanded. "You're supposed to stay here."

"I don't remember anyone saying that," I said.

"Well, I don't know," he said, flustered, pulling out a cell phone. "I have to call about this."

I wondered if we shouldn't tell Paula where we were going, just in case. After my adventures today, I wanted as many people as possible to know my whereabouts. But I could tell from Vinny's stiff posture that he wouldn't buy into this plan. He had a vested interest in finding Mark Torrey himself: a big wad of cash at the end of this roller-coaster ride from my mother's law firm. Having the FBI and the cops involved could only make his job harder. Kind of like the way I felt about Dick Whitfield stepping on my toes.

So I was sympathetic, but torn in my loyalty to my friend, the FBI agent who could kick the bad guy's ass, and to Vinny, who could also kick his ass while looking damned sexy at the same time.

Like any other woman would, I opted for the guy over my friend. Stupid, yeah, but it could be more interesting in the long run.

"Listen," I said to the cop, whose name tag labeled him as Morrison, "I'll call Paula from the road and let her know what's up. That way you won't get into trouble."

And before he could say anything, we were in Vinny's Ford Explorer and peeling away from the curb in front of my building.

We were halfway to Yale when my phone rang. I checked the number and saw it was Paula. I made a mental note to say something about Morrison to Tom; obviously he wasn't trustworthy.

"Where the hell are you going?" Paula didn't even say hello. "And it better be damned good to get me out of the interrogation room."

I told her quickly about Sarah and what Vinny had found.

"We're on our way over to her room to see if she's still there," I said.

"I'll call Tweed and Bradley and see if she's scheduled on any flights," Paula offered. "If she is, I'll make sure there's someone waiting for her to keep her from getting on the plane."

This was surprisingly easy. There had to be a catch.

"I'll send someone over to the dorm to meet you," she added. "This is really stupid of you two to do by yourself."

"Christ, Paula, she's a twenty-year-old college student. What the hell could she do to us?"

"Annie," and I was pretty sure a lecture was coming, but then, "Nicholas Curtin just told us Sarah killed Melissa Peabody."

Chapter 25

"Holy shit," I said softly. "Do you have proof?"

"No," and I could hear the fatigue in her voice. "He wants to cut a deal, so we're not even sure if it's true. But just in case, we were about to send someone over to pick her up. If you get there before we do, try to keep her there, but be careful."

"I'll call you when we know something," I said, ready to hang up.

"Wait."

"Yeah?"

"Something else about Curtin. That knife he held on you, he didn't cut you, did he?"

"No, he just pricked me a little but didn't draw any blood. Why?"

"There's blood in the grooves on the handle."

She hung up and I stared at the phone in my hand. If anyone had told me what my day would be like, I wouldn't have believed him. I'm a reporter, which means I usually just watch what goes on, then sit down at my little computer and write about it. That's the gist of it. I am not the news. I am an observer of the world. Christ, now I sound like Dick Whitfield.

But all of that was before Melissa Peabody's body was found in the street. Before Mark Torrey decided to rip off my mother and the publisher. Before the cows.

All of those things had set off a chain reaction that somehow was ending up in my lap, with my life hanging in the balance.

For a nanosecond I thought about calling Marty. This was one big fucking story, and that Pulitzer might well be within my reach if I approached it the right way.

But with my luck, someone would say I was lying, like that chick who wrote the story in the *Washington Post* about a heroin-addicted kid, or Jayson Blair, the *New York Times* reporter who made up shit about pretty much everything. Because this was all too weird to actually be happening.

"You okay?" Vinny was asking as we crossed State Street and went up Chapel.

I told him what Paula told me.

"Well, Melissa Peabody wasn't stabbed, so it isn't her blood," Vinny said.

"Yeah, you're right," I started, but then I knew. Allison. It could be Allison's blood on that handle.

And then another thought hit me in the gut like a lead balloon. Allison was killed after I talked to her. Maybe Curtin killed her because he found out she'd talked to me. Christ, I hoped that wasn't it. I didn't think I could live with the guilt.

I didn't have much time to dwell on that at the moment, however, because we were easing into a parking space on High Street. There were no cops in sight yet. We hopped out of the SUV, and I pushed all thoughts about Allison from my head. I needed to be focused on Sarah now.

The gate was propped open. Someone was expecting someone, and I hoped Sarah wasn't on to us. Vinny and I slipped through the gate and I led the way across the courtyard to Sarah's dorm. There were lights in every window except one. We stepped into the stairwell and heard a door slam somewhere above us. Vinny grabbed my arm and pulled me into the shadows.

Footsteps bounded down the stairs, and when we saw the figure in the doorway, Vinny and I stepped in front of her.

"What are you doing here?" Sarah looked from me to Vinny, shifting her backpack across her shoulder. If she was surprised to see us, she didn't show it.

"Going somewhere?" I asked.

"The library," she said.

"Saw you earlier, with Matt," I continued. "Had a little altercation with your friend Nick."

"I don't know who you're talking about."

"Nick. Nick Curtin. He's the one who killed Allison, did you know that?" Okay, so it wouldn't hold up in court unless there was more evidence, but she didn't have to know that right now.

This surprised her. The backpack fell off her shoulder and landed with a thud. I heard something roll across the floor, and I looked down at the small bronze Buddha I'd held in her room.

Vinny was faster than I was. "What's this?" he asked, picking it up.

Sarah reached for it, but he pulled it away and held it out to his side, inspecting it. "Pretty cool," Vinny said.

"Just give it back," Sarah said gruffly. "You know, you really should be talking to Matt."

"Why?" I asked.

She shrugged. "I didn't have anything to

do with this. It was Matt. It was all his idea."

"What was his idea?" Vinny was asking as I saw something else on the ground that had fallen out of her backpack.

I picked it up. "Airline ticket? Going somewhere?"

The light was dim, but my eyes aren't that bad yet, so I could still read it. "Tweed to Philadelphia to Paris?" I turned to Vinny. "Is Mark Torrey in Paris?"

Vinny shrugged.

"This has nothing to do with him," Sarah said, standing up a little straighter, her voice a little more self-assured. "My parents are there, I'm going for a week."

"But this is a one-way ticket." I leafed through the documents. "When are you coming back?"

"She's not."

The voice startled us, and Vinny and I turned to see Matt Minneo slumped against the wall.

It was enough of a distraction that Sarah grabbed the Buddha out of Vinny's hand, pushed me aside, and ran into the courtyard. But Matt was too quick for her, grabbing her around the waist and pulling her back to us.

"I can't believe you said it was all me,"

he growled at her. "Tell them the truth."

Her eyes moved from Matt's face to mine to Vinny's. "I don't know what he's talking about."

Sirens in the distance were getting closer, and I knew the cavalry was on its way.

"It was you guys, wasn't it, who mugged me that night," I said to both of them.

"If your stupid friend hadn't come to your rescue, we would've had all this over with a long time ago." Sarah couldn't keep the ugliness out of her voice. She really could do with a makeover.

"What threat am I to you?"

Sarah struggled, but Matt was strong. The sirens stopped just outside the gate, but we couldn't see anyone yet.

"Tell her," Matt demanded.

"She killed Melissa, didn't she?" I said.

Sarah's head whipped around and she stared at me. "Who told you that?"

"Nicholas Curtin told the FBI earlier. That's why the cops are here." And now they were coming, across the lawn, but it was too soon. I didn't have any answers yet.

"Nick?" Sarah asked in a very familiar way, and an image came into my head of Sarah leaning toward the Toyota, looking as if she'd lost something. Curtin must have been with her, saw me during her fight with Matt, and left her behind while he tried to kill me. That's why he didn't have his own car. That's why he said what he did about my not noticing him.

"What were you and Curtin doing near Wooster Square tonight? Were you going to kill me, too?"

Sarah frowned. "He was going to take me to the airport. When I saw he was gone, I figured I'd wait for him here."

"Because he must have gotten to me, right?" I asked sarcastically. "Get rid of me and then run his errands." She didn't contradict me. Something else dawned on me. "Are you the girl who set up me, Vinny, and Hickey last night at the diner?" I asked.

Sarah blinked a couple of times, and I knew she was.

I snorted. "You know, Sarah, I didn't suspect anything about you until tonight."

Matt took the Buddha from her and held it up. "She thought you knew," he said.

What the hell did the Buddha have to do with this? But as I stared at it, I remembered holding this little Buddha, turning it over in my hands, and it very likely may have been what had crushed Melissa Peabody's skull.

"Why? Why did you kill her?" I asked, although there was little time and I didn't expect her to be forthcoming.

But she surprised me. "They were in bed when I got to the apartment." She started to sob. "He was telling her he loved her. I thought he would be alone."

Tom and about four other cops heard her and stopped a few feet away. Sarah didn't seem to notice.

"Hickey didn't mention that you were part of the equation. How long had you worked for him?" I asked.

Her eyes flashed. "I didn't work for him. I met Mark when he came to pick Melissa up one night and she was late. We talked for a long time, and he really listened to me." Her voice got softer and she started twirling a strand of hair near her ear. "We met whenever we could. He told me he loved me, that I wasn't like Melissa, he could talk to me, and that made our relationship even better since it wasn't just sex." She blushed again, and I could see she'd been a virgin when Torrey decided to use her. Against my will, I began to feel sorry for her.

"Jesus, Sarah," Matt said softly.

Sarah sighed as she looked at him, and I could see she did care about this guy, too. But he never had a chance with her once Torrey came on the scene.

"So what happened that night?" I asked.

Sarah hung her head. "The door was unlocked. I heard them and waited," she said. "They came out of the bedroom, laughing. He looked so damned happy with her. So I grabbed the Buddha off the end table and went after her. I don't know what happened after that, she was on the floor, dead. It was his idea to dump her over the balcony, he thought people would think she committed suicide." Her arms hung limp at her sides.

Matt let go of her, a look of disgust on his face.

"And you thought I figured it out when I saw your Buddha? That's why you mugged me? That's why Matt pushed that note under my door?"

Sarah nodded. I had another thought. "Why keep the Buddha?"

She bit back tears. "My grandmother gave it to me. I gave it to Mark. He kept it at the apartment. He told me to get rid of it after Melissa died, but I couldn't."

Vinny began to laugh sarcastically. "Isn't this a sad story? Shame on you. Don't you know that Mark Torrey has been holed up in Europe with another woman while you're covering his ass here at home?"

Her eyes grew wide.

Tom stepped forward then. "That's right. He's not waiting for you in Paris. He was there, but Nick Curtin gave him up. He's in Madrid, being arrested there right now."

"You're lying," Sarah said, her face bright red.

Tom shook his head. "Sorry, but I'm not."

Her face contorted, tears spilling down her cheeks. Jesus, Torrey really fucked up her life. Even though she'd killed Melissa and tried to kill me, I did feel bad for her. She was just a kid.

Vinny stepped back in. "You know, I think Torrey set this whole thing up. He wanted you to catch them in bed. He wanted to see how far you'd go for him."

Her eyes were uncomprehending.

"Torrey's been using dummy accounts to shift his money from one place to another. That's where Melissa came in. Torrey would deposit large amounts of money in an account he set up for her. She thought all the money was for her, but then she discovered it was disappearing as fast as it was showing up. And she threatened to tell someone, so he had to get rid of her."

"This is on Hickey's tapes?" I asked.

Vinny nodded. "It was a little cryptic, but I put two and two together."

Tom moved toward Matt and Sarah, indicating they both should be handcuffed after he read them their rights. He turned to Matt. "You're an accessory, in that you knew about the murder and you threatened and tried to abduct Annie."

Matt nodded as a tear slid down his cheek. I could see that the enormity of what he'd done had finally caught up with him. He looked at me. "I can't believe I let her talk me into this. I'm sorry if we hurt you." He paused. "I couldn't let her take me down with her."

But he already had.

Tom sighed, and I knew what he was thinking. It's sad what trouble a guy's dick will get him into.

We watched them being led back across the lawn. I turned to Vinny. "So you also have copies of the deposits into all those accounts?"

"Yeah. They're in that envelope you've got."

"And Hickey? What's going to happen to him now?"

Tom chuckled. "Hickey's been around the block. Cooperating will probably help him, but he's looking at some jail time."

"So David Best was innocent all along," I mused.

Tom looked a little embarrassed at that, but I didn't blame him, since the evidence had pointed in David's direction.

"You might want to tell Paula to check if the blood on Nick Curtin's knife matches Allison's," I told Tom.

"It's the same blood type," he offered. "We'll be doing more tests to make sure, but it looks like it."

"She got killed after I talked to her," I said.

Tom nodded. "Yeah, I know."

I felt Vinny's arm snake around my shoulders. "That's not your fault," he whispered.

But I would always think it was.

I struggled again to put it out of my head. "So have you found Albert?"

Tom chuckled, although I could see he was keeping an eye on Vinny and didn't seem happy about how close we seemed to be. "He was packing up his stuff in his apartment when we went over there."

"Dumb as a box of rocks," I said.

"We'll need to talk to you," Tom was saying to Vinny, who nodded. "Tomorrow morning?" It looked like he wanted to say something to me, too, but after a second or two, he turned and walked away, leaving me with Vinny.

"You okay?" Vinny asked as we made our way back to his SUV.

I shrugged. I wasn't sure how I was.

"You know, now you have to call the cow doctor."

"Fuck you," I said, but my heart wasn't in it.

"You're feeling better, I see."

"So you're in kind of a pickle about Mark Torrey," I said as we climbed into the Explorer.

"What do you mean?"

"You didn't find him. The FBI did. So do you get paid?"

"There are other Mark Torreys around. By the way, Bill Bennett did not rape your pension fund."

I stared at him and said nothing, letting it sink in.

"Your mother had me do some checking. He apparently told her you'd virtually accused him of that, and she wanted to make sure. And I don't think it was just to help you out. She's being cautious."

"So he suspended me for no reason, took me off my beat, made me cover the cows. Why, if he had nothing to worry about?" I could hear my voice getting louder and louder as the indignation set in. "That just sealed it for me, made me think he was guilty."

Vinny shrugged. "He did invest some of his own money, and some money for some friends. Maybe he thought if you started publicly talking about it, other people would think the worst, too."

"So it was easier to get rid of me."

Vinny chuckled. "He should know it's easier to get rid of cockroaches."

He moved close, and even in my exhaustion, I could feel his heat. He touched my cheek, the side of my head that was tender from falling on the rock. I shook him off. "No, Vinny."

He ignored me and kissed me for what seemed like days before he finally started the engine and took me back to my brownstone, making sure my downstairs door had properly locked him out before leaving me alone.

So I was not only exhausted and beat up, but sexually frustrated and I had a date with the FBI and the cops tomorrow. Life's never easy.

* * *

Even though I was exhausted, I wasn't sure I could sleep. I pulled my robe around me as I padded into the kitchen in the dark, managing to pour myself a half glass of brandy. Sipping it, I moved through the living room to the window overlooking Wooster Square.

I'd forgotten about the damned cow, and the streetlight offered a pretty brutal sight. Pieces of cow were scattered like little bits of pepperoni on a pizza. I wondered if that cow doctor would come in a little white ambulance and take it away.

My mother's Mercedes was gone, and the yellow crime scene tape was flapping in the breeze. I drained my glass and turned away.

I'd barely gotten under the covers when the phone rang, startling me. I stared at it a second, wondering if I should bother. But it might be Vinny. I grabbed the receiver off the bedside table, but not without wincing as pain from my shoulder shot across my upper back. "Yeah?" I asked gruffly.

"Annie?" My mother's voice was soft, worried. Shit, I should've called her. "Are you okay?"

"I'm fine," I assured her.

"Vinny just called me, told me what happened. He also said Mark Torrey's been arrested in Europe."

"I hope you can get your money back," I said, staring at the ceiling. My bed was warm, the brandy was working, and I felt my eyelids drooping.

"I don't care about that, as long as you're safe," she said.

I smiled to myself, ready to hang up; then she added, "Bill's here. He wants to talk to you."

My eyes snapped wide open. Bill?

"Annie?" The publisher's voice resonated in my ear. I stayed mute, uncertain what to say, which was an invitation for him to keep talking. "I've spoken with Marty. Dick Whitfield's going to do a quick piece tonight about the arrest at Yale, but we'll do a bigger piece about Torrey for Sunday. Because of your involvement, and your mother's involvement, we don't want to risk any sort of impropriety, so you won't have a byline, but I'd like you to work closely with Dick on it. Marty tells me Dick may need some handholding."

That was an understatement, but I was back on the story, byline or not. I'm sure my mother had something to do with it, too, and I was still going to have to work with Dick, but as long as I wasn't going to lose my job, it didn't matter.

"Sure, no problem," I said nonchalantly, although my heart was racing with the thought of not having to entertain myself for an entire week. "Thanks," I managed to sputter just before I hung up the phone.

Richard Wells was going to shit when he saw this story. I smiled to myself in the dark, because even though Dick was getting the byline, this was my fucking story and everyone would know that.

I was almost asleep when the phone screeched again. I picked it up.

"Yeah?"

"Annie, it's Dick Whitfield. I just left the station house. They've arrested Melissa Peabody's roommate, and your name kept coming up."

I glanced at the clock. He had about half an hour to get the story to the copy desk. He didn't need me for this, it was cut-and-dried. I could see the headline now: "Yale Student Charged in Murder of Roommate." With the time constraint, he'd barely be able to write ten inches. Tomorrow I'd help him out; I just didn't have the energy right now.

"Can you give me a comment?" he asked

when I didn't answer. "I was going to swing by there, but I didn't think it would be a good idea."

He was right. And I showed considerable restraint by not telling him so in the manner that I wanted to. I merely hung up, rolled over, and stuffed my head under the pillow.

The employees of Thorndike Press hope you have enjoyed this Large Print book. All our Thorndike and Wheeler Large Print titles are designed for easy reading, and all our books are made to last. Other Thorndike Press Large Print books are available at your library, through selected bookstores, or directly from us.

For information about titles, please call:

(800) 223-1244

or visit our Web site at:

www.gale.com/thorndike
www.gale.com/wheeler

To share your comments, please write:

Publisher
Thorndike Press
295 Kennedy Memorial Drive
Waterville, ME 04901